THE
NIGHTMARE
CLOCK

THE
NIGHTMARE
CLOCK

DAVID LOGAN

Quercus

First published in Great Britain in 2015 by

Quercus Publishing Ltd
Carmelite House
50 Victoria Embankment
London EC4Y 0DZ

An Hachette UK company

A CIP catalogue record for this book is available
from the British Library

PB 978 1 78087 581 1
EBOOK 978 1 84866 827 0

10 9 8 7 6 5 4 3 2 1

Typeset by Nigel Hazle

Printed and bound in Great Britain by Clays Ltd, St Ives plc

For my gorgeous children, Joseph, Grace and Gabriel.
For my dogs, Harper and Milo.
For my lovely, wonderful, brilliant, beautiful wife, Lisa.

1

Junk Doyle sat on a bridge over the railway lines, watching as the train from Ballinasloe came screaming towards him. As he let himself drop into its path, he wondered if this wasn't a rather daft thing to do.

Three days earlier.

A Tuesday.

Junk was sitting in Dr Oak's dreary, stifling, oppressive office. It was a small but high-ceilinged room. The sun was shining intensely just outside but its rays struggled to penetrate the narrow windows, or maybe it was the frayed net curtains that were the real barrier. They were grey from being washed too many times. They seemed to absorb the golden light and spit out something milky and bland in its place.

'So how have weeeeee been feeeeeeeling?' said Dr Oak, sounding like a purring cat, elongating the occasional word as was his habit.

Junk wanted to say that he didn't know how the doctor was feeling – sorry, feeeeeeeling – but he was feeling terrible. Sad, depressed, his stomach was churning, his head was throbbing. He felt like crying all the time. But instead he said, 'Fine.'

'Gooooooood, good, good, goooooooooooooooood,' said the doctor, letting his voice trail away to nothing as he scribbled notes in an A4-sized leather-bound notepad. 'I think that new medication we're trying is showing some bully results.'

He used odd words like that. Bully? Junk had never heard anyone use it in that context. Doctor James Oak. 'Call me Jamie, like the cooking man. Bish-bosh-wibble-wobble.' Junk had no idea what that meant. Oak seemed fairly young for the position he held: medical director of St Jude's Psychiatric Hospital on the outskirts of Athenry, County Galway, about fifteen miles east of the city of Galway. He was a tall man, pole-thin with a pointed nose and a pointed chin. His hair was wispy and brittle-looking and what there was of it was a very pale blond colour. His scalp was prawn-pink and, thought Junk, always looked a little sore. Aggravated. He wore black jeans that were ironed in exactly the way jeans should never be ironed, and a series of polo necks. Junk knew it was Tuesday because today he was wearing a purple one. Tuesdays were always purple. Mondays brown, Wednesdays white, Thursdays blue, Fridays teal. Junk had called it green once and Dr Oak had corrected him, looking rather insulted by the aspersion that he would ever wear a colour as basic as green. Brown presumably wasn't brown but russet, and purple was probably lavender or amethyst. Junk wondered what he wore on the weekend. Did Saturday and Sunday have their own colour too or did he wear something completely different on those days?

'Soooooo, Colin,' said Dr Oak. He refused to call him Junk. No one had ever called him Colin. Not his parents, not his teachers. But Dr Oak said the nickname was an 'unhealthy remnant of his former life'. They had to 'reboot his motherboard' and 'give him a serious alt-control-delete sesh'. Junk didn't know what that meant either. 'Gok Wan your id' sounded painful. Dr Oak went on: 'Weeeeee've got you back, haven't we? You'rrrrrrre back in the room. Back in the room, out of your head, half the battle. Yes?'

'Yeah,' said Junk, his voice quiet. Oak didn't really need or want him to answer. Junk always had the impression that he was mostly superfluous to these one-on-one therapy sessions.

'But half the battle isn't aaaaaaall the battle, is it?'

'No, it's half,' said Junk.

'Exxxxxactly,' said Oak, nodding for slightly too long as he stared at Junk. 'What we want— what we need,' he corrected himself, 'is to focus on what is alllllllll the battle and that is how we win the war.'

'Sure,' said Junk.

'So today I want to talk some more about your fantasy world.' Junk sighed. That was all Oak ever wanted to talk about. 'Nnnnnnnnnnnnow, in your own words, in your own time, tell me everything.'

3

Junk didn't need to clarify what it was that Oak meant. 'Everything' meant everything that had happened since the night that twelve-year-old Junk killed his sister. Junk didn't have any memory of what really happened that night. However, he accepted now that Jacid Mestrowe, the three-metre-tall, hairless, silver-skinned, scarred assassin, evolved over millions of years from a shark, had never existed. He was a figment of Junk's warped mind. The same warped mind that had made him carry, probably drag, Ambeline, then just six-years-old, screaming and kicking and terrified, to the edge of the cliffs by their house and hurl her to her death in the roiling sea below. Junk was evil. He understood that. Dr Oak had explained it to him. He was an abhorrent human being. Except he didn't feel abhorrent. He didn't feel evil. But he guessed bad people didn't go around thinking about how bad they were.

So Junk accepted that Jacid Mestrowe had never existed. He, Junk, had done this terrible thing and created an actual 'monster' as a scapegoat. But he could not remember, however hard he tried, what he really did that night. He couldn't picture himself dragging little Ambeline from the bed and pulling her to the cliff-edge. Dr Oak assured him that he would remember in time. Thing is, Junk wasn't sure he wanted to remember. Ever. But he had to. He knew that. Remembering would be the cruellest penance. Being locked up in this place, maybe for the rest of his life, didn't come close to punishing him enough for what he had done. He was supposed to

4

have looked after Ambeline. Supposed to have been her knight. He had failed spectacularly.

Junk took a deep breath and recounted his 'story' again. They had been over this so many times now that Junk had lost count, but he assumed Dr Oak knew what he was doing. After all, they didn't let just anyone run a psychiatric hospital. Did they? So Junk dutifully recounted everything that had happened, or rather that he had imagined had happened, ever since the time he ran away from home nearly three-and-a-half years ago.

He talked about working his way around the world on different boats, searching for some clue to what had taken his sister. What he had found was the League of Sharks and a doorway to a room full of doors, a room of endless possibilities, a room connecting every point in time and space. Each time Oak got him to repeat it, it sounded ever more fantastical to him. He had stepped through a doorway that took him to the far future. Three million years into the future. Why he had chosen that time he had no idea. He talked about meeting Garvan and Lasel, Otravinicus and Cascér. He described finding the creature who killed his sister, only to discover that Ambeline was still alive in this future world.

Dr Oak made a clucking noise in the back of his throat and Junk paused to look at him.

'Is something wrong?' asked Junk.

'No!' said Oak shaking his head. 'No, no, no, no, no, no, no, no, nooooooo. Not at all.' Junk was about to continue when Oak spoke over him. 'It's just classic, that's all.'

'What is?'

'In your fantasy, your sister's not dead so you can undo the terrible thing that you did. Do you see? Textbook stuff. You see it in lots of psychopaths. Anyway, carry on.'

Psychopath. Oak dropped the word so casually. Is that what Junk was? He supposed he must be. His stomach cramped.

'Carry on,' said Oak more insistently.

So Junk forced himself to continue. He recounted his search for the Nine Emperors. He talked about the Antricle, a device that was both key and map to the Room of Doors, and how he had discovered its hidden properties and how it took him and Lasel to a space station manned by four-faced universe-building cyborgs.

'Why . . .' Dr Oak interrupted again, 'I wonder . . . why-why-why-why-why-why-whhhhhhhhhhhhhy did your mind conjure up this incredible contraption?' He had asked the same question dozens of times and Junk didn't have a better answer now any more than the first time he had asked. 'Don't stop,' said Oak. 'You've stopped. Don't stop.'

But that was pretty much all of the story. He had taken on an army belonging to the Nine Emperors and decimated it with the help of fighter planes from the Second World War and a herd of startled brachiosauruses from the Jurassic era. He'd discovered that one of the Nine Emperors, Foster Peck, had been his mother's boyfriend, long before she had married his dad, and he'd had Ambeline kidnapped to punish Junk's mother for breaking his heart. However, Ambeline had run away almost as soon as he got her, and Peck had no idea what had become of her.

The trail had gone cold, and then the new medication Dr Oak had prescribed had succeeded in bringing Junk back to the real world, where he had woken up in St Jude's and had started his never-ending therapy sessions.

When Junk had finished, Oak sat nodding his head for an extensive period of time while Junk listened to the ticking of the grandfather clock that stood in the corridor outside Dr Oak's office.

'Let's talk in some more detail about . . .' said Oak finally, and Junk knew what was coming – '. . . the Antricle.'

'Why do you always want to talk about that?' Junk said, failing to hide the irritation in his voice.

Dr Oak looked up sharply. He was not a man who liked to be questioned.

'Because,' he said, 'I think it is the key to unlocking the barriers that are damming your memory. In your fantasy world, it is after all a key. It unlocks your ability to go anywhere. It is staaaaaaaaaggeringly clear to me that the Room of Doors is you.'

'It is?' asked Junk.

'Oh yes. Your consciousness. Your mind.'

7

'A great empty space,' muttered Junk. 'Thanks a lot.'

'Except it isn't empty, is it? It's full of portals, and one of those portals is the pathway home. It'll bring you back. And in your mind you have created this Antricle, which is a key, a map, a guardian. Something you can manipulate with thought processes alone. If we can work out how you achieve that manipulation in your imagined world, what makes the connection between you and this device, then I think we can fix you.'

'I'm not sure I wanna be fixed,' said Junk, the words coming out before he could stop them.

Oak frowned. 'Of course you do, Colin. Don't be ridiculous. Why wouldn't you want to be fixed?' He looked genuinely confused.

'Because being fixed means remembering what I did,' said Junk staring at the green Crocs on his feet. He looked up at Oak. 'Would you want to remember that?'

'Yes. Yes, I would. Very much.'

'Why?' asked Junk.

Oak looked blankly at him and it was clear he didn't have a good answer.

'Time's up for today,' said the doctor. 'We'll pick this up tomorrow.'

Junk sighed and got to his feet. Oak had already turned to face his laptop and resolutely ignored Junk as he left.

2

The clock outside Dr Oak's office told Junk that it was almost six o'clock and therefore time for dinner. The hospital ran to a strict timetable, so Junk navigated the labyrinth of corridors to the dining hall. His Crocs squeaked on the cracked linoleum.

Oak cutting the session off so abruptly wasn't unusual. That was his default move whenever he was stumped for an answer. He was a man who didn't like to not have an answer, so he would simply change the rules whenever the situation called for it. Once he cut a session short after just three minutes, suddenly remembering he had to go to Galway or something.

When Junk had first found himself resident in St Jude's he did everything he could to deny the reality of his surroundings. After all, when he had been with his friends on board the Casabia or fighting the Nine Emperors, it had all felt just as real. He had tried to avoid taking his pills. A blue-and-yellow one in the morning and a green one in the evening. His hope was that without them he would just slip back into his imagined world and be reunited with Lasel and Garvan. However, it proved impossible to ditch his meds. His very first attempt was spotted straight away, and they were given by injection while two burly orderlies held him down. He didn't like that, so he had no choice but to take the pills.

Little by little, his defences had crumbled. The Room of Doors, Pirestus Octonary . . . all of it was unbelievable when he stopped to think about it. St Jude's with its stained floors, pockmarked Formica tables in the dining hall, the rickety beds with their painfully thin mattresses, none of that was unbelievable. That was all so depressingly normal that it had to be real.

As Junk reached the top of the staircase leading down to the dining room, he heard his name being called.

'Better get a wiggle on there, Junky.'

He turned to see one of the hospital's orderlies. He was a giant of a man. Somewhere around two metres tall and broad as a tree. He always had a smile on his lopsided face and the top of his head was crowned by a fiery explosion of tight, bright orange curls. 'Shepherd's pie tonight. Lotsy'll be on his thirds already.'

It was Dr Oak's assertion that Junk's fantasy world had been built using bricks that his subconscious had found in the real world around him, and when Junk looked at the big orderly he couldn't help but see Garvan. Even the orderly's name was undeniably similar.

'On my way there now, Gavin,' said Junk. The pair

walked along together, Junk having to almost run to keep up with the big man's gait. Just like he'd had to with Garvan.

'Been up with Dr Oak, have ya?' asked Gavin. 'How was that?'

'Same as always,' said Junk with a shrug.

'Ah, he means well and he's a clever fella, that man. There's no denying that.'

Junk wasn't so sure, but there was no point disagreeing with Gavin so he moved his head in a way that could possibly be interpreted as a nod and said, 'I guess.'

'And listen,' said Gavin, 'I've been here long enough to see that he's right more than he's wrong. I mean, I wouldn't go 'round telling him that to his face. We don't want him going off and getting himself a big head now, do we?' Too late, Junk thought. 'But it's a dumb ass who ignores good advice for no good reason. My father told me that. Which, ironically, was the only good piece of advice he ever gave me.'

'So I should only ignore it if I have good reason is what you're saying?' said Junk.

Gavin slowed to a stop as they approached the door to the dining room and frowned. 'Now what good reason could you have?'

'How does remembering the terrible thing I did help anyone? Does it bring my sister back? No. I think some things are probably best forgotten.' Gavin opened his mouth to speak but Junk cut him off. 'No matter

11

what Dr Oak might think.' Gavin closed his mouth again.

Junk could see the disappointment on Gavin's face. That hadn't been Junk's intention and he wanted to say something else, to make it better, but he couldn't think what. Then Gavin said, 'You better get in there before there's nothing left.' He gave Junk a reassuring tap on his shoulder and Junk watched as the big orderly plodded away. His girth almost filled the corridor. Junk sighed before opening the door to the dining room.

He was met with a wall of chatter that he hadn't heard outside. The soundproofing in the doors here was second to none. There were about forty resident patients in the hospital and they were all ages, from teenagers like him up to the Captain, an old merchant-navy man in his seventies maybe. Junk wasn't sure. The Captain was short but stout, a roly-poly barrel of a man, possessed of an utterly infectious laugh that started way down in the depths of his cavernous belly and ping-ponged all the way up until it burst from his throat like a foghorn. As if on cue, he heard it from across the room and turned to look.

On a round table in front of the window, the Captain was holding court as usual. Probably telling one of his many stories. He had a seemingly endless catalogue of them, but no one minded as they were never anything less than entertaining. Sitting around him were the friends Junk had made since coming out of his catatonia, and if Dr Oak's theory, that Junk had built his fantasy from the world around him here in the hospital, was correct, some of the parallels were all too obvious.

To the left of the Captain was an ex-boxer. At the age of fifty-two, Julius 'The Juggernaut' Campbell decided that he no longer wanted to live a lie, so he became Judith Campbell. Judith's wife and adult children couldn't accept the change and insisted she seek help. And although Judith made it clear that she didn't want help, she did like the peace and quiet at St Jude's. Unfortunately Judith was not the most feminine of women. In fact, Julius 'The Juggernaut' Campbell (who fought in the super-heavyweight class) had been about as masculine a man as a man can be. Now Judith wore a long blonde wig, which had a tendency to slip off her hairless head at the least provocation, and chunky pendulous earrings. It seemed clear to Junk that Judith had been his psyche's inspiration for Cascér.

To the right of the Captain was Roger. Though he shared very little in common physically with Brother Antor, the zealous monk who had sworn to protect the Antricle, Roger was also a devoutly religious man, who had been admitted to St Jude's when he became convinced that God was speaking to him through the medium of his kettle every time it boiled. The kettle (or God) had told him to go to the Body Shop on Shop Street in Galway and liberate all the bodies they kept there. Junk had never understood if these bodies were supposed to be alive or dead. Roger had become a little upset when he had been unable to find anything resembling a body on the premises, which had led to a small siege. Because Roger's only weapons during the incident had been a detangling comb and a tube of peppermint foot lotion, he had been swiftly sent to St Jude's for assessment rather than being sent to prison.

Next to Roger was Rory, a sweet, painfully shy young man who, from the age of fourteen, had been able to communicate to the outside world only through Dennis and Jean, a couple who ran a B & B targeted specifically at cats in the County Limerick area, but who were in reality Rory's hands. He had painted lips around his thumbs and curled forefingers and eyes around the knuckles. Whenever he had anything to say it was either through 'Dennis' (his left hand) or 'Jean' (his right). And almost everything they said would have some reference to cats even when not remotely appropriate: Would you pass the salt, please? We had a Japanese bobtail stay with us in June who loved salt on everything he ate. Terribly bad for their digestion, you know, salt. Would you pass the salt, please? It was next to impossible to have an actual conversation with Rory (or with 'Dennis' and 'Jean'). Junk thought back to a kitchen in his fantasy world. It had belonged to a couple called Yartik and Huppa. There he had drunk some tea, brewed for him by Garvan from the leaves of the nolic plant. It had caused him to hallucinate wildly and in his hallucination both of his hands had disconnected themselves from his wrists. One had turned into a seat for the other one, who spoke like Sean Connery and guided Junk through a vision of what was to come. It was obvious now that Rory had been Junk's influence there.

Next to Rory was a young woman with long coppery hair that snaked down her back, almost to her waist. She looked to be the same age as Junk but in truth she was three years his senior. Junk looked older than he was. He was tall and broad-shouldered. He shared his father's masculine build and people tended to assume he was an adult, when in reality he was still only sixteen. His last birthday had been just before he had come out of his catatonic state. The young woman with the long coppery hair was called Lisa. She was here because she was a kleptomaniac. She could not stop stealing. She was slim and graceful and moved with a dancer's step. She had dimples in her cheeks and incandescent blue eyes; she was so obviously his inspiration for Lasel. Junk was rather smitten, though he didn't know if he was smitten with Lisa or Lasel. Except Lisa was Lasel, and what's more there was no Lasel. Thoughts like that could send a person crazy, thought Junk. Lucky he was in here then.

Junk saw Lisa look over to him and smile. She nodded her head towards the empty chair next to her, and he knew she had saved it for him. He was pretty sure whatever feelings he had for her were reciprocated.

Junk crossed to the serving hatch, picking up a tray as he went. As Gavin had said, shepherd's pie was on the menu, along with hot rice pudding with a dollop of strawberry jam in the middle. He knew this was Lisa's favourite. He lay his tray down in front of the opening

15

and gave Mrs Flood, the sour-faced cook, a bright smile. She was puffing on an e-cigarette and glowering at him. He didn't take it personally; she glowered at everyone.

'I'm out of beans,' she said. 'If you wanted beans you should have got here sooner.'

'That's fine,' said Junk. 'I'm not mad keen on beans anyway.'

'What's wrong with me beans?' asked Mrs Flood, turning her glower to a scowl.

'Nothing,' said Junk. 'Just not a big bean fan. More of a carrot man.' He directed his gaze to a stainless-steel serving tray full of sliced carrots drowning in a lake of melted butter being kept hot under heat lamps. Mrs Flood seemed to go out of her way to keep the dairy industry afloat with the amount of butter she used. 'Those are some good-looking carrots, Mrs Flood.'

Mrs Flood sniffed and her scowl lessened, returning to a glower, and just a small one to one side of her face at that. 'Yeah, well, they are, as it happens. What I don't know about cooking carrots isn't worth knowing.'

'The same can be said for all your food, Mrs Flood.' Junk was laying it on thick, but he was hoping for an extra helping of the rice pudding. And it was working. Mrs Flood's glower faded even more and the hint of a smile considered appearing at the corner of her lips. 'It's never anything less than delicious. You could open your own restaurant.'

That did it and a smile exploded across her whole face. 'Do you really think so?'

'Are you kidding me?' said Junk. 'People would come all the way from Dublin for that rice pudding of yours alone.'

'Oh, go on!' said Mrs Flood, her cheeks reddening. 'Dublin's over a hundred miles away.'

'It'd be worth the trip for that rice pudding.'

Mrs Flood let out a little coquettish titter then and, glancing about, gave Junk an extra portion. 'It shouldn't sit there too long anyway,' she said, whispering conspiratorially. 'Starts to congeal if it does.'

Junk smiled and picked up his tray. 'You're the best, Mrs Flood,' he said as he turned away.

As he crossed to the round table in front of the window, he had to pass Neil Quigley and his gang of buffoons. He'd never used the word 'buffoons' before, least not that he could remember, but buffoons just seemed to be right for this bunch. Maybe it was because 'buffoons' sounded a little like 'baboons', and Neil and his friends resembled a pack of snarling, flea-bitten apes.

Neil was a former lollipop man who in full display of parents and pupils on their way to school had had a breakdown and decided he was a samurai battling attacking hordes. The attacking hordes were mostly cars and pram-wheeling mothers. Fortunately he was a rubbish samurai and didn't manage to hurt anyone, before the headmistress of the primary school, having heard the commotion he was causing, came out and tackled him to the ground. She had taken self-defence

17

classes. She sat on him till the police and an ambulance turned up.

When Neil arrived at St Jude's he still thought he was a samurai and went about assembling a group of like-minded individuals. The best he could manage was a group of simple-minded individuals who literally had nothing better to do. He insisted that there had to be seven in total because of some old black-and-white Japanese film, which as far as anyone could tell he had never actually seen. He got his seven, but then one of them insisted his room-mate be allowed to join them even though that made eight. Neil gave in and then someone else wanted their room-mate to join too, and because he had set the precedent with the first room-mate, Neil felt he couldn't say no. After that, however, he said absolutely no one else was allowed unless someone else left first. People didn't tend to leave St Jude's, and no one wanted to leave the group, so it stopped with nine members. It wasn't lost on Junk that in his fantasy world the Nine Emperors had kidnapped his sister and the only people he didn't like here were Neil and his band of pretend samurai. The parallels were all around him if he chose to see them.

As Junk passed their table, Neil pushed a chair out with his foot so it blocked Junk's path. Junk had no idea why Neil disliked him so much. The two had never actually spoken, at least not as far as Junk could remember. Since Junk tried to ignore Neil as much as he could, he simply stepped up and over the chair, blanking

Neil as he went. Junk wasn't intimidated by Neil, who was a rather diminutive man, a good foot shorter than Junk. Neil muttered something in Japanese as Junk passed, except it wasn't actually Japanese because Neil couldn't speak Japanese. It was a nonsensical made-up language that was merely Neil's idea of what Japanese sounded like. All nine of his gang spoke this made-up language, which was nothing but random noises, accentuated with short, sharp jerks of the head several times during every sentence. Watching them from a distance, one would think they were a table of nine people plagued with uncontrollable twitches. The group spoke like this all the time unless they actually wanted something, in which case they would revert to English so they could be understood.

When Junk reached the round table, the Captain was telling a story Junk hadn't heard before. Junk was sorry he'd missed the start but knew it wouldn't be long before he'd be able to catch the repeat. He sat down next to Lisa, who had already finished her meal and was leaning back listening to the Captain speak. Junk slid the extra rice pudding in front of her without a word. Lisa smiled but didn't look at him. She grabbed her spoon from the empty bowl of her first dessert and stabbed it into the jammy red heart in the centre of the translucent white rice. As she moved to take a bite, she brushed against Junk and a jolt of excitement shuddered through him. His mind whirled as many thoughts vied for supremacy all at once. The winner was one that said he had started this infatuation with someone else, someone who didn't exist, admittedly, but it still made him feel like he was being disloyal to Lasel. But how could he be disloyal to a figment of his imagination?

Just then, the Captain's woody baritone found its way into his consciousness and he heard something that was familiar.

'. . . swore blind . . .' the Captain was saying, '. . . he was descended from a chap called Bernard O'Higgins Requelme.'

'Bernardo,' said Junk as a discarded memory resurfaced. All eyes turned to look at him. 'Sorry, Captain, didn't mean to interrupt. I missed the beginning of the story.'

'I was telling everyone about the time I was in Valparaíso in—'

Junk finished his sentence: 'Chile.'

The Captain frowned. 'That's right. Have I told this story before? I don't want to go repeating myself.'

'No, no,' said Junk. 'Finish the story. Please.'

It took little encouragement. 'So I found this scruffy little dive bar on the waterfront. Met this crusty old timer. Salvador de Valdivia his name was.'

Junk mouthed the name along with him. He could see the wrinkled-prune of a man now. Junk had met him in that same bar. Salvador had been the first person to tell Junk about La Liga de los Tiburones, the League of Sharks. Except of course he hadn't, because Junk had never been to Chile. Despite knowing that to be true, he could see Salvador's face as clearly as he could see the Captain and the others sat around the table. He could remember vividly the pungent smell of the old man's tobacco, the stink of cheap alcohol on his breath, the rough skin on his gnarled hands, his expressive leathery face, the button missing from his faded maroon waistcoat, his crooked brown teeth, his ragged yellow fingernails. He could see all that in his mind's eye but none of it was real.

'General Pinochet had a Scottish Fold called Mr Miaow Miaow.' All eyes turned to Rory and then swivelled down to look at his right hand, 'Jean', which was peering up over the lip of the table.

'A what?' asked Lisa, addressing the hand directly; they all did it.

'Scottish Fold. It's a cat, dear,' said 'Jean'. 'Big eyes, bent ears. Funny-looking little things.'

'Doted on that cat, he did,' added 'Dennis'.

'General Pinochet?' asked Roger, raising an incredulous eyebrow. 'The dictator? Had a cat called Mr Miaow Miaow?'

'That's right,' said 'Jean'.

'Hitler had an Egyptian Mau and Pol Pot had a Selkirk Rex,' added 'Dennis'. 'Very popular pet among dictators.'

A canopy of silence hung over the table. There was little anyone could say to follow that, not even the Captain, who was rarely at a loss for words. Just then, Gavin entered and announced it was time for everyone to retire to their rooms for the night. St Jude's had a somewhat monastic policy of quiet, solitary contemplation after dinner.

As everyone rose with a clatter of metal chair legs scraping the parquet floor, Junk saw Lisa palm a stainless-steel salt cellar, sliding it discreetly into her pocket. The salt cellar was worthless and not even particularly attractive. It was egg-shaped with a flat bottom and looked like any number of other salt shakers. Lisa had stolen sixteen identical ones from this very room since she became resident at St Jude's. Or rather she had possibly stolen the same salt cellar sixteen times, because she always brought them back. Her stealing was a compulsion and had very little to do with any desire for a particular object. It was all about the act itself. Junk said nothing and filed out with everyone else.

Junk lay in his bed looking out, across the courtyard, to the huge old clock tower. It was almost as high as the surrounding buildings and had four separate faces, one on each side. Junk wondered if the clock tower had been his blueprint for Espa and the giants of Pirestus Octonary. He didn't feel remotely tired and assumed he would be awake for a few hours, but before he knew it the sun was shining on him and it was a new day.

3

The next morning Junk was walking through the hallways on his way to Dr Oak's office for yet another one-on-one session. It had occurred to him already that not everyone could get the same level of treatment he was receiving. He had seen Dr Oak every day, sometimes more than once, since coming out of his catatonic state. If Oak did that for all his patients he would have to work all day every day, and even then he still wouldn't be able to fit everyone in. Junk assumed he was a special case, seeing as how he had been here for three years and had been about as talkative as a chair before he woke up. There were a lot of missed sessions to catch up on. Or maybe it was because of the terribleness of what he had done. It occurred to him then that the other patients were mostly harmless. Lisa had a compulsion to steal, Judith wanted some peace and quiet, Rory was just a confused young man. In contrast, Junk was a murderer. He was the odd one out. He didn't belong here. He should be somewhere much worse.

Suddenly he realized how very quiet everything

was. He listened for sounds of life but there was nothing. No birdsong or traffic noise. No sounds of laughter or crying or screaming or anything from the other patients. It was like he was completely alone. Just then, as if the building itself could read his mind, he heard whistling. The sound began abruptly and grew closer and closer until Gavin appeared from the adjacent corridor and walked towards him.

'There you are,' he said. 'Been looking for you.'

'I'm just on my way to see Dr Oak,' said Junk.

'Yeah, change of plan,' said Gavin. 'It was Dr Oak what sent me to find you. You've got a visitor.'

Junk was shocked. That was the last thing he had been expecting. He hadn't had a visitor in all the time he was here. Even when he was catatonic. (He had asked.)

'Who is it?'

'It's your ma,' said Gavin, and Junk shivered involuntarily. His mother? He hadn't seen her for over three years. She had never visited him as far as he knew. So why now? Why today?

'Why?' he asked.

Gavin looked surprised by the question. He shrugged and shook his head. 'I don't know. Does she need a reason? She's your mum after all.'

Junk looked down at his hands. They were shaking. His mouth felt dry and his stomach was shrinking and twisting to the size of a walnut. Junk realized that he was scared. The last time he had seen her had not gone well, having ended with him leaving his house in the middle of the night and starting a journey that . . . He stopped mid-thought. He hadn't considered this before, but now he wondered if that last time with his mother, in the kitchen of their house when her rage had overflowed and made her destroy everything that wasn't nailed down and a few things that were, had that actually happened? When had his 'break from reality' – an expression Dr Oak was fond of repeating – actually started? It would make sense if everything from the moment he had seen Jacid Mestrowe in his bedroom was all in Junk's mind. Which would mean that that last terrible interaction with his mother in the kitchen had never actually taken place.

'Junk?'

It took Junk a moment to realize that Gavin was talking to him.

'Sorry,' said Junk. 'Mind wandered.'

'Come on,' said Gavin. 'She's waiting.' He gestured for Junk to walk with him. Junk hesitated. He couldn't think of a way to avoid seeing her other than point-blank refusing. He knew that would probably lead to Dr Oak becoming involved, and Dr Oak being involved would inevitably lead to a long and wordy lecture until Junk gave in. At the same time, Junk wasn't entirely sure why he was trying to find ways to avoid seeing her. Part of him wanted to see her and part of him was scared to see her, but there wasn't a part that didn't actually want to see her.

'Junk!' Gavin was more forceful this time.

'Yeah, sorry,' said Junk. 'I'm coming. I'm coming.' And he and Gavin set off.

St Jude's was a sprawling eyesore of a building. The oldest part of the house had been built in the late-eighteenth century; it had been added to half a dozen times since then, but with little thought to the aesthetics. It was like some great lumbering deformed creature trying to drag itself into the sea, probably in an attempt to end its miserable existence.

The west side of the building opened out on to unkempt, overgrown lawns that led down towards a broad flat beach of yellow shingle and this was where, Junk assumed, Dr Oak had suggested he and his mother meet. Junk liked it there. There wasn't a lot to look at, but with his back to the hospital he could pretend he was somewhere else entirely. He could stare out at the distant horizon and on a calm, dull day, like today, the sea and sky were cold and grey and featureless. He found it easy to clear his mind then and think of nothing at all. The silence brought a state of serenity.

Gavin walked with Junk along a snaking path of trodden-down grass to the brow of a hillock beyond which was the beach. Time slowed down for Junk as they came over the rise. He saw a lone figure dressed in a long red coat standing by the water's edge, looking away from him. If he didn't know who it was he wouldn't have recognized her. She looked smaller and thinner, not that she had ever been particularly big. Since the age of eleven Junk had been taller than his mother.

Junk stopped walking and stared down at her. He could feel Gavin looking at him.

'Well?' said Gavin softly. 'Go on.'

'What if she hates me?' said Junk, more to himself than to Gavin, but he said it out loud. His voice sounded young. A child's voice.

'Course she doesn't hate you. She's your mother. Mothers can't hate their children.' That wasn't true of course, and Junk knew Gavin didn't actually believe that. It was just something to say. 'I'll be right here if you need me.'

The beach levelled out at the foot of an embankment and Junk started trudging down to the shoreline, each footfall sinking into the stones as they spread out under his weight. He was glad then that the beach was made of pebbles and not sand. It meant that his mother could hear him coming. He saw her head cock slightly as she heard the approach of his footsteps but she didn't turn around. Junk kept walking until he reached the lapping waves and stood level with his mother but not too close. Janice Doyle didn't speak or move. She just kept staring ahead. Junk would have liked her to acknowledge him first. He would have been able to assess her mood.

'Hi,' he said finally when the silence grew too loud for him to bear. He kept his eyes looking out to sea, fixed firmly on the horizon.

His mother took a deep breath then and slowly

turned her head. When she saw him she let out a sharp gasp.

'Look at you,' she said, her American accent a little more hidden than he remembered. 'You're all grown up. You're a man. You look like your father.'

Junk turned his head towards her, but hesitantly. He kept his eyes looking down at the stones. He saw her shoes first: chestnut-brown boots. The toes were scuffed and the leather scarred. They stopped just below her knees. There was a gap between the top of the boots and the hem of her red coat where he could see a strip of denim jeans. His gaze kept rising, taking his time. One of the gold buttons of the coat was loose, dangling by a precarious thread. He wondered if she knew and thought about warning her that she was in danger of it falling off, but he didn't want that to be the first real thing he said to her after all this time. Then he noticed that the end of her sleeves were frayed. A decorative button on the left cuff was missing altogether and there was a stain on the lapel. It was something dark, like red wine or coffee. It was an old stain. Someone had tried to rub it out but only managed to smudge it, causing it to spread out more. It had been scrubbed until the material of the coat beneath had started to bobble. That wasn't right. Junk's mother had always been a very stylish woman. She was one of those people who made looking good seem effortless.

Junk raised his eyes further and looked at his mother's face. It was a shock. She looked ten years older, maybe more. Her face was thin, gaunt even, and deeply lined. Her skin was pale and blotchy. There were charcoal-grey bags beneath her eyes and her hair was lank and greasy. She wasn't wearing any make-up other than some cheap lipstick that was patchy and caked in the corners of her mouth. Their eyes met but only for a moment before Janice turned away. She reached into her pocket and pulled out a packet of cigarettes. The writing on the front was Polish or something like that. She never used to smoke, but Junk noticed the middle finger of her right hand was now stained yellow. She took out a cigarette, lit it and took a deep drag, running her fingers through her hair.

'Do you . . . ?' She held out the packet. 'Do you want one? I guess you're old enough now.'

Junk shook his head. 'I don't smoke.'

She coughed. It was short and sharp with a gurgle of phlegm behind it. 'Very wise. Wish I hadn't started again. My friend Luka brings these over from Romania. There're cheap as anything. Real cigarettes cost a fortune these days. You can take some if you want. Don't you use them for money in here?'

'This isn't prison, Mum.' The last word got stuck in his throat. It sounded odd to say it after all this time, but Janice didn't seem to notice. She didn't react to the word in any way.

'What's it like here?' she asked.

'It's, you know, OK, I guess. It's all sort of new to me.'

'Yeah,' said Janice. 'I spoke with your doctor. What's he called?'

'Dr Oak.'

'That's him. Seems nice. Bit full of himself. He said you've had a major breakthrough. The drugs or whatever.'

'Yeah.'

'Said you'd created this whole other world for yourself in your head.' Junk shrugged. He didn't want to talk about it. 'What were you doing?'

'What?'

'In this other world, what were you doing?'

Junk didn't want to answer that question. He knew he would have to answer truthfully. He knew he couldn't lie. He wanted to go back to his room. Even though it was a dull day, it felt too bright and the excess of light was giving him a headache. Or maybe it was something else.

'I was looking f . . .' His voice trailed off.

'What were you looking for?'

'Ambeline.' His voice was almost a whisper.

'Oh,' said his mother. She took a long final drag on her cigarette and ground it into the shale beneath her foot.

Junk needed to change the subject, and fast. 'How's Dad?' he asked.

'He's . . .' She hesitated. 'He's OK, I guess. I mean, I don't really know. I've not seen him for a while.'

'What? How come?' The question escaped before

Junk could stop himself, though a moment of thought probably would have answered the question without having to vocalize it.

'Well, we're not together any more. It was too difficult. There was a lot of anger after what you d—' She stopped herself. 'After what happened. We blamed each other for not seeing the signs.'

What signs? thought Junk. How could anyone else have seen them when he wasn't even aware of them?

'He's got a girlfriend. Annie or Amy or something like that. I've never met her. She's young. They've got a kid.'

'What?' Junk was finding it hard to process all this.

Janice nodded and lit another cigarette, pausing to pick strands of tobacco off her tongue. 'A boy. You've got a little brother. Half-brother. Dermot, I think he's called, something beginning with D anyway. I forget.'

There was a lot to take in. His father had moved away and seemingly moved on.

'That's kind of why I came here today,' his mother said.

'What is?' asked Junk.

'Your father. He's . . .'

'He's what?' said Junk anxiously. It sounded bad. Was he ill?

'Settled.' She made it sound like a bad thing. 'He's happy. He's moved on. It's not right.' Junk could tell that that wasn't quite what she meant. 'It's not fair.' That was what she meant. 'I want to move on. I want to be happy again.' She sucked hard on the cigarette and her drawn cheeks tightened. Her skin was paper thin and Junk could see the outline of her teeth.

'What do you want me to do?' asked Junk.

'I need to know what happened that night.'

'I don't remember what happened.'

'Then I need you to remember.'

'I can't.'

'Dr Oak said that's not true. You can. You just don't want to. I have to know, Junk.' She finished her second cigarette and this time flicked it into the sea. 'Dr Oak said there's something from your fantasy that's the key to unlocking your memory. The Antricle, I think he called it.'

'That's just a dumb thing I made up.' Junk focused on the sodden butt of his mother's discarded cigarette bobbing on the surface of the water.

'Well, Dr Oak says it means something. I don't know. I don't know how your head works. I don't know how my head works. I'm not the expert. He is. He says that if you can remember that, then it'll unlock all your other memories and then you can tell me why you did what you did. I need to know if it was my fault.'

'No, Ma, it wasn't—'

She cut him off. Her voice rising. 'How do you know? If you can't remember, how do you know?' She calmed down a little and lit another cigarette. Junk wanted to make her stop. This wasn't his mother. What had he done to her? 'I have to know the truth and I think

32

you owe me that.' A tear ran down her cheek. She wiped it away and Junk noticed her chipped, torn fingernails. His mother had always had immaculate nails. Always shaped, always painted. 'I should go.'

'Will you come back?' Junk asked the question without thinking about it. It just tumbled out of his mouth.

'Do you want me to?' asked Janice.

'Of course,' said Junk.

She nodded. 'OK,' she said. 'We'll see. Maybe.' She threw her half-smoked third cigarette into the sea and turned. 'Well, you take care of yourself. Do what the doctors tell you. Remember they have your best interests at heart.' She paused for a moment then and Junk thought she was about to hug him and it wasn't until that moment that he realized how desperate he was to feel his mother's arms around him. But she didn't hug him. She creased her thin mouth into the semblance of a smile, but there was no warmth behind it, and then she nodded her head and walked past him, heading up the beach, her footsteps crunching on the pebbles as she went. Junk watched her make her way up the small embankment. It wasn't easy. The stones fell away beneath her and she had to use her hands for extra purchase. However, she made it to the top and kept going. She didn't look back and quickly disappeared from view.

Junk was in no hurry to return to the hospital so he turned back to look out across the water, sitting down where he stood. The tide was coming in and the water ran up through channels snaking through the millions of small stones. It bubbled just in front of him before retreating so it could regroup before it appeared again. Junk hung his head.

4

That afternoon, Junk sat across from Dr Oak. The physician was perched stiffly behind his desk, his fingers pressed together and resting just under his nose as if he was praying. His pale grey eyes stared at Junk.

'I want to remember,' said Junk.

Dr Oak smiled with his mouth but his eyes remained cold. 'Exxxxxcellent,' he purred. 'No more holding back.'

'I wasn't holding back before,' Junk said defensively. 'I don't know how to remember something like the Antricle. It's not a fact or a name. It's a feeling. You don't think about using the Antricle when you use it. It's like –' Junk struggled to find a good analogy – 'it's another limb. It's like, I don't know, clapping your hands. You don't think, I need to put this hand there –' Junk held out his right hand in front of him – 'and this hand there –' he held out his left hand, his open palm facing the right one – 'and then bring them together!' He clapped his hands. 'You just do it. Right?'

'Right,' said Oak.

'Well, the Antricle's like that.'

'It's like clapping?' said Oak with a deep scowl on his face.

'Well, no. Well, yeah.'

'Which is it?' Oak sounded testy.

'What I'm trying to say is, I didn't need to think about using the Antricle. I just used it. It was like it was part of me.'

'Yes,' said Oak with a sneer. 'Another limb.' He closed his eyes and slowly rubbed at his temples with his index and middle fingers. The action reminded Junk of a teacher from his old school: Mr Pope, a rather sadistic English teacher, who would do that very same action whenever a pupil read aloud in class. Mr Pope would make strained groaning noises in his throat as if the delivery was causing him physical pain.

'Imagine . . .' said Dr Oak, 'that you needed to . . . teach me to manipulate the Antricle. How would you go about instructing me?'

Junk frowned, struggling to know how to answer the question. 'I would say . . . you would need to clear your mind.'

'Good,' said Oak, making a note in his pad. 'What else?'

'You would need to picture what it is you want from the Antricle. What you want it to do. Where you want to go or whatever.'

'Very good, very good. Go on.'

'And then it would happen. Whatever it was you

wanted.' Junk saw Dr Oak grimace. His jaw clenched as he ground his teeth together.

'Let's try something different,' said Oak hoarsely. 'A memory exercise. I want you to close your eyes.'

'OK,' said Junk. He did as instructed.

'Get comfortable on your chair,' said Oak, and Junk made a show of fidgeting, making it appear that he was following instructions, but in reality the chair was hard and unforgiving: there was no getting comfortable.

'Now I want you to think back to a time when you used the Antricle. From your imagined world; it can be anywhere, any time. First place that comes to mind. Tell me where you are.'

'On a battlefield.'

Oak nodded and raised his eyebrows in an expression of interest. 'Describe it to me. What can you see?'

'OK. Behind me is the Palace of Versailles,' said Junk, keeping his eyes closed.

'So you're in France,' said Oak.

'No,' replied Junk.

'No? Last time I looked the Palace of Versailles was a short distance outside of Paris.'

'It had been moved,' said Junk.

'Moved? The entire palace? What, brick by brick? We are talking about the actual Versailles? The royal residence of the French monarchy from Louis XIV?'

'The Magpie Emperor stole it.'

'Ah yes, the Nine Emperors.' Junk had previously

talked about the Nine Emperors, telling Dr Oak all about who they were and how they chose their names, how they created their empires, how they died. Clearly he hadn't mentioned where they had chosen to live. 'How do you steal a building?' asked Oak, sounding incredulous.

'The Antricle. The way it was explained to me was it could open two doorways, one into the other, connecting two different points in space and time and then closing the first or something. To be honest, it was an insane person who explained it to me.' Junk paused. He was talking about Danny, the Pigeon/Peacock Emperor, but it occurred to him now that Danny was a figment of his imagination and he was the insane one. Except Dr Oak didn't like the word insane, or crazy, gaga or fruit loop for that matter. He called them dangerously pejorative. Junk didn't know what that meant. Junk opened his eyes then. 'Sorry,' he said.

Oak shook his head. 'Keep your eyes closed. Go on,' he said, exaggerating an exasperated tone in his voice. 'You're doing well,' he added as somewhat of an afterthought. Junk closed his eyes again. 'So if you're not in France, where are you?'

'Cul Mallia,' said Junk.

'Tell me where that is. In your future world, I mean.'

Junk knew what he meant. 'It would be part of South America. The grass plains of Argentina, I think.'

'Interesting. Carry on telling me what you can see.

Go into as much detail as you can. I want you to lose yourself in the memory.'

'So the palace is behind me, lots of manicured lawns and topiary and things like that. Ahead of me and to the sides are open plains. Flat, featureless. It stretches all the way to the horizon. There's a breeze. Warm air. It smells sweet. I think it's jasmine, but I'm not sure.'

'Jasmine,' Oak repeated. Junk could hear the scrape of Oak's nib writing on his pad. The doctor's scrutiny made Junk analyse his every word. He wondered why he had said jasmine. Was the smell lodged in his subconscious somewhere? Did it refer to something from his real life? Maybe his mother wore jasmine-scented perfume. His mind was beginning to wander when Oak pulled him back.

'Are you alone?' he asked.

'No,' said Junk.

'Who else is there?'

'Soldiers.'

'Soldiers? Why?'

'The Nine Emperors built an army.'

'Where did they get an army from?'

'Everywhere. They collected them from different points in time.'

'How did they do that?'

Junk opened his eyes again. 'How do you mean?'

'Eyes closed,' demanded Oak. Junk sighed but did as he was told. Oak explained himself: 'I mean, how did they persuade these soldiers to work for them? Did they say, We're time travellers – come and join our time-travelling army?'

'I don't know,' said Junk, frowning. 'Maybe.'

'OK, it doesn't matter. Continue. Where have the soldiers come from? Describe them. How many are there?'

'Lots. Twelve hundred, fifteen hundred, maybe more, I don't know. I just see a lot of people. There are Romans. From like ancient Rome. A cohort or a legion or whatever it's called. There's a few hundred of them. Four, five hundred maybe. They're wearing breastplates and their little leather skirt-y things and they've got shields and helmets and swords and spears and what-have-you.'

'Who else?'

'Pallatans.'

'What are they?' asked Oak.

'They're like the person who took Ambeline, Jacid Mestrowe, but they come from a different part of the world to him so their skin's a darker colour. Brown, like milky coffee.'

'Are they dressed like the Romans?'

'No. They just wear clothes. No armour. Their clothes are pretty tatty-looking.'

'But they're from the future,' said Oak, 'why aren't they wearing spacesuits or something?'

Junk opened his eyes again, scowling. After all the conversations he had had with Oak, all the time he had spent in this room, Oak still didn't seem to understand what Junk was talking about. Oak made a snapping gesture with the fingers of his right hand, like a crocodile, that Junk understood meant he should close his eyes again, so he did.

'No. No spacesuits. It's not that sort of future.' There was a weariness creeping into his voice now.

'Who else?'

'Roundheads and Cavaliers. Samurai. They've got elaborate scary masks covering their faces and long, thin swords.'

'Is that all?' asked Oak.

'No, there are others but I don't know who they are. One group looks a bit futuristic maybe. They've got bits of metal all over them. Like with pistons and stuff, you know, to help them move.'

'And the rest?'

'Olde worlde,' said Junk. 'They're wearing chainmail and they've got axes and spiky balls on chains.'

'They're called morning stars,' said Oak. Junk nodded, though the thought occurred to him that although Oak had said that quite definitively, he hadn't been there so how could he know? After all, Junk's description (spiky balls on chains) was a little vague.

'Any more?' asked Oak.

'No, that's it,' said Junk.

'So you have the palace behind you and all these soldiers in front of you. Are you alone?' Junk nodded. 'What about the Antricle? Do you have it with you?' There was a pleading tone to his voice, like he wanted desperately to get to the meat, and for him the

Antricle represented the meat. 'Is it on your wrist?' he asked.

'No,' said Junk. 'I'm wearing it, like armour. It covers all of me from the neck down.'

'How? Tell me how you make it do that? How do you make it cover you?'

Junk focused his mind. He thought back to a few moments before he stepped through a portal on to the battlefield that day. The Antricle had been coiled around his wrist like a fat, dozing coppery serpent. Without a word he had made it spread out, flowing like mercury up his arm, spreading out across his torso and back, cloaking his shoulders, spilling down the opposite arm and cascading down his legs until it encased all of him. How had he done it? What was going through his mind as it was happening?

'I can hear it breathing, the Antricle. It's like it's alive. My breathing falls in time with it. There's a heartbeat. Boom-boom. Boom-boom. That's the Antricle. Mine's the same though. Like, perfectly synchronized. Then I see it spreading out. Picture it in my head flowing all over me. Thinning out. Joining up. Encasing me, and it does it.'

'Just like that?' asked Oak.

'Just like that,' said Junk, opening his eyes. Oak didn't tell him to close them again. He nodded thoughtfully.

'We'll leave it there for today.'

*

Oak had turned his chair and his back on Junk almost immediately and Junk had left his office without another word being spoken between them. Junk supposed he must have been distracted by the session, because all of a sudden he found himself sitting in the TV room. He didn't remember going there, even though it was all the way over on the opposite side of the hospital to Dr Oak's office and was therefore quite a trek. What's more, he rarely ever went there, so it was a surprise to find himself in the unattractive room with wood-panelled walls and mismatched, threadbare furniture, two sofas and four armchairs. All had lopsided cushions and smelt strongly of mildew and dried-in sweat. The lighting was glaringly bright; two fluorescent strips flickered and buzzed intermittently. The TV, which was attached to a metal arm jutting out from the wall just under the picture rail, was old and bulky and the screen was small. The reception sucked and the picture ghosted. As a result of all those factors, the room was usually empty.

Now Junk was aware of where he was, he found himself staring at a horse race on the boxy television. There was a lot of white noise and every horse had a shadow. The monotonous commentary was just a lot of words strung together so closely as to be practically incoherent. Junk managed to pick out every third or fourth word. Someone was apparently coming up on the outside. He didn't know who and he didn't care.

As he moved to get up, one of the armchairs moved

too and Junk cried out in surprise. It took him a moment to realize there was someone else in the room with him. Lisa uncurled her slim legs.

'I was looking for you,' she said. 'Found you in here of all places. Almost didn't check in here. Where were you?'

'What do you mean?' asked Junk.

'When I first got here, I spoke to you but you weren't listening. Your head wasn't in the room, so where were you?'

'I don't know. I'm not sure why I came here. I don't remember coming here.'

'Tar cunnunca ba dusco,' said a woman's voice. The words were Jansian, a language of his imaginary future world. Junk spoke it more or less fluently. The words meant, 'I brought you here.' Junk jerked his head up and looked at Lisa. She was looking back at him.

'W-what did you say?' he asked.

'I said where was your head at? Are you OK?' She looked at him with genuine concern in her eyes.

Junk wasn't entirely sure he was. He was certain he had heard something, but as he looked around the room it was apparent that he and Lisa were the only ones here, and it couldn't have been her. For one thing, it hadn't sounded like her, and what's more, how could she possibly know Jansian? A fictional language from a fictional land that existed only in Junk's insanity. He looked up at the TV screen. The race had finished and the horses and jockeys were sauntering back to the paddocks or wherever they go after a race. The commentator was still speaking, but his voice was less frenetic now. It must have been him and Junk had misheard. That was the only explanation. Unlikely as it was.

'I was going to go for a walk along the shore,' said Lisa. 'I thought you might like to come with me.'

'Umm . . . yeah . . . sure,' said Junk. He was still thinking about the voice he had heard.

'You seem really stressed,' said Lisa. 'Are you sure you're all right? Do you want to talk about anything?'

'Yeah, if you like,' said Junk, only half listening to her at best. 'What do you want to talk about?'

'Did something happen?' asked Lisa.

Junk looked at her. 'Why? Did you hear something?' he asked.

'No,' she said, 'but I know you went to see Dr Oak earlier. What was that about?'

'Oh,' said Junk, realizing she was talking about something else entirely. Of course she was. 'He wants me to remember something.' He hadn't spoken to Lisa or anyone other than the doctor about his fantasy life, and he really didn't want to have to go into details now.

'Why?'

'Why what?'

'Why does he want you to remember whatever it is?'

'He thinks it's important to my . . .' Junk wasn't sure what word to use. Recovery? Mental health? Guilt? He plumped for the former. 'Recovery.'

'Then you should do what he says.'

Junk frowned. Lisa had always struck him as somewhat of a rebel. A rebel without a cause maybe, but a rebel nonetheless. He liked that about her. It seemed strange for her to be toeing the party line so readily, advocating that he follow the orders of the man in charge. 'I should?'

'Sure you should,' she said. 'I'll help you.'

'How would you do that?' he asked.

'Did I ever tell you about the time I joined the circus?' she said, and Junk had to laugh. In her short life – she was only just nineteen years old – Lisa had had more jobs than most people three times her age. She had been a dancer on a Turkish cruise ship and in a South Korean karaoke bar. At an Australian amusement park she had dressed up as Cathy the Kangaroo and entertained three-to-eight-year-olds six times a day, which would involve at least one child a day vomiting into her pouch. She had almost been a hairdresser in Berlin, after lying about her experience of styling hair (she figured, how hard could it be?). Her own hair had been dyed every colour of the rainbow numerous times over the years and she considered that training in itself. So she fabricated some letters of recommendation from three of the best hair salons in the world and talked herself into a tryout. It had turned out to be much harder than it looked and she ended up climbing out of a bathroom window midway through the trial and leaving Berlin twenty minutes later, never to return. She wasn't sure if the hair

46

of the poor student who had agreed to be a test subject in return for a cut-price hairstyle had ever grown back. She'd been a tour guide in New Delhi. It was a job she had managed to talk herself into an hour and half after arriving in India for the first time. Suffice it to say, she knew nothing about New Delhi when she first started, but as her clientele were mostly German and Italian tourists she figured it didn't really matter. She was a firm believer in the idea that if a person says something with enough conviction then it must be true. There are possibly still a handful of Germans and Italians who believe the Taj Mahal was built by Napoleon Bonaparte as a gesture of his love for Anna Karenina, despite the facts that Anna Karenina was a fictional character, that Napoleon had been dead for more than fifty years before Tolstoy's book came out, and that the Taj Mahal itself had been around for about a hundred and twenty years before Napoleon was even born.

'No,' said Junk. 'You've never mentioned the circus.'

'It was while I was in Bulgaria a few years ago. I met a couple of circus people in this bar one night: Bogdan and Elisar. They did aerial work. You know, trapeze, high wire, that sort of thing.' Junk nodded, listening intently. Part of him wondered if Lisa's endless stories were all just a tissue of lies, but he didn't really mind. They were always entertaining, and he liked the idea that she had led such a varied and stimulating life before coming to St Jude's. 'Well, it turned out that there were supposed to be three of them in the act. There had been a girl, but she had gone and got herself in the family way with one of the clowns. She did the aerial silks. You know what that is?' Junk shook his head. 'You climb up these silk ribbons hanging from the ceiling . . . it's not really silk. They just call it that. "Aerial tricot nylon" doesn't sound nearly so exciting. There are no safety wires. You have to twist the silks around you and let yourself drop and catch yourself and things like that. Anyway, they needed a replacement, the pay was all right and I didn't have anywhere to stay, so I joined the circus.'

'Just like that?' said Junk, the corner of his mouth curling into a smirk.

'Most of my life's been just like that,' said Lisa with a sigh exaggerated for effect. 'The point is, while I was there I made friends with the woman who mucked out the horses. Her name was Petra. She was, like, full-blood Romany, like fifteenth generation or something. And she had the Gift.'

'The Gift?' said Junk, giving it even more emphasis than Lisa.

'The Gift, a gift, I don't know. Thing was, she could see into a person's deepest darkest thoughts and she taught me how to do it.'

'Whoa, whoa, whoa, whoa,' said Junk, holding up his hands. 'You're saying this woman was a mind-reader and she just up and told you how to do it?'

'That's right.' She paused, frowning as she realized there was a hint of incredulity in Junk's tone. 'Is that OK?'

'Well, it's just I would assume it takes years to learn how to do something like that. I mean that's if it's even possible. I'm not a big believer in such things.'

'That's OK. It doesn't make what I have to do any harder, and as it happens it doesn't take years to learn at all. She taught me how to do it in an afternoon. Over tea and cakes.'

'Huh!' said Junk, because he couldn't think of anything else to say.

'Ku nenga juut set!' It was the same voice. A female voice. Speaking Jansian again. Junk spun around to look at the TV, but the racing had finished and a commercial was playing. An animated toilet roll was singing about the joys of wiping bottoms. Junk was certain the voice hadn't come from there. So where had it come from?

'Did you hear anything?' he asked Lisa. She hadn't reacted at all to the voice.

'Like what?'

Junk looked blank, not wanting to have to explain. He considered what he had heard: Ku nenga juut set. It meant, 'Do not let her.'

'Are you sure you're OK?' asked Lisa. 'You seem awfully distracted.'

Junk shook his head. 'I've just got a bit of a headache is all.'

'Oh, well, this technique the Romany horse woman showed me works wonders for headaches too. It's just a relaxation thing, but it can help you remember anything. Even if it's something you don't know you know. One time I saw her help Karl, the circus's strongman, find his wedding ring even though he had no memory of taking it off.'

'Well, this is a bit more involved than a missing ring,' said Junk, his mind whirling. He felt a little nauseous. Why was he hearing voices? And why were those voices speaking Jansian?

'Well, of course it is or you wouldn't be here. I was just using that as an example, like. Do you want to give it a go then?'

'Junk, harrutum,' said the voice. Junk, look up.

'Well?' said Lisa, but Junk wasn't listening to her. He raised his head slowly till he was looking up at the ceiling. He didn't see anything out of the ordinary.

'Dusco tar ti,' said the voice. Here I am. Junk tilted his head, turning to look at the TV once again. He froze. His mouth gaping open, his eyes widening with the sight that greeted him. The commercials had finished and the horse racing had resumed. However, in front of the galloping horses, as if superimposed on the screen, was Lasel.

5

Lasel continued speaking in her native tongue. Junk had always had a keen ear for languages and Jansian had been one of the most widely spoken in Jorda, as Earth was known in the future of his imagination. Junk had been quick to learn it as he had travelled with Lasel, Garvan and the others. 'Don't say anything, don't react to me,' she was saying. Junk looked at Lisa, who was staring at him, frowning. 'She can't see or hear me,' said Lasel. Of course not, thought Junk, on account of your being a figment of my imagination.

'But if you react to me,' Lasel continued, 'she'll know something's wrong. You need to get rid of her without making her suspicious.'

Junk wanted to sit down, lie down or fall down. He didn't really have a preference. He was regressing. He knew that. His meds must be failing. It was the only explanation. He knew he should tell Lisa and get her to alert Dr Oak, but part of him was desperate to talk to Lasel again, even if she was imaginary.

'What . . . errr . . . ?' Junk struggled to know what to

say. His mouth was rough and dry, like he'd been gorging on salted peanuts. 'Why did you leave the circus?' It was all he could manage.

Lisa scowled but answered his question nonetheless.

'It didn't end well. Bogdan and Elisar both fell in love with me. Which was a surprise because they had been in love with each other when I met them. Things turned a bit nasty and they ended up shooting each other. Didn't kill each other though. But I thought it was best if I moved on. Went back to India and got involved in Bollywood but that's a whole 'nother story. So anyway, what do you think? Can I probe you?'

'Yeah, sure,' said Junk. 'But not right now, OK?'

'Why not?' said Lisa, a little hint of petulance sounding in her voice.

'I just need to get my head around everything, you know?' Junk kept grabbing swift looks at the TV screen to make sure Lasel didn't vanish. 'Maybe in, like, an hour or so. Why don't you go and have your walk and I'll see you when you get back. I'll have got my . . . thoughts together by then and we can try out whatever it is you learned from your horse-poo lady.' Junk could see Lisa considering his suggestion, playing it through in her head. Finally she shrugged.

'OK,' she said. 'That's fine, I guess. It'll make you more receptive, more open. I think it'll really help . . .' then added as an afterthought: 'you.'

*

52

The moment Lisa left the room, Junk locked the door behind her and spun round to look at the television. Lasel was still there. Junk felt a flutter of excitement in his belly. He crossed the room, staring up at her with a big stupid grin on his face.

'I thought I'd never see you again. I mean, I know you're not really there and I'm having an "episode", but it's really good to see your face.'

'Junk, you need to listen to me,' said Lasel. He had never heard her sound so stern. 'We don't have very long. You're not back home. You're not in a hospital.'

'Ah, come on, my meds could kick back in any second and you'll disappear. I mean, it'd be great if I knew you'd come back every now and then. I know you're a hallucination and everything, but—'

'Junk!' The severity of her voice startled him. 'You have to listen to me. You're on Espa's ship. You're on Pirestus Octonary. Everything you see around you isn't real.' Junk considered this. Pirestus Octonary, Espa's ship, was a space station that, in Junk's imagination anyway, sat silent and invisible in the depths of space.

Junk looked around at the drab TV room. 'How do you mean?'

'After the battle, you disappeared. We didn't know what had happened to you. You just vanished. Then a few days ago, Espa managed to get in touch with us. He said you had been taken, transported from Cul Mallia to the space station. You've been there for weeks.'

'What?' Junk was a little confused. Was his

hallucination hallucinating? Was his crazy head going off in an entirely new direction?

'Listen, I'm with Espa now. He can explain this better than me.'

There was movement next to Lasel and a portion of one of Espa Hara-kayan's four enormous faces filled three-quarters of the screen. Junk couldn't imagine what bizarre and contorted position Espa was in right now to be able to appear next to Lasel. His face alone was, after all, about four metres from crown to chin.

'Hello, Junk,' said the cyborg, speaking perfect English. Espa was one of a race of universe builders called the D'Krinians. They had built this universe, Junk's universe, and thirty-six others (with planning applications pending on nine more). Espa had told them that life on Earth had been unplanned but that when it was discovered Espa had been overjoyed and had embraced every aspect of the evolving life forms on the third planet. He spoke multiple languages and knew much of Earth's long (almost five-billion-years long now) history. 'This is all my fault,' said Espa. 'I'm so sorry.'

'How do you mean?' said Junk again, with a sneaking suspicion it wouldn't be the last time he asked this.

'I told someone, someone I thought was a friend, about you and Lasel. His name's Dras Sbey. He's a scientist here on Pirestus Octonary. I thought he would have been as excited as me to find out about you.

Anomaly dwellers using the Rammaniac.' Anomaly dweller was the term Espa used for Junk and Lasel and any other life form from Earth. The Rammaniac was what his people called the Room of Doors. 'But he wasn't. What excited him was finding out you could manipulate the Antricle. There are now so few of our race who still have that ability that Dras wanted to know how you are able to do it. Instead of just asking you, he's created everything you can see around you right now in order to trick you into telling him your secret. It's nothing more than a computer simulation. You understand that term?'

Junk nodded. 'Yeah, I understand.' Except he didn't understand. He understood the words but the concept was making his head throb. 'But why didn't he just ask me?'

Espa looked uncomfortable before he answered, 'You're . . . primitive.'

He was quick to qualify that statement: 'That's what some people think. Some of my people. Dras, for example. He assumed you wouldn't understand the question unless he framed it in such a way that your limited brain could comprehend.' Espa considered the words he had used for a moment. 'You realize I used the word "limited" to describe Dras's opinion, not mine.'

Junk smiled. He liked the big cyborg, who had a thirst for knowledge and was infectiously enthusiastic about all things to do with the third planet from the sun. 'It's OK, Espa. I'm not offended.'

Espa looked relieved. He continued: 'Right now you're on Pirestus Octonary, in a laboratory, wired up to a machine.'

'Wait! Stop. No, that doesn't make any sense,' said Junk. 'The . . . the detail . . .' Junk looked down at a table lamp next to him. The shade was covered in green velvet, worn and patchy in places, and there were gold-coloured tassels hanging from the rim. It was torn on one side so four tassels hung down lower than the rest. That level of detail was incredible. It couldn't be fake. Could it?

'The detail comes from you,' said Espa. 'It'll take too long to explain, but Dras sets the parameters of the simulation, tells you where you are, what you're doing, and then gets you to fill in all the colour by asking you what you would expect to see. That's why you believe everything around you. It's what you think should be there.'

Junk's head was reeling. He stared at the lamp. Had he seen that lamp somewhere before? He had a half-remembered image of a lamp just like that in the hallway of his grandmother's house when he was a child. Now he couldn't tell what was real and what wasn't. He thought about his mother. If what Espa was saying was true and the details had come from him, from his subconscious, then why had his mother looked the way she had when they met on the beach? Why had he thought of her as so raggedy and broken? Because that's what he'd expected, he realized. The woman on the beach was an extension of the grief-stricken, traumatized woman he'd seen in his kitchen that last night before he left home. Lasel's voice pulled him from his thoughts.

'Look, Junk, we don't have long. I'm on Pirestus Octonary too. Espa's hiding me, but we can't get to you. You're in part of the ship he doesn't have access to. You're going to have to get out yourself and come to us. Then Espa can get us both back home.'

'How do I do that?' asked Junk.

He saw the look of concern on Lasel's face even as she tried to hide it. She glanced at Espa. 'There's only one way,' he said. 'You have to overload the system.'

'What does that mean?' asked Junk.

'If you were to do something to utterly shatter the illusion of reality, then the simulation would have no choice but to turn off.'

'How d'you mean?' said Junk. 'What do I have to do to "shatter the illusion"?'

Espa paused before answering. 'You have to die,' he said and then added: 'violently.'

'What now?' Junk felt very cold all of a sudden.

'You have to shatter the illusion, literally. Then the simulation won't be able to maintain its pretence of reality and it'll switch off. You'll wake up in the laboratory.'

'You're telling me to kill myself?' said Junk.

'Violently,' Espa repeated, his massive face nodding for emphasis. Then he looked at something off screen. 'We have to go. Any longer and Dras might notice we're tapping into this simulation. He'll know we've talked to you. Do what I've told you and do it quickly. If he works out you've spoken to us, he'll just reset the whole program. You'll wake up and you won't remember this conversation. If he gets to us too, then you'll be stuck here forever, or at least until you give him what it is he wants. And after that you'll just be a liability.'

Junk had so many more questions, but before he could say another word Lasel and Espa disappeared from the screen, leaving just the galloping horses and their brightly attired jockeys. The volume of the commentator's voice rose and Junk realized for the first time that he had been silenced while they had been talking.

Had any of that been real or just all in his head? Junk didn't know what to think. Lisa, when she was here, hadn't heard or seen anything, but if Lasel and Espa were the real ones then Lisa was nothing more than a character in the world's most detailed video game. He realized he had had enough of this room. He needed some air.

Lisa had said she was going to go walking down by the shore and Junk didn't want to bump into her or anyone else so he went in the opposite direction, over the boggy fields to the dark woods. He needed time to think and the woods were a good place to do that. The trees were dense and very little outside noise managed to seep in. There were birds sitting unseen in high branches, screeching, warbling and cawing back and forth. There was movement or the sounds of movement in the bracken and ferns that dominated the forest floor either side of a thin, rutted path that had been worn into the flora by ramblers and dog walkers.

As Junk walked he remembered a trip to Wales maybe six or seven years earlier. An old friend of his dad's, a former teammate from his days of playing competitive hurling, owned a Christmas-tree farm a short distance outside of Cardiff. His dad's friend had a wife, two children – a girl about Junk's age and a boy almost exactly the same age as Ambeline – and two gorgeous Golden Retrievers called Honey and Breeze. They had stayed for a long weekend and Junk had a woolly memory of walking the dogs over a wide lawn, through the Christmas-tree plantation (Christmas trees as far as the eye could see; all shapes, sizes and shades of green and blue), over a stile and into a forest. The way Junk remembered that woodland in Wales, it was identical to where he was now.

Of course, he was savvy enough to acknowledge that maybe forests tend to look much the same. Maybe he would be able to tell the difference between a forest in California and one in Wales or Ireland, but woodland in the British Isles was probably much of a muchness.

It was hard to organize his thoughts into a coherent whole, but he did his best. What it came down to was that either Lasel and Espa were real and telling him the truth, or he was much crazier than he thought and he needed to run not walk to Dr Oak and tell him exactly what had happened. Dr Oak would probably up his meds and he'd turn into a zombie. There were a few patients at St Jude's who were kept permanently doped up because they were a danger to themselves or others. Junk's heart thumped and his head spun as he realized he might well fit into that category. If he believed Lasel and Espa and did as told, then he was about to very much be a danger to himself.

How could he know what was real and what was not? Was there a way? Sure the forest looked like one he'd been to before, and the lamp in the TV room and the way Dr Oak rubbed his temples when listening to Junk speak and a hundred other factors that had parallels in his former life but none of that was definitive proof that he was imagining all this, filling in the blanks from his subconscious, and that Lasel and Espa were real. It was so much more probable that Lasel, Espa, Garvan, Dr Otravinicus and the dozens of others he had met over the last three years were the delusions of a damaged mind, the mind of someone who could throw a helpless young girl to her death.

But there was the rub. If he chose the more likely explanation, then he was a murderer and he couldn't believe that. He wouldn't believe it. He knew deep down that he just wasn't capable of hurting anyone like that, let alone his little sister.

Without making any sort of conscious decision or plan, Junk had followed the path through the woods until it came to a fork. Without hesitation he took the route to the right, which brought him out from under the trees to a towering fence topped with rusting barbed wire. Junk didn't even think about going over. Instead he dropped to his knees and started tunnelling down. The ground was dusty and the soil fine. It scraped away with relative ease until there was a shallow channel that Junk was able to wriggle through to the other side, where there lay a broad expanse of rapeseed fields. The bright yellow crop danced in the afternoon breeze and Junk ran his hands gently over the tops of the plants as he walked on.

Beyond the fields he saw a bridge: a double-arch stone bridge that spanned two parallel railway lines. He could hear the express train from Ballinasloe approaching long before he could see it. He sat on the parapet of the bridge, his legs dangling over the side, and saw the train appear as the track curved a short distance ahead. Now it was straight on, all the way to him. It was moving fast and he could feel the whole structure shuddering as the train thundered onwards.

Junk took a deep breath, closed his eyes and shuffled forward on his buttocks until there was more of his rump not touching the wall than touching it and then, as gravity took over and Junk found himself falling to the train tracks below, he wondered for a moment if he had just made a horrible mistake. What if this was all part of his madness and none of it was real? No Lasel. No Espa. No escape. What if this was reality? What could be worse than a lifetime incarcerated in St Jude's?

A lifetime as a vegetable hooked up to machines after a speeding train had shattered his body.

But, too late now. He landed hard on the tracks and tilted his head up to see the train just centimetres away from him. It had no intention of stopping. Suddenly the breath was sucked out of him as the train hit.

6

Junk was surrounded by pale pink light. He pictured himself sitting in a meadow, eyes closed, head tilted up towards the sun. He was warm and wet. Floating. Was this heaven? As his senses returned, he realized he was suspended in some sort of gelatinous liquid. As he moved his arm, the substance surrounding him gave a little resistance. He had once worked for a company that took people scuba-diving in the Dead Sea. The sensation here was similar to the high salt content of that water.

Out of the corner of his eye he noticed something pale and snakelike near to him. He reacted on instinct and jerked away from the creature. It took him a moment to realize that it wasn't a snake but a tube. It took him another moment to realize the tube was connected to him. With difficulty he moved his hand to his face and discovered the whole lower half was shrouded in a rigid mask. The tube projected from the mask. It drooped downward and disappeared into the pink murk below him. He inhaled and understood that it was breathing apparatus. Air was running through the tube into the mask. He started to suspect that this wasn't heaven. He didn't know what heaven was like, but he felt confident that it wouldn't involve excessive amounts of gunk and oxygen masks.

He shifted his weight and moved less than half a metre before his hand touched glass. He was in a tank. It was like he was a fly caught in a vat of hair gel. Light shone in from outside but the viscous substance was just the wrong side of translucent for him to make out any details of what lay outside the tank.

His head was becoming clearer by the second and he was sure he must be in the lab on board Pirestus Octonary. Espa and Lasel had been real. The hospital had been fake, just as they'd said. Everything he had believed, and then believed he was mad to believe, was true. He hadn't killed Ambeline. She was still alive. He felt a moment of pure elation blooming inside him, but then his thoughts turned to where he was and he realized Espa and Lasel had failed to warn him that he would be leaving one prison for another.

He quickly decided escape lay either up or down. It wasn't here floating uselessly in the featureless middle. He tried going up first and started to kick his legs in order to power his ascent, but it didn't work. Nothing happened. He stayed exactly where he was. The hold of the gunk was too great.

So his only option was down. He caught sight of the air tube snaking away beneath him and realized that because there was air coming through the hose, the other end had to be connected to something. He had the same issue with swimming down that he had with going up. However, the hose gave him one advantage. He took a tight hold of it with one hand and then the other and started to pull himself down to the base of the tank. The air tube was longer than he had originally assumed, and his descent took more time than he would have thought possible. The tank was narrow but deep, as if he was imprisoned in a test tube.

And the deeper he went, the thicker the substance encasing him became, slowing his progress further. He had to pull even harder on the air hose and his muscles started to burn. Every time he wrapped his hand around the hose he blocked the airflow, and he quickly became lightheaded through lack of oxygen. He went deeper and deeper. The light and his surroundings never changed. It stayed consistently pink and bright.

And then suddenly he felt a jerk and the air tube came away in his hand. He took in a sharp, involuntary inhalation of breath. Unfortunately he also inhaled some of the glutinous pink substance. It tasted vile: bitter and medicinal. It stung the back of his throat and he had to fight an almost overwhelming desire to cough. He squeezed his eyes shut, and the determination it took to stop himself retching made him shudder. He wrapped his hand tightly around the bottom of the tube, which was about two metres in length, and squeezed it shut. He fought the building panic and knew that he had to focus on his predicament. He had only a few short, shallow breaths before the air lodged in the tube would be all used up and then he would suffocate. He had seconds to live unless he did something. He had to get out.

With one hand choking off the end of the hose, he reached out with the other, praying for a miracle. His hand groped blindly but he couldn't feel anything. His eyes were beginning to sting now and his lungs were burning. He took another half a second's gulp of air and with it came more of the pink gel. Junk knew that was his last breath. There was no more air to be had in the tube.

And just as all hope seemed futile, his fingertips brushed against something metallic. His middle finger found a hole and he managed to hook it inside. It was the opening that the hose had been connected to. He could feel the oxygen still being pumped in through this gap. Another second and he was able to get three fingers in the hole. He curled his digits around the edge and that gave him just enough purchase for a decent grip. He pulled himself down towards the hole. He could feel the cool air blowing in and bubbles rising through the gel. He manoeuvred his mouth to the orifice and got his lips against it. He gulped down as much air as he could take.

Feeling with his fingertips, he could tell that the metal plate where the hose had been connected was about ten centimetres square. On closer examination, Junk realized it wasn't screwed on. Some sort of adhesive bonded it to the glass wall. Struggling to hold his breath, Junk worked fast and desperately. He dug his fingernails into a tiny crack at the point where the casing met the glass. He pulled and wiggled and forced his fingers down behind the plate until it came away in his hands. As it did so, a valve on the exterior of the tank dropped away and the pink gunk started to spurt out. That meant the tank would empty, but it wouldn't happen quickly enough, and now that his air hole was spewing out goo, Junk couldn't take another breath. What he had in his lungs right now was all he had unless he was able to break the glass. It was his only hope.

Using the metal plate he had yanked off as a tool, he started to strike the surface of the tank near the opening with the corner. His first blow made no impact on the glass, but the rough edge of the metal slashed a cut across the heel of Junk's right palm. The pink gel stung like hell but Junk ignored that pain and kept striking. His vision was failing, great storm clouds of angry blackness gathering on the periphery. His head was throbbing as if someone was inflating a balloon made of granite in the centre of his brain. His eyes felt as if they were expanding to the point where he was sure one or both of them was about to pop. And just as it was about to overwhelm him and he was going to pass out, the glass cracked. Junk didn't have the strength to hit it again. His lips started to part as his body was forcing him to take a breath. Then suddenly the crack doubled, then tripled. More cracks spread out from the first. A thousand angry fissures rippled outwards, circumnavigating the entire structure until they met up and the tank exploded.

Junk was free in less than a second. He ripped the mask from his face, opened his mouth as wide as he could and consumed as much oxygen as his lungs could hold in one go. He lay panting at the base of the shattered tank as shards of broken glass rained down on him and thick globules of pink gunk splattered the floor, walls and ceiling around him. His blurry vision was starting to clear. The throbbing in his head dissipated slowly and his pounding heart decided to stay inside his chest after all.

Junk allowed himself almost a full minute of stillness before he even considered moving. When he did, his limbs felt stiff as if through lack of use, and the slightest movement was agony. With some difficulty he sat up and took in his surroundings. The room was vast: wide, high, long, much like all the rooms on the space station, which were built to accommodate the cyborgs, who were fifteen or twenty times the size of an average human. It looked like a laboratory was supposed to look. There were floating monitor screens that appeared to hover independently. Each was transparent and bursting with data: diagrams, charts and reams of information written in a language that Junk could not read. He noticed a small red light flashing on some of the monitors. He paused, wondering what it was, but then he realized that something was wrong: he couldn't hear anything. There was no sound around him at all. Total and utter silence. He grimaced as he raised his left hand to his ear, sending spikes of pain shooting through his entire body. He touched his ear and discovered a rubbery substance clogging up his ear canal. He felt the right side and that was the same. He used the fingernail of his little finger on each hand to gouge out the rubber. After a moment of probing he was able to get his fingers behind the blockage and both slipped out with ease. He discovered they were stoppers that were shaped precisely to the contours of his ears. It was then that he heard the alarm. A klaxon was blaring: monotonous, repetitive and deafening. The rubber bungs had been so effective that he hadn't heard a thing. Now he could hear nothing else. The sound drilled straight through him. He knew he had to get moving. He knew the alarm was because of him.

If raising his hands to his ears had hurt, then getting to his feet and actually walking was sheer torture. He had no idea how long he had been in that tank, but clearly he had not had to use any muscles for a while and now they protested. It didn't help that he was dressed in a thin, shiny bodysuit, plastered with the gunk from the tank. It made his feet slip out from under him as he tried to get up and he quickly found himself on his back again and spinning helplessly like an inverted turtle.

He tried again, more slowly, and with much difficulty was able to stand upright. He took a moment to be sure of his balance. He saw a massive door, which appeared to be the only way in or out, but then he spotted another problem. He was barefoot and the floor all around him for at least two metres if not more was a sea of broken glass. He couldn't take one step without slashing the soles of his feet to ribbons. But did he have any choice? He couldn't just stand there. Someone could be here any second in response to that alarm. It was a miracle they weren't here already.

The closest floating monitor was within reach. It was about four metres wide but thin, no deeper, front to back, than a magazine. Junk stretched out and got a hand to its smoothly rounded edge, drawing it closer to him with ease. It felt surprisingly robust. He had no notion how it managed to stay airborne, but whatever was powering it was powerful enough to stop him pushing it all the way to the ground. As he pushed down on it he felt it resisting, like two magnets repelling one another. Junk had an idea, but it was going to be difficult. It would require him to use strength in his arms that he didn't possess right at that moment. However, he couldn't think of another way so it quickly became his only option.

Standing on tiptoe, wincing as his calf muscles engaged, Junk hooked his fingers over the top edge of the monitor. Once he had a firm grip, he jumped and pushed forward in the same movement. The suspended monitor sailed out over the broken glass with Junk hanging on to it for all he was worth. It started to slow down when he was only halfway across, but Junk thrust his body forward in an effort to drive it on. And it worked. Just. Junk let himself drop down with the jagged glass behind him.

He raced to the door, his feet slipping as he went. He fell more than once, but each time he managed to stand up again and keep going. He had seen these same fifty-metre-high doors before, in the transporter room, which had been the place he and Lasel had entered on arrival the last time they were here. The mechanism for opening it was some twenty metres or more off the ground. While he was still contemplating his next move, he heard the sound of someone approaching. He wondered if it was Espa and Lasel come to rescue him, but then he remembered they couldn't get in. They needed him to get out. Deciding it was more likely to be foe than friend, Junk hid, and just in time. The door shot upward, smoothly and silently, as he ducked behind a towering metal container, which after a moment he realized was Pirestus Octonary's version of a waste-paper basket.

A cyborg entered and Junk got his first look at his jailor: Dras Sbey. Just like Espa and the other cyborgs Junk had seen, he was huge: twenty-five, thirty metres tall. Instead of legs, however, his bottom half consisted of wheels housed in caterpillar tracks. Like Espa's mechanical legs, they were scuffed and industrial-looking. They had once been red, but most of the paint had been scraped off so the dull metal beneath showed through. His top half was more organic. He had two flesh and bone arms where arms should be as well as two sleek, red robotic arms reaching around from his back. These projected from a bandolier-like contraption that criss-crossed his torso. He also had two much smaller arms sprouting from his belly. These were organic too and looked almost like a baby's arms. They were typing speedily at a keyboard situated at his waist, and the alarm was soon silenced. Like Espa's, his head had four faces, but in Sbey's case, each face was different. Though the dome of his head was bald, one face sported a shaggy, soup-strainer moustache, another a trim goatee, the third had a full beard and the fourth was freshly shaven. As with the other cyborgs, Sbey's eyes moved from one face to another at will.

He looked at the remnants of the tank for several moments as if trying to process what he was seeing. Then his eyes flicked to his right face, then the back face, then his left face. He was looking all around the room.

His stumpy little arms typed at the keyboard and one of the floating screens hummed as it crossed to hover in front of him. He reached out with one of his red robot hands and performed a series of gestures in the top corner of the screen; fingers splayed, his index finger turning in tight concentric circles. From Junk's hiding place he could see right through the monitor as recorded footage of his escape from the tank started to play. He watched from a whole different perspective as Sbey saw the tank disintegrating, leaving Junk panting and shaking like a fish whose aquarium had suddenly disappeared from around him. Sbey continued to watch as Junk got his bearings, avoided the glass-strewn floor with the help of the floating screen and hid as the main door opened. Sbey's eyes flicked to his bare left face, looking straight at Junk's hiding place. He knew exactly where he was. Junk knew he should run, but he was frozen with fear and indecision. Run where? There was no way out. He couldn't open the door. He knew that. There was no way he could reach the control panel.

'You have nowhere to go.' Dras Sbey had a booming baritone voice. Junk could feel the sound reverberating deep inside his chest. He peeked out and saw Sbey pivoting to face him, but he made no move towards him. 'How did you know how to get out? I wonder. Was it just luck? An accident?'

Junk looked around for something, anything, that he could use as a weapon, but there was nothing, and what sort of weapon could inflict any damage on a being so much bigger than him?

'You may as well come out. Don't make me come and get you.'

Junk's shoulders dropped. He had nothing. There was no escape. However, just as he was about to step out, the huge main door shot upward once more and another cyborg entered. His additional limbs were all dark blue and he wore a visor that wrapped around all four of his faces. This was one of Pirestus Octonary's security guards. Junk had seen them on his previous visit to the station. Dras Sbey barked something at him in their quick, incomprehensible language, probably telling him to close the door, but the guard didn't move and barked something back. The main door stood open behind him and Junk knew it wouldn't remain like that for long. It was now or never. He shot out from his hiding place and ran as fast as he could.

Sbey saw him immediately and shouted. The guard swivelled his four-faced head and froze as he saw a tiny creature darting across the floor. From the security guard's stunned reaction, Junk was certain this was the first time he had ever seen an anomaly dweller up close. Sbey came trundling towards him, shouting, but the guard just stared, giving Junk time. He drew ever closer to the door. He was going to make it. But then the security guard snapped out of his shock and reached out towards the control panel with one of his thin, sculpted dark blue arms. He pressed the button to close the door and it started to come down rapidly. Junk ran for all he was worth and at the last moment let his slippery legs fall out from under him. His lubricated body slid across the smooth floor and under the rapidly descending door just as it slammed down into place with a resounding and definitive crack, missing Junk's head by just a few centimetres. He was out and on his feet in seconds, running without pause.

7

Junk kept running without looking back. He didn't know if the door to Dras Sbey's laboratory had risen again, and he didn't want to know. From his diminutive perspective, the corridor ahead seemed almost endless. It stretched out before him like a football stadium. He kept moving his legs, ignoring the spasms of pain that tore through them with every step. He focused on nothing more than the next thing he had to do, and the next thing he had to do was to find Lasel and Espa, but it occurred to him then that they hadn't actually told him where to find them. All they had said was he had to get out under his own steam. He had done that. Now where should he go?

After running flat out for several minutes his body protested so forcefully that his legs buckled, demanding he stop by making him collapse. He was gulping down air. He looked back but no one was following him. Maybe they hadn't seen him. Maybe he had got out of there so quickly that their eyes were on a different face, looking in the wrong direction. Maybe.

Junk tried desperately to focus. Had Espa said where to find them? There had been so much new and mind-blowing information coming at him that he couldn't remember any specific instructions. Plus Pirestus Octonary was so vast that to go anywhere would take him such a long time. Even longer if his legs continued to refuse to cooperate. And it wasn't as if he could ask someone for directions. He needed a plan of action. He didn't have one. What would Espa and Lasel do? Maybe they would go to the transporter room? Junk knew that room. Maybe they would assume that was where he would head. Except he didn't know where that room was located in relation to where he was now. It would be like saying, I'll meet you at the bench, when you're at Disneyland. Lots of benches. Lot of places for benches.

So he thought about it from a different angle. Lasel was smart. She'd use what she knew they both had at their disposal. She would know, from Espa, where Sbey's lab was. She would know that once Junk got out as they had told him to, he would run forward because it was the only way to go. That meant he only had to go on, and somewhere ahead of him would be Lasel, Espa and freedom.

He struggled back to his feet. He was exhausted and his muscles screamed. They wanted him to lie down, but he couldn't do that. The corridor stretched on. To his left was a massive wall of glass that looked out into open space. In any other circumstances he would have stopped to marvel at the sight that presented itself: the solar system, his solar system, displayed like a postcard. The sun roared proudly just a few million miles away, though the glass, or whatever it was, made it appear so much closer. He recalled seeing a similar view from Espa's cabin the last time he was here and he knew the window augmented what he was seeing. Had the ship been as close to the sun as it appeared; they would all burn to death. Beyond the sun were planets: Mercury. Venus. Earth. It was just a speck but he could make it out. This vessel was designed for the people who had created this wonder to marvel at their achievement. They created universes for a living, but it wasn't like manufacturing a car or building a house. This was the work of gods. But Espa and his race weren't gods; they were designers and architects and builders, but on an unimaginable scale.

Junk reflected on the ridiculousness of him taking this, all this, in his stride. Three years ago he had left his comfortable, normal home to find his sister's killer. Back then he had just been an average sort of kid, thinking the same thoughts as everyone else. Now he had found so much more. He had discovered how his world worked. Why it was there. How it fitted into a much larger picture, a much larger universe, multiverse even. For decades, humans had questioned whether there was life anywhere other than on Earth. More than twenty years before Junk was even born, a vessel had been sent out looking for life on other planets with instructions on how to find Earth and what its dominant race was like.

No one had ever responded, but it was mind-blowing to think that the planet, and the system of planets, and the galaxy that that system was part of, and the universe that that galaxy and its stars and planets and Earth and its inhabitants were contained in, were all a product of another race. We went looking for someone else, never realizing that we were here because of someone else and they had been watching us all along.

Junk forced himself to turn his thoughts back to the present and the pressing issue: getting out of there. The only thing he could rely on was Lasel's smarts. She was smarter than Junk. She would be one step ahead of him. Whatever he did, she would already have predicted, so Junk decided not to over-think. He asked himself what he should do, and the answer was run. So he ran.

The corridor leading away from Dras Sbey's lab curved gently to the right. Pirestus Octonary was not teeming with life, so Junk didn't see anyone else until he reached a dizzyingly high flight of stairs. Each step was over a metre high, but Junk was relieved to see that there was a ramp to one side, which he assumed was for Sbey and any other resident of the space station who had wheels instead of legs but ultimately it didn't matter why it was there. It was there and Junk was still greased up. He hit the slope hard and slid with abandon. If the circumstances had been different he would have let out a holler of excitement. It was like an amusement-park ride. The world's tallest slide. He realized he was being reckless. He had no idea what was at the bottom so he tried to control the speed of his descent by pushing the heels of his hands down but all he managed to do was start himself spinning. He came off the end and kept going, spinning in slowly decreasing circles until he stopped. Then he looked up and saw, to his horror, twelve blue-limbed security guards directly ahead of him. Junk's stomach clenched. He knew he was caught.

As he slowed to a stop, he was desperately trying to think of ways to outrun the guards, but he knew that was futile. There were too many of them and they were too close. Should he mention Espa's name? Would they just imprison Espa alongside him if he did? There was nowhere to hide and nowhere left to run.

For a moment, nothing happened. The guards didn't move and Junk didn't move. And Junk realized that not one of them was looking in his direction. Then there was movement behind him and a massive pair of mechanical legs stepped over him. They were teal in colour or had been once. Now they were old and worn and faded. Junk had a brief image of Dr Oak and his teal-coloured Friday polo neck, but this most definitely was not Dr Oak. It was Espa. The legs stopped with a resounding clang right in front of Junk and the guards' eyes flicked to their rear faces, but it appeared that not one of them could see Junk.

A doorway opened in the back of the left leg and Lasel was standing there. She beckoned urgently and Junk did not hesitate. He scrambled towards her on his hands and knees and she pulled him in. The moment he was inside the panel behind him closed again and the pair of them were thrust together in the dark. Their faces were only centimetres apart. Junk could feel Lasel's breath on him. It smelt sweet. He felt her arms curling around him, pulling him to her.

'I thought I'd lost you,' she said softly. 'I didn't know where you had gone. I was so worried.' She squeezed him tightly and he squeezed back. He pushed his face into her long red hair and breathed in her scent. It was a smell he knew well. It hadn't changed. She smelt of sweat and smoke and a dozen other odours but dominating them all was something else. Something that was uniquely Lasel. Junk couldn't describe it. Not even to himself, but it was an aroma that made his thumping heart calm down.

'We're not safe yet,' said Lasel. 'Espa can get us back home, but Sbey might still come after us. After you. Espa will explain.'

Their stomachs rose into their throats then as Espa turned and walked away. His steps were smooth but they felt them. For a moment they would be weightless, huddled together in their bubble, then Espa would bring his foot down and they would feel the forces of gravity pressing down on them. The compartment they were in was too tight for them to move, let alone sit down, so they just held on to each other and waited for the ride to end.

It did eventually and the door behind Junk's back opened. He stepped out into the light, reaching for Lasel's hand and leading her out with him. He wasn't ready to let go of her just yet. They were in the transporter room. With a wheezing of pistons and chugging of mechanical parts, Espa leaned down. He held out his big hand and Lasel skipped on to his palm without hesitation, curling one arm around his erect thumb and pulling Junk with her. Espa raised them up so it was easier to speak.

'Junk, I'm so sorry,' he started.

Junk shook his head. 'Stop,' he said. 'It wasn't you. It wasn't your fault.'

'I thought Dras was my friend,' said Espa. 'I thought he would feel the way I did about you. Excited, curious. I couldn't have been more wrong. He just sees you as fodder for experiments.'

'Why? What have I ever done to him?'

'Nothing. If I can put it into some sort of context from your time: human scientists would experiment on rats and not think twice about the rats' feelings in it all.'

'So I'm a lab rat?' said Junk.

'Comparatively speaking,' said Espa.

'Why me?' asked Junk.

'As I said, it's because of what you can do with the Antricle. The Antricles are a remnant of a different time in my people's history. Once there were hundreds, maybe even thousands, of D'Krinians who could use an Antricle to its full potential. Now there are hardly any. Maybe none. I've never met anyone before you who can interact with them as you can. Just like Dras, I would love to know how you can do it, but I would never do to you what he has done.'

'I know.' Junk smiled. He could see the sincerity on the cyborg's massive face and found it rather touching.

'We haven't got long,' said Espa. 'If the station goes into a security lockdown I won't be able to get you off at all. It'll only be a matter of time before you're found and then we'll all be in trouble. Here.' A concealed compartment in his thigh hissed open to reveal a bag. Junk opened it and found his clothes and the Antricle. It was frozen in a shape similar to an archer's bracer and he slipped it over his left hand, where it covered most of his forearm. He knew it wouldn't do anything here on the space station but he felt more confident with it on his wrist.

'How did you get it?' asked Junk. 'Won't Dras notice it's gone?'

'No,' said Espa. 'He had just returned it to supplies. There's nothing unique about your Antricle. You're the unique one.' Junk chuckled at that.

'Now listen,' said Espa, 'whenever you use it, Dras can track it. The reason he was able to get you before was because you used it so much. It made it easy for him to lock in on you.'

'I can't use it?' Junk sounded disappointed.

'Well, that's up to you,' said Espa. 'I'm just telling you what could happen if you do. And Dras is extremely bright. Even if you don't use it, he might still find a way to get you back.'

'Can he do that?' asked Lasel. 'Are there no laws against it? You have laws, right?'

'We do of course,' said Espa, 'but you're just an . . .' His voice trailed off.

'Inferior life form from the anomaly?' offered Junk. Espa didn't respond. He didn't need to. The shameful look on all four of his faces said it all. Junk nodded. 'I understand.'

'Decide where it is you want to be,' said Espa. 'I can take you there. You want to go and be with your other friend? Garvan – is that his name?'

'Where is Garvan?' Junk directed the question at Lasel.

'Cantibea. Being king brings a lot of responsibilities.'

'I can imagine,' said Junk.

'He sent his whole army out looking for you and Ambeline. And Cobe is—'

Junk cut her off: 'Cobe? Who's Cobe?'

'Oh, of course you don't know yet. That's what Payo–Mestrowe call themselves now. Their coming together is complete. They aren't separate any more. They're one united being, so they decided they needed a new name: Cobe.'

That was a strange concept for Junk to get his head around. To be honest, he had never really understood what was happening with Payo and Mestrowe. Jacid Mestrowe was a Pallatan, and once a member of a group of mercenaries, the League of Sharks, proud of the fact they had evolved from such a fierce and resilient

83

predator. Mestrowe's race only had one natural enemy they feared: Twrisks. Strange little worm-like creatures who created stumpy fake bodies for themselves until the time came when they could do what they were created to do: burrow deep inside a Pallatan and become pilot to their host vessel. The Twrisk who joined with Mestrowe was called Payo, and when they became one – parasitic worm clamped on to a shark-man's brain stem – they called themselves Payo–Mestrowe. They had two voices sharing one mouth, two personalities vying for dominance. They were two separate beings sharing a single body. However, over time the bond between them grew stronger and the individuals started to merge into a single combined consciousness. Payo and Mestrowe vanished and the result was one unified being, the sum of both creatures. All Pallatan on the outside, but inside the courage, ferocity and determination of the Pallatan was tempered by the intelligence, decency and compassion of the Twrisk.

Lasel continued. 'After Espa contacted me and we found out what had happened to you, Cobe went looking for Tolfke. We thought he might have some idea of where Ambeline went.'

Tolfke was a mysterious employee of the Nine Emperors. He had been a sort of middleman passing on the emperors' instructions to Jacid Mestrowe. He had worn a mask to cover a hideously scarred face, but Junk and the others had never found out what had happened to deform him so badly.

'Did they . . . he –' Junk corrected himself – 'find him?'

'I don't know. We're to meet him in a place called Tojek. It's about fifty miles northwest of the Magpie Emperor's palace.' She turned to Espa. 'Can you send us there?'

Espa nodded. 'Of course. I'll keep an eye on Dras and if I can I'll warn you if I find out he's coming after you.'

'What about you?' asked Lasel. 'Will Dras know you helped us?'

'I don't think so,' said Espa. 'I was careful to cover our tracks when we hacked into the computer simulation. Don't worry about me. I'll be fine.'

The transporter on Pirestus Octonary put Junk and Lasel down on a dusty stretch of road in the middle of nowhere, right where Lasel had requested. The terrain around them was dry and rocky, butterscotch earth under a cloudless blue sky. Junk, now wearing his own clothes, went down on one knee and picked up a handful of stones and grit. He let them fall through his fingers and then stood brushing his hands.

'It's good to be back,' he said. 'Now, which way's Tojek?'

Lasel gestured by pointing her head. 'That way,' she said. 'Not too far.'

Junk nodded and they started walking. They walked in silence for a while. It was Lasel who spoke first.

'I'm not going to ask you about what you went through, but if you ever want to talk about it, I'm happy to listen.'

'Thanks,' said Junk, not looking at her. The truth was, he didn't want to talk about St Jude's and what had happened to him in the time he had been Dras Sbey's prisoner. It occurred to him then that he didn't actually know how long that was.

'How long have I been gone?'

'Twenty-seven days,' said Lasel.

'Oh,' was all Junk could say in response. To him, it had felt much longer. He thought it had been about six months since he had woken up in St Jude's. Clearly Sbey had been able to manipulate his sense of time. Probably not that hard, when Junk considered it. He had had many moments when he had lost track of time. Like on that last day, when he had left Dr Oak's office and found himself in the TV room without any memory of getting there. He wondered why he hadn't questioned that more. He had thought it was weird after all. But he shook the thoughts away. He had spent enough time in St Jude's. Enough time thinking himself a killer. He would waste no more time or thought on that place.

Junk and Lasel walked for about twenty minutes before they reached the brow of a steep hill and found themselves looking down into a sprawling valley below. There was a small town that, much like Corraway, the town where Junk had first met Lasel, was built around a land-ship station.

86

'Here we are,' said Lasel. 'This is Tojek. Hopefully Cobe will be here.'

'Did you arrange where to meet?' asked Junk as they started down the hill.

'No,' said Lasel, 'but it's a small town. It won't be hard to find him.'

At the centre of the town was the huge land-ship station. It towered over two dozen or so smaller buildings that Junk knew only existed to service the passengers and crews passing through on the land-ships. He had been to several similar outposts on his travels.

Tojek had the feeling of a temporary settlement, even though it wasn't. Little thought had been put into town planning and there was no uniformity to the buildings. The land-ship station, for example, seemed to have been constructed in stages from whatever materials were available. The bulk of it was made from brick, but one wall had been finished in metal sheeting, as if, having run out of bricks, the builders just cobbled together an alternative. Then there were three extensions, each made of wood, with more metal sheeting used for the roofing. It had been an ugly building from a distance, but up close it was much worse. It was both ugly and precarious. There was something worryingly insubstantial about it and Junk got the impression that a strong wind could blow the whole thing away. Possibly the whole town.

The surrounding buildings were mostly single-storey shacks that looked as if they had been thrown together by people who had only a vague idea about architecture or construction. Nothing looked planned or finished. No pride had been taken when making them. Corners didn't quite match up. Paintwork had been started but abandoned. Temporary solutions to problems of plumbing or heating had become permanent, so buckets collected water dripping from pipes, and hoses channelled that water back into the dwelling.

The streets between the houses were broad. There was no lack of space here. Children and animals roamed freely.

No one gave Junk and Lasel a second look. Tojekians were used to strangers. Their entire existence was built around strangers.

The land-ship station was the hub of the town, so that's where Lasel and Junk headed. Junk saw Cobe first, but it took him a moment to recognize the Pallatan he had hated for so long. The last time Junk had seen Payo–Mestrowe, he had been dressed like all the members of the League of Sharks, in a mishmash of leather and other animal hides that appeared to be strapped together in a sort of Viking chic. Now, as Cobe, he couldn't look more different. He wore a pale blue tailored suit. The jacket was three-quarter length, the trousers crisp and freshly ironed. He wore leather boots that were highly polished and a white shirt with a long thin tie hanging in two loops, like something from an old Western. The left side of his face had always been heavily scarred, the eye milky and useless. Now he sported a brand-new tattoo that to Junk looked vaguely tribal. It covered his scars with delicate whorls that did a fine job of distracting from his injury.

He was sitting drinking from a tall hourglass-shaped beaker while people-watching. As he saw Junk and Lasel approaching, his wide, thin slit of a mouth burst into a warm infectious smile that lit up his face in a way Junk had never seen before. Even his terrifying collection of hundreds of jagged little teeth didn't detract from the pleasant countenance. He stood, rising to his full and dwarfing height.

'I had almost given up hope,' he said, offering his hand. Junk took it without thinking and was taken by surprise as the big man pulled him into a hug. 'Almost.' The hug lasted a little longer than was comfortable for Junk, but finally they parted and sat at the table. Junk stared. He couldn't get over the changes. Even Cobe's voice sounded different. It was deep and smooth. Relaxed. He took his time enunciating each word clearly.

'You look . . .' Junk searched for what he wanted to say, but there was so much he could say he plumped for the most obvious option: '. . . different.'

Cobe laughed. It was neither the cruel, mocking laugh of Jacid Mestrowe nor the happy, enthusiastic laugh of Payo. It was a confident, comfortable, honest laugh.

'Lasel tells me you've changed your name,' said Junk.

'No,' he said.

'No?' Junk looked confused. That *was* what she had said.

'Not changed. I didn't have a name before. Payo had a name and Mestrowe had a name, but neither of them was me.'

Oh good, thought Junk. Another ridiculously complicated concept to get my head around.

'There was no me,' he continued.

'Right . . .' said Junk. 'That is Mestrowe's body though, yeah?'

'Used to be. Now it's mine. Allow me to introduce myself properly. I am Cobe.' He held out his hand. This time Junk didn't take it. He frowned at it instead. Cobe didn't retract it, but he lowered his voice. 'I did not take your sister, Junk. Though I do recall the deed. I know everything that Mestrowe did. Everything.' Junk understood what he meant by that. He meant that kidnapping Ambeline was just one of many terrible things that Jacid Mestrowe did in his lifetime, and Cobe knew them all. 'He was a vile creature. But I am not to blame for his deeds, any more than I can take credit for Payo's good character. Payo was not vile. He was not anything. He waited. A lifetime spent waiting. And he was old when he joined with Mestrowe. He would have died had that not happened. He would have died without ever fulfilling his purpose in life. But that didn't happen. Because of you and your friends. And they made me. In much the same way your parents made you.'

'Payo and Mestrowe are your mum and dad?' said Junk, trying hard not to laugh at the idea.

'In a way,' he said. 'I have life because of them. Their choices inform mine to a degree, but I have my own will so I can make my own choices, and not necessarily what they would do. Is that not the same for you?'

'Well, yeah, but . . .' Junk didn't know how to finish. His mouth hung open, waiting for the words to come, but nothing did so he relaxed and let out a sigh. 'I suppose,' he said. The palm of his left hand started to itch. He gave it a good scratch.

'So, Cobe,' said Lasel, 'any luck finding Tolfke?'

Cobe smiled. 'He was on foot, we knew that.' He was saying this for Junk's benefit. Junk hadn't been party to the thinking behind Cobe coming to Tojek. 'There weren't many places he would go, and this seemed the most obvious. After all, it's a land-ship hub. Without access to the Room of Doors, he would have no choice but to travel by more conventional means.'

'He was here,' said Lasel, reading the smile. It wasn't a question.

'He was here,' agreed Cobe, 'and he still is. And what's more –' he fixed his eyes on Junk – 'he says he knows how to find your sister.'

8

Tolfke knew the good times he had experienced in the employ of the Nine Emperors were over when he watched Junk destroy Foster Peck and Ed Cresswell's patchwork army on the plains beyond Versailles. He skulked away before the battle was even over and headed north-west to the nearest town with a land-ship station, a place called Tojek. He had a few days to wait for the next transport and he took that time to ponder his future. He wasn't sure if he was going to return to his little house on the island in Ollamah Bay. He thought maybe he had had enough of the cold. He'd always thought about retiring to somewhere exotic like Tayana. He had enough money to live out the rest of his life in luxury in a place like that.

He was walking down a quiet street thinking these thoughts when a large man in a pale blue suit had stepped out in front of him. It took Tolfke a moment to realize it was Jacid Mestrowe. They had met many times over the last few years on a zit of an island in the middle of the Glarn Arka Sea, where Tolfke had relayed instructions from Foster and Ed.

Tolfke remembered Mestrowe had attacked him on the balcony. Well, OK, he had attacked Mestrowe first. It seemed like the right thing to do at the time. Tolfke wished he hadn't bothered now. The Pallatan attacked him again then, making the first move this time, knocking him unconscious with a single punch.

When Tolfke woke up he discovered he was locked in a cellar. There was straw on the floor and he was manacled at his ankle to the thick stone wall. There were no windows and only one door on the very far side of the room. The only source of illumination was a small light-well that fed the room with air and, occasionally, a cooling breeze that would jostle the straw on the ground. Mestrowe stopped by several times a day with food and water. Tolfke could see immediately that there was something very different about him now, and not just the way he was dressed. The Jacid Mestrowe he knew of old had been a thug. An ill-educated killing machine who would do whatever he was paid to, no matter how unsavoury, without question or hesitation. Now he was talkative and inquisitive. He would sit and converse each time he came, interested to learn more about Tolfke. At first, in an effort to show him how irritating he found his imprisonment, Tolfke was resolutely uncommunicative, but this never dampened the Pallatan's enthusiasm and he would natter away despite getting no response. Tolfke discovered he was a new man with a new name, Cobe, and a new outlook on life and the world in general, mostly because of the parasitic worm lodged in his brain. It takes all sorts, he thought.

On the fourth day of his captivity, Cobe had brought him a small box of Mallian flatoushes, small slug-like creatures that were inhaled into one's nasal cavity, where they would feed off the host's blood and in return release an intoxicating and pain-numbing odour. Tolfke had been flatoushe-less for almost two weeks so he was particularly grateful, and the barriers between them came down a little more then. Anaesthetized and feeling more relaxed than he had in ages, Tolfke finally started to talk back.

They talked about some of the jobs Tolfke had sent him on back in the day, back when he was Mestrowe, and finally Cobe understood some of the things he, or Mestrowe, had done. Mestrowe had never cared enough to question what he was being asked to do. All he wanted to know was where he had to go and what he had to do there. The reason why had never been important to him. Some of the truths Tolfke told him made him feel ill, but not with remorse. It was as if they were talking about another person. As if Mestrowe had been someone Cobe knew once but hadn't seen in a long time and was unlikely ever to see again.

Talk turned to the subject of Ambeline and they discussed what had happened after Mestrowe had delivered the girl to Tolfke. When they had arrived on the tiny island in the Glarn Arka Sea the girl had been understandably terrified and traumatized. She was wide-eyed with fear and always seemingly on the verge of bawling her eyes out but, Tolfke recalled, she never did. Not once. He had paid Mestrowe and watched him return through the portal without looking back. Mestrowe had had zero curiosity about anything. He never questioned, never cared, never enthused.

Once Mestrowe was gone, leaving Ambeline, Tolfke didn't loiter. He took the girl by the hand and pulled her back into the Room of Doors. Their path had been pre-determined by Foster Peck, as always, and the Gatekeeper lit a line for Tolfke to follow. Less than a minute after stepping off the little island, they were stepping into the gallery in the Palace of Versailles: the room that housed the bulk of Ed's stolen art collection. Ed and Foster were waiting for them.

Tolfke had been paid for his services even though his duties weren't over. He was to take the girl home in two days' time, so he was given a room in the palace and he made himself comfortable. However, no one explained to the little girl that that was what was going to happen. Had they done so, then maybe things would have turned out differently for everyone. The next morning, Tolfke awoke to much shouting and activity. The girl had somehow escaped from a locked, top-floor room and vanished.

Tolfke had already explained all this to Cobe, who then had him repeat it, practically verbatim, to Lasel and Junk. Junk listened intently, hoping to hear a new piece of information that would help in his search, but there was nothing. He already knew all that was relevant to finding Ambeline from talking to Foster Peck before he died.

'So you've got no idea what happened to her either,' said Junk, failing to suppress his frustration. His left hand was still itching like crazy. It wasn't the gash he'd received trying to escape from Dras Sbey's tank on board Pirestus Octonary. That was on his right hand and was healing quickly. This was becoming distracting. He dug his fingernails into his palm and scratched until the skin was red raw.

'No,' said Tolfke, 'but I do have a suggestion about how you could find her. Have you heard of the Valuda?' Junk looked blank; he had not. 'They are a group of mystics. They live north of here – about a day's journey by land-ship. They have the Gift.'

Junk frowned some more. 'The Gift?' he sounded sceptical. Last time he'd heard that phrase was from Lisa in the TV lounge at St Jude's.

'The gift of sight,' said Tolfke.

'I have heard of them,' said Cobe. 'They are supposed to be remarkable, but they're recluses. They lock themselves away and have nothing to do with the outside world. Ever.'

'That's true,' said Tolfke, 'but I happen to know their leader. In return for my freedom, I will get you in to see them.'

*

After much debate, it was decided that they would give this plan a shot. Cobe had vouched for Tolfke, citing the fact that he had got to know him over the last few days. Junk thought it strange that he was relying on the judgement of the man who took his sister to endorse the man who hired him to do it. He had to keep reminding himself that Cobe didn't take her, Mestrowe did, and although Cobe used Mestrowe's body, he was not Mestrowe. Not any more.

There was a land-ship heading north that afternoon, and Lasel managed to procure them a first-class cabin, just as she had done once before, on Junk's first trip by land-ship, from Corraway to Arrapia. Junk didn't ask her how she did it then and he didn't ask now. Cobe kept a close eye on Tolfke so he couldn't slip away, but the scarred man in the red mask assured them that he had no desire to abandon them. He wanted to help. Junk didn't believe him for a second, but he couldn't see any better options.

After almost a month in captivity, Junk's sleep patterns were all screwed up, which was probably a result of Dras Sbey's making him think he had been at St Jude's for more than six times as long as he actually was. He had probably put him to sleep three, four, five times a day in order to mess with his mind, to weaken his defences and have Junk tell him how to use the Antricle.

Junk looked at the copper sheath covering his forearm. He held it to the light, turning it slowly, watching it glitter. He wished he could open it up. He longed to be back in the Room of Doors. The Gatekeeper there wasn't much more than a disembodied voice but Junk actually missed him. However, he knew he couldn't risk Dras Sbey finding him. He closed his eyes and drifted off.

It felt like he had only been asleep for minutes when Lasel shook him awake to tell him they had reached their destination. It hadn't been minutes. He had been asleep for hours. Almost immediately he became aware of his maddeningly itchy left hand. He started to scratch at it, but stopped when he spotted something bright yellow right in the centre of his palm, under the skin. It was almost glowing. It wasn't big, only about the size of a pinhead, but he was certain it hadn't been there before. He wondered if he had some sort of virus, but apart from the itchy hand he felt fine. Then it was time to disembark and he pushed the yellow mark from his mind.

They alighted in the middle of nowhere. There wasn't any sort of settlement built around a land-ship station here because there was no station. There wasn't very much of anything that marked the stop, only a very basic image of a ship chiselled into a rock.

'It's this way,' said Tolfke, pointing. 'Not far.' They started walking. The landscape was parched. Orange sand and stone littered the craggy steep ground. There was no vegetation to be seen.

'So tell me about these Valudas,' said Junk, eyes on

the back of Tolfke's covered head. He had meant to quiz him on board the land-ship but having managed to sleep through the entire journey that opportunity had been missed.

'The Valuda,' Tolfke corrected.

'Whatever,' said Junk. 'How do you know them?'

Tolfke didn't reply immediately. He didn't acknowledge Junk's question in any way and Junk was just about to repeat himself when Tolfke answered: 'I used to be one of them.' Cobe and Lasel exchanged surprised looks. 'A novice anyway.'

'What is it they do exactly?' asked Junk. 'You said they have the gift of sight. Does that mean you do?'

'No, not any more,' said Tolfke. The regret in his voice was obvious. 'Not ever really. I never finished my training, you see, so whatever little tricks I could do faded in time.'

'Tricks? What does that mean?' asked Junk.

'The Valuda can see all: past, present, future. They can talk to the planet, the animals, the stones and the sea.'

'The sea have much to say for itself?' asked Junk with a smirk.

'No, not much, apparently,' said Tolfke ingenuously.

'Why didn't you finish your training?' asked Lasel. Junk noted that she didn't have the same cruel, mocking tone to her voice that he did, and he suddenly felt ashamed. He wasn't sure why exactly. After all, Tolfke was one of the bad guys. He worked for the bad guys.

He was instrumental in Ambeline being taken. Junk had every right to mock the man and Lasel should have been mocking him too, but she wasn't. She sounded genuinely caring.

'I failed the test of Fiarni Samor.'

'What's that?'

'It translates close enough to Scorched Room.' No one pried any further, allowing Tolfke to continue only if he wanted to. He did. 'A room in a cave is set alight and a novice must enter. The entrance is sealed and the novice must survive. He must talk to the fire and convince it not to burn him.' No one spoke. Junk and Lasel had both seen under Tolfke's mask. They had seen enough of his scarred, melted flesh to understand what must have happened. 'I was not able to persuade the fire.'

Junk considered this. He realized that they possibly should have had this conversation before they travelled for ages to get here. Now he understood that he was on his way to see a bunch of crazies who talked to fire. This wasn't going to help him find Ambeline. Just how desperate was he? Very, he thought. Tolfke was still talking and Junk wondered if he had ever talked about this with anyone before. Every utterance sounded like it was accompanied with a brief sigh of relief.

'I was five years old,' Tolfke was saying, 'when I joined the Valuda.'

'Five?' Lasel sounded astonished.

'I trained for the next thirty-eight years and then I thought I was ready to move up.' He paused for a long time and no one else spoke. They all walked on in silence. 'I was not ready,' Tolfke added eventually.

'What happened afterwards?' asked Junk. 'How did you go from that to being a henchman for the Nine Emperors?'

'Henchman? What is "henchman"?'

'Doing their dirty work for them,' said Junk. 'Hiring the likes of –' He looked at Cobe and was about to point to him when he thought better of it. He turned away before finishing his sentence: 'Mestrowe or whoever.'

'I had spent most of my life working towards something else. Afterwards, when I didn't die, I didn't have very much else I could do. I had spent my life here.' He gestured to the barren, arid world around them. 'I thought I might as well travel. See some more of the world. I met Foster Peck by chance in a town in Glarn Mallia. He offered me employment. No one else had, so I agreed. Then he introduced me to the hall of connection.' The others understood he was referring to the Room of Doors. 'I saw many places.'

'And how did the things you had to do for the Nine Emperors sit with your religious upbringing?'

'The Valuda have no religion. They are not about a higher plain. They are about this one. And we are here.'

Tolfke stopped on the edge of a ridge where the ground sloped away fiercely towards a vast hole, an entrance to an underground cave system. He set off towards it. Junk, Lasel and Cobe hesitated before following.

They reached the lip of the hole and peered down, looking into utter, impenetrable blackness. Junk dislodged a rock with his toe and let it fall. It was quickly swallowed up by the dark and he strained to listen, turning his ear, but heard no sound of it hitting the bottom. Maybe there wasn't a bottom.

'How do we get down there?' asked Lasel.

'It's easy,' said Tolfke with a smile in his voice. He was home. Then he turned his back to the hole, spread his arms and allowed himself to tip backwards. Lasel, Junk and Cobe all cried out and reached out to grab him, but it was too late. He had gone, vanishing into the gloom. He didn't scream, and as with the rock there was no sound of him hitting the bottom.

'Now what do we do?' said Junk.

'Well,' said Cobe, with a contemplative furrow to his heavy brow, 'it seems unlikely that he would bring us all this way just to watch him die.'

'Man tried to convince a room of fire not to burn him,' said Junk, not even trying to mask the mocking in his voice now. 'I'm not sure his stairs go all the way to the top.'

'I do not know what that means,' said Cobe brightly. Then he turned his back to the hole just as Tolfke had done, spread his arms wide and without a moment's hesitation he let himself topple backwards into the hole. Unlike Tolfke, Cobe did let out a cry as he fell. It didn't last long. Only two or three seconds and it was suddenly silenced.

'Oh God!' said Junk. He couldn't believe what Cobe had just done. He looked at Lasel and she looked as thunderstruck as he felt. Junk opened his mouth to ask what she thought they should do now but was cut off by a thin voice emanating up from the hole. It was Cobe.

'Come on,' he shouted. 'It's quite safe.'

Junk and Lasel looked questioningly at one another, wondering how hurling oneself into a black hole could ever be deemed safe.

'Actually, it's fun,' shouted up Cobe.

Lasel shrugged, turned her back to the hole, aping the actions of Tolfke and Cobe, and, before Junk could stop her, allowed herself to pitch back into the pitch black. She cried out too and, as with Cobe, her cries didn't last long.

'Come on, Junk,' she shouted up. 'It's wonderful.' Junk did not know what to do now. Every sensible fibre of his being was telling him not to hurl himself into the black pit. As he considered this dilemma he became aware of his itchy left palm. He looked at it and discovered that the pinhead of yellow had spread considerably. It was now about a centimetre long and it seemed to be pulsing, growing brighter, then dimmer, brighter, dimmer.

'Are you coming?' he heard Lasel call, and turned his mind away from the sensation in his hand.

'Oh well,' said Junk to himself, before he turned and let himself fall.

*

Junk felt his stomach rush up through his body, trying hard to escape from his mouth. He roared as he watched the entrance of the cave shrink to a mere speck far above him. In his peripheral vision he could make out some vague source of light below him, but before he had a chance to work out what it was he was suddenly caught in a warm updraught of air. His descent slowed rapidly until he was being lowered ever so gently to the ground as if an invisible giant was setting him down on his feet. He landed on soft mossy earth, beaming with exhilaration. Lasel and Cobe had the exact same look on their faces.

'I want to do that again!' said Junk with a wild grin.

'We both said the same,' said Cobe, laughing.

'Come on,' said Tolfke. 'It's this way.' Junk turned to see him heading off towards a nearby tunnel. The walls were phosphorescent, emitting a hazy orange glow that lit their way, and Junk was reminded of the time he went diving with Cascér. The commust jelly that had covered and protected them released a similar kind of bioluminescent light, although that had been a cool shade of blue rather than fiery orange.

The tunnel was only a dozen or so metres long and it curved slightly before opening out into a vast space that descended for hundreds of metres below them and was almost fifty metres wide. The walls were riddled with caves drilled into the rock, all connected by a series of walkways, ladders and pulleys. Water dripped from the roof of the cave high above and was collected in reservoirs and channelled through miles of pipes, conveying the water all around the interior. There were taps placed in the pipes every few metres. There was a thriving community of men, women and children down here, all going about their business. There were cooking fires here and there. Music played. Children squealed and laughed. Goat-like animals skittered back and forth, yickering.

'This way,' said Tolfke. Junk, Lasel and Cobe followed the man in red down ladders, over bridges and along walkways. Many of the residents recognized him despite the mask and stopped him to shake his hand or embrace him, welcoming him home. Junk looked at a group of small children running around wildly. They were only four or five years old and Junk thought about infant Tolfke living here.

Towards the bottom of the cavern they approached a cave mouth that was larger than most. It became apparent that this was where they were heading. As they neared it, a wizened old man, sitting at a desk writing in a heavy book, glanced up, and his toothless mouth broke into a grin as he spotted Tolfke. He pulled himself to his feet, using the desk to steady himself, then shuffled out from behind it with his arms spread wide.

'Ma marna na,' he said, repeating the phrase over and over again in a language Junk didn't recognize. He threw his arms around Tolfke and hugged him tightly. 'Ma marna na.' His voice was weak and cracked, his breathing laboured. Junk thought he might be the oldest man he had ever seen. 'Ha munna babanda?' said the old man to Tolfke when he broke the embrace. Tolfke answered him in the same tongue and then turned to the others.

'This,' he said proudly, placing an arm around the old man's shoulders, 'is the great-father. He is the oldest of the Valuda.'

'I'd bloody hope so,' muttered Junk under his breath. No one heard him.

'I have told him we wish to see,' continued Tolfke. 'We must follow him now.'

'Puna, puna,' urged the old man, beckoning them on. He led them into the mouth of the large cave.

It was slow going. The great-father led the way, which meant they all had to walk at his plodding pace. The walls of the tunnel were smooth and exuded the same orange phosphorescent glow. It was a warm, calming light.

The end of the tunnel opened out into a wide low-ceilinged room. The great-father held up a hand, indicating everyone should stay where they were.

'We need to wait here,' said Tolfke, somewhat unnecessarily as the great-father shuffled forward, disappearing from view. Tolfke touched Junk's arm. 'A word of warning,' he said, 'talking to the Valuda is not like having a conversation. They will answer any question, but once they consider it answered you can't ask it again.'

'OK.' Junk frowned. He didn't really understand what that meant.

'So be sure to phrase any question carefully. And whatever you do, don't touch them. That goes for everyone.'

Junk nodded. 'OK,' he said again. He shifted, stepping to his right so he could see further into the room. What he saw was a shallow pit in the centre, and in the pit were bodies, alive not dead, curled and balanced on top of one another, more at the base than the top. Junk couldn't be sure how many there were. More than five, less than ten, he guessed. They were just a mass of twisted, interconnected limbs, heads and torsos. It almost looked like a game: a cross between Twister and Jenga.

He watched as the great-father spoke to the human pyramid. Then a head flicked out from the pile, looking straight at Junk. The face had no eyes. In their place were two deep, black, empty holes.

9

The old man ushered Junk, Lasel and Cobe into the room. Then the great-father and Tolfke stood apart from them. Up close, Junk could see the Valuda were indeed a jumble of intertwined people. He counted seven heads. Their bodies were naked but their skin was painted a lustrous gold colour. Now he could see that their eye sockets were not gaping, empty holes but their eyelids had merely been painted black, which gave the impression from a distance that they were horrifically vacant. However, it soon became apparent that they never opened their eyes.

'Bubo Valuda.' All seven spoke as one, in perfect harmony. Their voices were melodic, but at the same time strangely inhuman; robotic even.

Tolfke translated: 'We are the Valuda.'

'Ha trunna kamanana,' said the seven voices.

'What would you have us see?' said Tolfke. He gestured for Junk to step forward.

Hesitantly, Junk did. He cleared his throat.

'I . . .' he started, but stopped. Should've rehearsed what I was going to say, he thought.

'Facha dunto,' said the Valuda.

'There is no need for that,' said Tolfke.

Junk frowned, thinking, Can they read my mind?

'Zo,' said the Valuda.

'Yes,' said Tolfke.

Junk shuffled nervously then, trying hard to think of nothing at all, especially nothing embarrassing. Of course it's impossible not to think of something whenever one tries to not think of something so Junk asked his question without formulating the words.

'Sister,' he said abruptly. 'My sister. Ambeline. Where do I find her?'

'Dajja,' said the Valuda.

'What's that mean?' asked Junk, looking at Tolfke, suddenly excited.

'It's a town,' said Tolfke. 'South-west of here. Not far. Less than a day.'

'She's there?' cried Junk. 'You're sure?'

'Vebo tarnotsir,' said the Valuda.

'We see a field,' translated Tolfke.

'Lijna wesil.'

'A tree upside down.'

'Vebo camasir.'

'We see a marker.'

'Maws sunsee.'

'It is a circle.'

'Nu soot susu.'

Tolfke hesitated before repeating. Junk looked at

him with eager, expectant wide eyes. 'She is beneath,' said Tolfke finally.

Junk was breathing hard, playing the words back and forth in his head. Then he caught a look at Lasel and Cobe. Neither was looking at him, in fact they were looking away. Junk looked at Tolfke and the great-father. Both had their heads bowed. Also not looking at him.

'What does that mean?' asked Junk, suddenly scared and not sure why. 'What's the marker? The circle?'

No one spoke for a few moments, and then Lasel took Junk's hand. He saw tears in her eyes. He felt goosebumps on his neck.

'It's a grave, Junk. The circle is a marker for graves. It represents life. How it keeps going round.'

Junk was finding it hard to process the words. 'She's beneath the . . . She's in a grave?' She's dead?' He spun back to face the Valuda. 'Is my sister dead?'

'Ho nabe,' said the Valuda.

'What?' said Junk.

Tolfke spoke quietly. 'The Valuda consider your question answered. I did warn you. You can ask a different question on a different subject but—'

'No!' Junk railed. 'They haven't answered. Tell them they haven't answered. Is Ambeline dead? That's a different question. That's a different question!' And then he reached out his hand towards the Valuda. It was an unconscious gesture of emphasis, nothing more.

'Goge!' cried the great-father in alarm.

'No!' yelled Tolfke, moving towards Junk to stop

him, but he was just too late and Junk's hand grabbed one of the arms in the Valuda pile.

A rush of images flooded through Junk's mind. He saw a town painted in blood. Skulls loomed out of the darkness. Hideous, contorted faces cackled, twisted with rictus grins showing crooked, dirty teeth. He saw a graveyard. He saw a tree and the grave as the Valuda had described with a circular marker on top of it. And then everything went black.

King Garvan III leaned against the balustrade bordering the south garden of the Edrin palace. From here he could look down on the town and out over the bosky hills of Cantibea to the thrashing sea beyond. He loved this view. He would sit here for hours as a child. He would read and write and draw. He would concoct wild plans for his future. For travelling the world when he was older. As it happened he did get to travel the world, but in all those years sitting here as a child he had never imagined he would be travelling it the way he had: with Junk and Lasel, on board the *Casabia*, on land-ships, through the passageways leading from the Room of Doors. He had fought with carnivorous birdmen, battled crazed monks, enlisted Twrisks, narrowly avoided freezing to death and being beheaded by his own brothers. He had died and been brought back to life. He had killed his own father and then with Junk's help 'unkilled' him. He had watched his friend take on an entire army and decimate them without really breaking a sweat. He had then lost his friend. Inexplicably. Junk had just vanished from the face of the planet.

Garvan knew he shouldn't be here. He should be with Lasel and Cobe looking for Junk and Ambeline. Even though Junk had disappeared, his friends had chosen to keep on with his search. After all, they had followed him halfway around the world, tracking the Nine Emperors to find Ambeline. No one was going to give up now. Garvan had sent his brothers out. He had had Jadris head north, Kyril went east, Toodar and Hanch went south, Paran and Bantil west. Only Cortree, the youngest, stayed behind, much to his own annoyance but their mother's gratitude. Each brother took a platoon from the Cantibean army. They were to search out any clue to the whereabouts of either Junk or Ambeline. Garvan received daily reports, but so far they had found nothing at all.

His advisors were with him, talking, but he wasn't listening. They did nothing but talk. He had found out early on that most of what they droned on about was meaningless. At the very first of these meetings there had been a three-hour discussion about whether or not the water fountain in Habalt Square in the east part of Edrin should be moved twelve paces to the left so the dowager Munca, the matriarch of one of Edrin's oldest families, could enjoy the setting sun of an evening while sipping a drink at her favourite cafe. Garvan had decided against that one.

These were the duties of a king. It was not what

Garvan had been expecting. He thought it would involve more important matters, matters of state rather than town planning and meet 'n' greets. Tomorrow he was to travel to Jerra, a town in the north, for the opening of a bakery. How had he never noticed that this was what his father and mother used to do? They were always rushing off somewhere. He had never paid enough attention to what it was that happened when they got to that somewhere.

Just then there was movement at the door and Garvan turned to see a messenger quarrelling with the royal guards standing duty.

'What's going on?' called Garvan, talking over the Secretary of the Treasury who had been listing the country's many debits and credits over the last several hundred years in order to bring Garvan up to speed. Garvan had not taken in a single detail.

The guard turned to address Garvan: 'Messenger, Your Majesty. I told him he has to wait for the committee to take a break as per protocol.'

'Who's the message for?' asked Garvan.

'It's for Your Majesty, Your Majesty.'

'Good, let's take a break, shall we?' said Garvan, crossing to the messenger.

'But I still have 214 years of finances to list for Your Majesty.'

'If something's worthwhile it's worth waiting for,' said Garvan.

His advisors looked at one another, frowning. They

all jerked their heads in the Chief of Staff's direction, gesturing for him to speak on their behalf. The Chief of Staff was a glum-looking man called Movon.

'Is that an official decree, Your Majesty?'

'What?' asked Garvan, looking back just as he reached the messenger.

'"If something's worthwhile it's worth waiting for"?' repeated Movon. 'Is it official? Should we have it added to the Cantibean charter?'

Garvan scowled. 'What are you talking about? No, of course not. It's just something I said. We're all taking a break, OK. Talk among yourselves.'

His advisors shared some more frowns, wondering if that was an order. Each struggled to think of something to say to the others.

'Splendid day,' said the Secretary of the Treasury, looking pleased that he had thought of something to say first.

'Yes, splendid,' said the Secretary of Welfare. 'As pleasant as yesterday if not slightly more so.'

'I like the music of the Pothro Throat Singers,' said the Secretary of Defence.

Garvan rolled his eyes and turned his attention to the messenger. 'What is it you have for me?' he asked. The messenger beamed as he held out a letter addressed to King Garvan. Garvan took it and snapped the wax dot holding the folded sheet of paper closed. He unfolded it and started to read. As he did so a broad smile of pure joy spread across his face.

'Gentlemen,' said Garvan to his advisors, 'meeting adjourned for the day.' They all started to protest but Garvan didn't give them the opportunity as he marched away.

There had been much debate on what title should be bestowed on the old king, Garvan's father, Cadrew. There had never been a living ex-monarch before. Garvan's mother, Adilla, would become the Royal Mother, so it seemed sensible that Cadrew should be the Royal Father, but he wasn't keen. Truth was he wasn't keen on any title, because anything other than king was a step down in his mind. He had never expected to be alive so long and now he struggled to find things to occupy his time.

Garvan found him down by the old jetty, fishing. His father hated fishing, but it was something that took up quite a lot of time, albeit with very little activity involved or anything to show for it.

'Fish aren't biting today,' he said.

'There are no fish,' said Garvan, sitting down next to him.

'I know. Don't spoil it,' said his father. They sat in silence for several long moments. Golden-winged monca flies whizzed over the smooth surface of the water, pausing now and again to hover over potential food before zigzagging away again.

'I'm going away,' said Garvan.

'Are you?' said his father, crumpling his brow in thought. 'I don't remember any official visits planned.

Apart from the opening of the bakery up in Jerra tomorrow, but you can be there and back in a day.'

'It's not official. It's Junk. I got a letter from him. He's back.'

'Where was he?'

'It would be almost impossible to explain.'

'When are you leaving?' asked Cadrew.

'Now.'

'What? You can't. The Itris delegates are arriving the day after tomorrow. You have to be here for that.'

'I know. I thought about that. You're going to take my place.'

'What? No. I can't. That's a king's duty.'

'You are a king, Father. It's not like you can stop being a king.'

'No, Garvan, this is not acceptable.'

'If I decree it, it's acceptable.'

Cadrew chuckled and looked at his son with undisguised pride. It was a look he had never given Garvan before. 'Never thought I'd hear words like that coming from you.'

'As I said I would, I have had the law changed. Our duel will be the last. In future, a firstborn will succeed the old monarch when the old monarch chooses to step down or dies of natural causes. No more beheading one's parent.'

'Times change. Never questioned it in my day. Lopped my old dad's head off and never thought anything of it.'

'I've made all the arrangements. You are to occupy the throne in my absence. Your voice is the voice of the king.' Garvan paused, feeling that wasn't enough. 'Still,' he added.

'How long will you be gone?' asked Cadrew.

'I'm not sure. Can I rely on you, Father?'

'If you weren't king, I'd smack your legs for asking that question.' Garvan smiled. 'Well then, I suppose I won't have time for any more fishing.' With that he tossed his fishing rod into the lake. 'Thank God for that.'

Cadrew got to his feet and Garvan did the same. 'Your throne will be safe and waiting for you when you return.' Then he put his hand on his son's arm and looked him in the eye with earnest seriousness. 'I do understand why you're going, but you know you shouldn't, right? Different rules apply now, Garvan.'

There was a gentleness in his father's eyes that Garvan wasn't used to seeing. Cadrew had always been a stern and authoritarian father. Cold even. And for the first time Garvan saw how old his father was. He suddenly looked ancient and frail, just for a moment, and then Cadrew straightened his back and spread his shoulders and his regal presence returned.

'Right then,' he said. 'This place isn't going to rule itself.' And with that he marched back up the jetty towards the palace.

10

Junk woke and it took him several moments to get his bearings. He was on a land-ship again. He looked around and saw Lasel and Cobe nearby. There was no sign of Tolfke. Lasel was asleep, but Cobe stood staring out of the window. Junk became aware of his left hand almost immediately. The itching sensation had given way to a fierce throbbing. He massaged it with the thumb of his right hand, but when he looked at it he let out an involuntary cry, sitting bolt upright. This caused Cobe to spin around and Lasel jumped up, suddenly awake and a little disorientated.

'What? What is it?' she said. Breathing hard, trying not to give in to panic, Junk held up his hand, showing them both his palm. Cobe and Lasel edged closer, both frowning.

'What's that?' said Cobe.

What had been a centimetre-long smudge of yellow pulsing under his skin the last time he had looked was now something quite different. It had now stretched diagonally across the whole of his palm, about ten centimetres in length. It still appeared to be just under the top layer of his skin, but now instead of a nebulous shape it had divided into four very distinct symbols. The first was a diamond over a square with a circle in the middle. The second was an eight-pointed star made up of interlocking isosceles triangles. The third was a series of circles overlapping each other to create one large circle. The final symbol was made up of eight thin lines that seemed to move at random, creating different patterns, like a mini-Rorschach test.

'I don't know,' said Junk, rubbing at it again. 'There was a mark there earlier. It was just a bit itchy. I didn't think much of it. Now it hurts. It throbs. What happened back there?'

'They were upset,' said Cobe. 'Because you touched them. Tolfke said not to touch them.'

'You blacked out,' said Lasel. 'The Valuda separated and moved away. On all fours, like animals. It was weird. There were holes in the wall. They went inside. One for each of them. The old man was very angry. He told us to leave. Pretty sure we're not welcome there any more.'

'What happened to Tolfke?'

'He stayed. We couldn't think of any other reason why we'd need him.'

'No, I guess not,' said Junk. 'You think they did this?'

'No,' said Lasel. 'We would've noticed.'

'When did you see it before?' asked Cobe. 'You said there was a mark there earlier.'

Junk cast his mind back. 'It was on the way there. Just before we jumped into the cave.'

'Then it couldn't have been them,' said Lasel, 'if you already had it.'

'But it didn't look like this.' He considered it. There was only one other possible explanation. 'It's Sbey. He did it to me.'

'You don't know that,' said Lasel. 'Don't go jumping to conclusions.'

'Can you think of another explanation?' asked Junk.

Lasel considered the question with a frown. 'No, but that doesn't mean you're right.'

'What does it mean?' asked Cobe.

Junk's mind raced. What did the symbols mean? He didn't recognize them.

'I don't know. Maybe some sort of brand? A logging number maybe? Maybe I was just one of lots of experiments.'

'When we hear from Espa,' said Lasel, trying to sound reassuring, 'we can ask him about it.'

Junk nodded, forcing a smile designed to reassure her in return, but he was faking and they both knew it. He focused in on the first symbol: the circle in a square over a diamond. The circle was divided into eight equal parts and one eighth was pulsing rhythmically in time with the throbbing pain. He stared at it, closer and closer. And then an announcement came over the tannoy, jolting him from his thoughts. He didn't recognize the language.

'What was that?' said Junk. He rubbed his palm and then curled it into a fist, putting it out of his mind.

'I think it was telling us we're almost there,' said Cobe.

'Almost where?'

'Dajja,' said Lasel. 'Figured that's where you'd want to go.'

Cobe turned back to the window and gazed outside.

'There it is,' he said. Junk and Lasel joined him by the window. The landscape was flat and mostly barren. There was the occasional sorry-looking tree or bush, but they appeared to be dead. Animals that looked like steroid-pumped rabbits about the size of dogs raced alongside the land-ship in packs of fifty or more. Suddenly a huge eagle-like bird flew down, trying to snatch one up. The rabbit-creatures scattered but the bird was persistent. It swooped again and this time managed to wrap its talons around one of the infants. Immediately the fleeing über-rabbits stopped fleeing and turned to attack. They swarmed over the bigger, nastier-looking predator bird. Junk's last view of it was its beak open wide, screaming in distress, as it was overwhelmed.

'There,' said Cobe, and Junk turned to look ahead.

'Oh my God!' he gasped, unable to stop himself when he saw the town of Dajja. It was a sprawling, striking-looking settlement that consisted of around a hundred separate buildings all plastered in a blood-red render and raised about four metres off the ground on stilts. Junk remembered the images that had swamped his senses when he touched the Valuda. He remembered seeing a town bathed in blood. It wasn't blood but it was Dajja that he had seen. Most stilt houses Junk knew of – he'd come across a few in Thailand and Myanmar while working on boats – were generally built over water. Here they had just been raised above the level, rocky ground.

When they stopped, the three of them disembarked the land-ship, the only passengers to alight. They headed towards the stilt town as the sun was beginning to set.

The red buildings were in no discernible pattern. They appeared to have been built randomly and then connected to their neighbours by the means of narrow walkways that had also been painted the same shade of red. Junk, Lasel and Cobe stood in a flat open square of land, surrounded on all sides by the stilt buildings. It had the feel of a town square maybe. They listened. There was no sound of life.

Junk looked at the other two: 'You think anyone's here?'

Lasel shrugged.

'ANYONE HERE?' yelled Cobe, without warning, at the top of his booming voice, taking Lasel and Junk by surprise. There was no response. He tried a few more times in various languages but still nothing. 'I guess there's no one here,' he said finally. Just then they noticed that every walkway had a ladder but all were stored on the walkways, as if they had been put away before the residents had retreated into their homes. 'I think it's deserted,' said Cobe.

122

'I don't know,' said Lasel. 'It doesn't look neglected.'

'Then where is everyone?'

'Good question. Give me a boost,' she said to Cobe. He put his hands on her waist and raised her into the air as if she weighed nothing at all. He raised his arms above his head, holding her aloft and then propelled her upward. Lasel rose in a controlled arc and landed on the side of one of the walkways, grabbing the top railing immediately and pulling herself up and over. She made her way to the nearest ladder, unhitched it and lowered it over the side for Junk and Cobe.

When all three were up they started to explore. They peered through windows into the rooms beyond. All did indeed look cared for. Nothing was overtly dusty or decrepit. It was as if the occupants had simply dematerialized and floated away into the ether.

Junk tried a few doors. The first four were locked but the fifth was not. He hesitated momentarily before going inside. It was someone's home: a living room and kitchen, a bathroom and a bedroom. The bed was unmade. There was a book on the side table. It had been left upside down, its pages spread out. Junk picked it up but couldn't read a word of it. It was in a language he had never seen before. He put it back and continued with his search.

He returned to the walkway and saw Lasel on the parallel one. He called over to her: 'What language do they speak here?'

'The same as the Valuda back in the caves. It's called Bujolo. This whole area is the Bujol Peninsula.'

'We should have brought Tolfke with us.'

'Why?' she asked. 'There's no one here to speak to.'
It was a fair point.

Just then, they heard Cobe calling to them both and
hurried to find him. They followed the sound of his voice
to the westernmost walkway, skirting the outside of the
town. When they got to him he didn't say anything. He
just directed them to look at a small hill a short distance
away. Atop the hill was a strange-looking tree. It looked
like it was growing upside down, just like the one the
Valuda had described. A chill of dread ran through Junk.

The three of them lowered another ladder and
climbed down. The land rose steeply and it was a
punishing climb to the top of the hill. Junk's leg muscles
were burning, every step was torture, but eventually the
ground plateaued. It was indeed a graveyard. Flat slabs
of rough-cut silver-grey stone, a metre in length and
half a metre wide, marked each grave, and on each slab
was a circle, again just as the Valuda had said, chiselled
into the stone. There were about a hundred graves, but it
was the one under the upside-down tree that Junk was
interested in. He approached it slowly, solemnly, until
he stood looking down at it. It was exactly as had been
described. Exactly as he had seen in the moment when
he had touched the Valuda on the arm. *Did that mean
Ambeline was under the stone, lying in the grave?* All their
other predictions had been correct.

Junk looked at the weird tree. It wasn't growing
upside down, it just looked like it was. It was thinner at

the bottom and the foliage that sprouted from the top was long and thin, looking more like roots than leaves. Junk hung his head and could feel tears starting to rise up inside him. His throat tensed, making it hard to swallow. He covered his face with his hands and was on the verge of giving into the emotion he felt when he heard singing. They all heard it. The three of them turned to look back at the blood-red town. They couldn't see anyone, but they could distinctly hear a woman's voice singing a lilting, haunting refrain.

They moved back down the hill to the ladder and climbed up to the outer walkway. Then, with Lasel leading, they headed back the way they had come when they first arrived. As they turned the corner that led to the buildings around the open square, they were shocked to discover the town was suddenly fully populated. The walkways were bustling with men, women and children hurrying to and fro. More children were playing some sort of bat-and-ball-based game down at ground level in the town square. Residents were hanging washing on clothes lines outside their homes. One such resident was a plump, pear-shaped woman with long pigment-less hair that ran down her back, tied in a ponytail, reaching almost to the ground. She was the source of the singing. Her voice was exquisite and rose above everything else.

The residents were all shapes, sizes and colours. So far no one had noticed the three strangers in their midst, but that was about to change. A ball came bouncing along the walkway and rolled all the way to Lasel's feet, but it was Cobe who bent down and picked it up in his vast flat hand. Just then a young boy, short blond curls atop a chestnut brown face, hurried towards them. He stopped when he saw them and stared open-mouthed with surprise. Then Cobe took a step forward, holding out the ball to the boy. This was all too much and the boy suddenly found his voice.

'Nungra!' he hollered, turning and running. 'Nungra!' Everyone turned to look, and after a brief lull where everything was plunged into silence as the townsfolk processed what they were seeing – interlopers in their midst – panic broke out. Parents grabbed children and hurried them up the ladders and indoors. The town's militia, or maybe just some of the braver residents as they didn't wear anything that resembled a uniform, rushed forward, coming from all directions and converging on the one walkway, all armed with tools similar to pitchforks and long-bladed machete-like knives. Cobe stepped in front of Lasel and Junk, shielding them, but at the same time holding his hands up, trying to make it clear they were not a threat. However, that was easier said than done. Cobe was twice the size of anyone in Dajja and his heavily scarred and tattooed face wasn't designed for putting strangers at their ease.

The armed men and women shouted. From the inflection in the words, it was apparent they were asking questions. *Who are you? What are you doing here? What do you want?* or something along those lines. Cobe tried replying in the various languages he spoke, but he was met with blank looks. Lasel stepped forward and did the same. She spoke several languages that Cobe did not, but still not one of them was met with anything other than fear.

Lasel looked to Junk.

'You try.'

Junk thought it pointless. He didn't speak any languages that Lasel didn't speak apart from a few from his own time, and the people here were unlikely to be fluent in a dialect that hadn't been popular in three million years. He tried Italian, Spanish, French, Russian and finally English:

'We don't mean any harm. Please, put down your weapons.' Junk paused and silence hung over the entire town. Then he heard a voice, a child's voice, calling out.

'N'yask!'

There was movement in the crowd. Someone small. Too small to see. Junk was able to follow his or her progress by the way the adults moved to let the child through. 'N'yask!' he heard again. 'I understand,' the same small voice said, but this time in English. The voice was that of a girl, quite young, and Junk spotted a blonde-haired child rushing forward. His heart throbbed. He knew exactly who it must be. He would recognize her anywhere.

'Ambeline?'

11

The child reached the edge of the town square and was lifted to the ladder. Still Junk couldn't see her properly from where he stood. He stepped forward, moving around Cobe, and watched as a small tanned hand reached up and grabbed the railing, pulling herself up. A head of blonde hair came into view. *Ambeline!* thought Junk again and then the child rose above the railing and Junk saw her face. His heart sank. It wasn't Ambeline.

The girl gasped as she spotted Cobe and her eyes widened in alarm. Junk smiled at her, drawing her attention away from Cobe and on to him.

'Hi,' he said. 'My name's Junk. These are my friends. We don't mean you any harm. Do you understand?'

The little girl was only seven or eight years old. She frowned, playing his words over in her head. When she spoke it was slowly and deliberately, enunciating each word as clearly as she could. 'Me name Tualla.'

'That's a pretty name, Tualla. How is it you speak English?'

She cocked her head to one side, frowning. 'Ing-lish?'

'The words we're speaking,' said Junk, trying to think of the simplest way to explain what he wanted to say and waving his hands around in an attempt to utilize some sort of makeshift sign language to help him, 'are called English where I come from.'

Tualla considered this and took her time answering. 'Friend my,' she said eventually, 'say me how I speak.'

Junk replayed her words, reordering them till they made sense. 'A friend taught you how to speak English? Was your friend a little girl like you? With long blonde hair like you.' Junk pointed to Tualla's own hair, but the movement startled the girl; she flinched and two of the men with weapons lurched forward. Junk held up his hands. 'It's OK, it's OK.'

The moment passed and Tualla grew brave again. She came closer once more and took hold of a handful of her own hair. 'Friend my,' she said, 'yell-o.' She shook the handful of hair, looking pleased with herself that she had remembered the word.

'Your friend had yellow hair?' Junk took a deep breath. He was hesitant to voice his next question. He was dreading a negative response. 'Your friend . . . was her name Ambeline?'

Tualla's face broke into a bright smile, fuelled by recognition of the name. She nodded her head vigorously. 'Zo, zo . . . Ambeline. Ambeline.'

Junk let out a joyful sob. Somehow, against all the

odds, he had found his sister's trail. But then the joy faded and he remembered the grave under the upside-down tree. 'Where is Ambeline?' he said softly to Tualla, waving his hands in wide circles, the universally acknowledged gesture for *where*. Then despite himself he turned to look up at the graveyard on the hill and pointed. Tualla's face fell and she nodded sadly.

'Zo,' she said, and then her little face creased into a thoughtful frown and Junk could see she was searching her memory for the right words. 'Bone . . . face,' she said, and punctuated the end of the phrase with a sharp nod, as if to say, *Yes, that's right*.

'Bone face?' said Junk, looking to Lasel to make sure he had heard correctly. He turned back to Tualla. 'What's that? What's bone face?'

Tualla squeezed her eyes tightly shut, struggling to find the right words to articulate what she was trying to say, but finally she shook her head in frustration. The words wouldn't come.

Junk, Lasel and Cobe were invited to stay and Tualla did her best to act as interpreter between them and the town elders. The initial suspicion and fear that had greeted the strangers seemed to have faded away and the people of Dajja proved themselves to be friendly and generous. However, the language barrier was frustrating. Junk managed to glean that Ambeline arrived one day out of the blue. She was scared and sullen, which Junk could well understand. She was only little. This was over three years ago when she had been only just six, younger even than Tualla now. She had been taken in by Tualla's family and the girls became the best of friends. Ambeline had learned to speak Bujolo a lot better than Tualla could speak English, but she had been unable to explain where she came from. They showed her maps of the world, but she couldn't point out her home. Of course Junk knew that in this time Ireland wasn't there any more. It had been consumed by the sea. There was nothing left to point out.

With no idea of where Ambeline's home was, no one in Dajja knew how or where to return her so it was decided that she would stay with them. Tualla's family as good as adopted her. As far as Junk could tell, she was happy. It is said that children that age are resilient. Junk couldn't learn much more. Tualla's limited grasp of English and his non-existent Bujolo stymied the majority of his questions.

They were given beds for the night, longer if they wanted them. Junk lay awake staring through the window at the bright half-moon floating in the sky. He kept remembering what Tualla had said: *bone face*, and he thought he understood. She meant death. She was saying what he already knew: that Ambeline was dead. That she was just a skeleton in a grave. A face of bone. A bone face.

He thought ahead now to what he would do next. With Ambeline confirmed dead, he had reached the end of the road. Originally he had been thinking about

131

taking Jacid Mestrowe back home to show his parents that he'd been telling the truth. He could still do that with Cobe. He knew Cobe would come with him. But then he considered Dras Sbey. Would Sbey be able to snatch Junk the moment he entered the Room of Doors? But without using the Room of Doors Junk could never get home. That would mean he was stuck here, in this time. Junk turned his head a little to look at Lasel. That might not be so bad. He had good friends here. He knew he could go and live in Cantibea with Garvan. He could track down Hundrig Shunt and the *Casabia* and live a life on the ocean waves. Or he could explore the world with Lasel maybe. Or maybe he didn't have to worry about the future because he didn't have one.

He looked at the symbols on his hand again. His thoughts had kept returning to them over the last few hours and he would snatch glimpses frequently, constantly trying to work out their significance. The throbbing had eased off and he was hardly aware of it now. The symbols had changed. The section of the circle that had been pulsing at a faster rate than the rest had now stopped pulsing entirely and was just a faint empty outline. It had just gone. As had the next eighth, its neighbour, and the one after that. The fourth was now blinking faster.

And in that moment, Junk had an epiphany. He knew what the symbols meant. It was so obvious. After a period of time that fourth section would also vanish, followed by the rest, one by one, until the circle was gone completely. Then the next symbol, then the next. Until they were all gone. It was some sort of countdown. A type of clock. He guessed it wasn't a countdown to something good. Instead it was probably a countdown to something worse than he could imagine. A countdown to a nightmare. A nightmare clock.

What was going to happen when the last symbol faded? Would he die? Be recaptured? Something he couldn't predict? Probably the last one. It made sense that Dras Sbey would have a back-up plan. Though why not just pull him back now? Or kill him? Why draw it out? He would have a reason. Junk was sure of it.

Junk was tired. He had been searching for such a long time. First for Mestrowe, then for the Nine Emperors and finally for Ambeline. But now that was all over. Ambeline was dead. There was nothing else to search for.

He looked at the symbols again and did some quick calculations in his head. It had taken about two hours for each eighth to vanish. If each section was consistent, and he had no reason to think otherwise, then each symbol would last for sixteen hours. That meant he had about two and a half days left before the clock would run out. He felt oddly calm about the whole thing, when rationally he shouldn't. He should be freaking out but, after everything he'd been through, was freaking out going to help? Did freaking out ever help? And anyway, what did it matter now? He had failed. Ambeline was gone.

Suddenly the door to their room burst open and Tualla raced in, looking panicked. Lasel and Cobe both woke.

'Tualla,' said Junk, 'what is it? What's wrong?' Tualla grabbed Junk's hand and tried to pull him up. She looked terrified.

'Puna! Puna! Puna!' she said, yanking at him. Junk had heard that word before, but he didn't know what it meant.

'Calm down,' he said, keeping his voice level. 'Tell us what's wrong.'

'Goge!' she said, shaking her head. 'Puna!' She was almost in tears now. Junk looked at Lasel and Cobe.

'I think she wants us to go with her,' said Cobe.

Still the newcomers weren't moving so Tualla fought through her panic and searched her head for the right words.

'Bone face,' she said.

Junk frowned. Did she mean Ambeline? Tualla was still pulling at him and now Junk got to his feet. He could see the relief on the little girl's face. Lasel and Cobe rose too and all four left.

When they got outside they were astonished to see that the entire population of the town was streaming out of their homes in their nightclothes. No one was speaking. The silence was eerie. They were all converging on the very centre of the town square, where Junk saw a hole in the ground that he was sure had not been there before.

It was no bigger than a manhole, and the residents of Dajja were descending into it one at a time in an orderly and clearly much practised fashion. Tualla still had a tight hold of Junk's hand and she led him to her parents, joining the line.

'What's going on, Tualla?' asked Junk, and everyone around him shushed him urgently.

Tualla worked out what she wanted to say and whispered to Junk: 'Bone face coming.' And with that she looked to the graveyard on the hill. Junk looked too and saw the upside-down tree and then he saw a figure of a man rising up out of the topmost grave. Ambeline's grave. And in the light of the half-moon he saw his face was a skull.

And then it was Junk's turn to enter the hole in the ground. He was guided forcefully, moving on autopilot, and he found a set of narrow steps and went down into a low-ceilinged underground room. He couldn't stand up straight and had to bend his neck and shoulders. Cobe had no choice but to crawl on all fours and sit. There was no light apart from the moonlight coming through the entrance but they had been among the last to enter and the hole was soon closed, plunging them all into total darkness. The only sound was breathing and the occasional muffled cough.

They stayed like that for a long time, Junk wasn't sure how long exactly. At one point, he glanced at the palm of his hand and he could see the yellow symbols shining in the darkness. Another section had gone out and the next was blinking. He balled his hand into a fist, smothering the light, as if trying literally to hold on to time. Then they heard footsteps overhead and even the sounds of breathing stopped as everyone held their breath. The footsteps were heavy. Clumping. And there was more than one set. More than one person up there. Junk strained to listen. He could hear voices, but the sound was highly muffled. He couldn't make out what was being said and probably wouldn't have understood even if he could. Was this where the townsfolk had been when he, Lasel and Cobe had arrived earlier? Had they all been down here listening to them walking overhead? The footsteps moved away and quickly faded. Breathing resumed.

After another maybe ten minutes, someone climbed the steps and opened up the entrance. Still no one made a sound. A scout slipped out and the covering was replaced, sending them back into darkness. More minutes passed and then the entrance reopened from outside.

'Durt zha!' the scout called down. It was evidently the all-clear, because the residents of Dajja relaxed and started chatting as they filed up the stairs and out of the shelter.

'Tualla,' said Junk, as they were going, 'what was that? Who was up here?'

'Bone face,' said Tualla, sounding confident in her pronunciation, having said the words several times now.

'I thought Ambeline was bone face.'

'Zo, Ambeline bone face,' said Tualla.

'Ambeline was here?' asked Junk, pointing to the dusty ground beneath their feet.

'Goge,' said Tualla, which Junk had by now worked out meant 'no'. Tualla concentrated, choosing her words. 'Bone face take . . .' and she mimed someone snatching something. 'Take, zo?'

'Take, yes,' said Junk, nodding.

'Bone face take Ambeline.'

'Take Ambeline where?' said Junk, and Tualla pointed to the hill and the upside-down tree and the graveyard.

Lasel and Cobe raced to keep up with Junk as he scrambled up the hill to the graveyard.

'Slow down, Junk,' Lasel shouted. 'What are you doing?'

'She's not dead. Ambeline's not dead.'

'That's not what Tualla said.'

'She said she was taken by the bone face – whoever he is. I saw him standing by the upside-down tree, just before we went down into that cellar.'

They reached the graveyard and stopped by the grave under the tree.

'We don't know what he is or even if he's alone,' said Lasel.

'I'm telling you, I saw him. It wasn't a ghost. It was a man,' said Junk. 'A man with a skull for a face but a man nonetheless.' Junk grabbed the corner of the

137

stone slab covering the grave and put all his strength behind trying to move it. It would not budge and he exhausted himself in seconds with nothing to show for it. He looked imploringly at Cobe. The big man nodded and crouched down, forcing his fingertips under the slab and then lifting. He roared with the exertion but it started to move. Little by little he was able to move the slab to the side until it unbalanced and toppled to the ground with a resounding thud. The three of them crowded around to look into the grave, except it wasn't a grave at all. What they found instead was a broad flight of stone steps descending into the earth.

12

It was a glorious summer's afternoon in Paris. Dr Sznarzel Otravinicus was sitting outside the Café de Seine, situated on the bank of the river of the same name and across the water from Notre-Dame de Paris. The year was 1828 and his companion was a young Frenchman in his twenties.

'I mean, take the cathedral for example,' Otravinicus was saying, his French flawless, 'the beautiful stained glass . . . gone! And for what reason? More light!'

'More light,' echoed his companion.

'It is obscene,' announced Otravinicus.

'I couldn't agree more, Doctor.'

'You should write something, Victor, something to stir the passion of the masses and have them put an end to this ridiculous regime of destroying the beauty of Parisian architecture and building these modern monstrosities in their place.'

'It's uncanny. It's like you can read my mind, Doctor. I've started toying with an idea for a new book dealing with that very subject.'

'No!' exclaimed Otravinicus, feigning surprise.

'Yes,' cried the young man. 'It's even called *Notre-Dame de Paris*.'

'Here's a suggestion for you – make the protagonist a hunchback.'

'A hunchback?'

'Yes, a man who is ugly on the outside but beautiful within.' Otravinicus's young companion considered this for a few moments and then smiled.

'I like it!' he announced.

That morning, which happened to be an autumnal morning sixty years later than the afternoon, Otravinicus had been in the south of France in a small town called Arles. He had breakfasted at a little cafe next to a yellow house. Across the street sat a troubled young man with red hair and a straggly ginger beard. He wore a tatty straw hat that he would gnaw at out of habit as he drew. He was starting his initial sketches for his latest composition. The troubled young man was an artist. Otravinicus stayed sitting outside the cafe until the young man had finished and left.

Using the Antricle he had purloined from the Nine Emperors, Otravinicus left Arles and jumped about a century or so into the future and appeared in Amsterdam, where he paid his admission fee to enter a modernist building on Museumplein and strode through the museum dedicated to the work of Vincent van Gogh until he found what he was looking for: a painting known as *The Yellow House*. He saw several small, indistinct figures sitting outside the neighbouring cafe and he smiled to himself. No one else would know one of them was him maybe, but he knew and that was enough for him.

It was a cold wet night in 1960. Otravinicus sat at the back of a bus as it pulled up to a stop outside a Hamburg night club called the Kaiserkeller. Five scruffy young English men jumped aboard, paid their fare and took their seats, each sitting separately. It was late and they were all tired. The bus trundled through the city.

Without drawing attention to himself, Otravinicus got up from his seat at the back of the bus and moved forward so he was sitting directly behind one of the men, a good-looking teenager with a mop of black hair. His head was leaning against the window and his eyes were closed. Otravinicus started to sing quietly to himself.

'Yesterday, all my troubles seemed so far away . . . Now it looks like they're here to stay . . . Oh, I believe in yesterday . . .'

The young man with the mop of black hair didn't react. It's possible he was asleep, but Otravinicus finished the song and got off the bus with a satisfied curl to his lips.

In the time since Otravinicus had stolen the Antricle, he had travelled the world. He considered he was making much better use of it than its previous owners, two of the Nine Emperors: Foster and Ed. They used it merely for stealing art and recruiting an army. Otravinicus had moved through history. He concentrated on what was to him the distant past: Junk's time and a few hundred years either side. That period had always been a personal favourite for Otravinicus ever since the time he spent travelling with Foster.

Foster Peck, the Falcon Emperor as he had dubbed himself, had told Otravinicus all sorts of things that had stuck in his mind. For instance, Paul McCartney initially thought he had plagiarized the song 'Yesterday' because he woke up with it almost fully formed in his head, so assumed he must have heard it somewhere first. Hamburg in October 1960 was around five years before McCartney would actually write the song, but Otravinicus liked to think that he had laid the foundations for it, even if he was singing McCartney a song McCartney wrote.

Otravinicus had befriended Abraham Lincoln when he was a young man, in his early twenties, working in a general store in New Salem, Illinois. He had then stayed in constant touch with him over the next fifteen years, which had only taken up a couple of days of Otravinicus's time, and had got himself invited to the White House when Lincoln became president. He had also done this with eleven other presidents and sixteen British prime ministers, several German chancellors, including Hitler, many French presidents and heads of state from all over the world and throughout time.

As well as Van Gogh's, Otravinicus managed to position himself into 126 other paintings. The one he was most pleased with was Édouard Manet's *Music in the Tuileries*, where he is staring forward, out of the painting, standing next to a tree and wearing a top hat. Go and look at the painting and to this day you will see the face of Sznarzel Otravinicus.

He also managed to appear in the background of seventy-nine movies, from early ones by the likes of D. W. Griffiths through to films Junk would have seen as a child and beyond.

Other than Victor Hugo, Otravinicus befriended a whole host of authors and positioned himself just right so he could offer them the spark of inspiration that launched a hundred different books. He was thanked in the acknowledgements of ninety-three classic works.

None of it amounted to anything more than vanity on Otravinicus's part. None of it was real. He wasn't really giving the writers and musicians their inspiration, he was merely telling them what they had already thought of just before they had thought of it.

Otravinicus had been fascinated with the Room of Doors for the best part of two decades, since he'd come across a vague reference to it in an obscure and dusty old book. That fascination turned to obsession, when he wrote his own book about it, and that obsession got somewhat out of control when Junk and his friends crossed his path. Now that he had what he had longed for, his very own Antricle, he discovered there was nothing he really wanted to use it for other than frivolous excursions through time. He didn't have any megalomaniacal tendencies that might lead him to seek world domination, though that was surely possible with such a powerful device at his disposal. He had no desire to accumulate wealth, as the Nine Emperors had done. Money had never been a motivating factor in Otravinicus's make-up. He didn't want to change history, his or anyone else's; he just liked to see things for himself, which most people would probably say was actually a pretty wonderful use of the Antricle.

The only thing Otravinicus really lacked was to have someone to share his travels with. He was lonely. He had watched the Great Pyramid of Giza being built. He had stood in the middle of Trafalgar Square, very briefly, during the Blitz, as the Luftwaffe rained bombs down on the British capital. He had been to the Colosseum in Rome and watched gladiatorial games. He had stood at a safe distance to watch the Battle of Hastings in 1066. He had been one of the few to witness and survive the reawakening of the supervolcano underneath Yellowstone National Park in Wyoming, North America, in the early thirty-first century. The USA had taken centuries to recover after that. He had stood on the deck of the *Titanic* as it ploughed into the iceberg. He had been racked with guilt after that, because of course he could have stopped that from happening, saving everyone on board, but the implications of such an action were too great even to contemplate. He had met Alexander the Great, Mao Zedong on his Long March, Emperor Nero, Billy Wilder, William Shakespeare and Orville and Wilbur Wright, but always alone. He had no one to share these experiences with. No one he could talk to about the wondrous things he had seen. It very quickly became a lonely existence.

He had thought about trying to find Cascér, which wouldn't have been too hard, but she was too angry for his liking and too rough. He knew he had the whole of history at his disposal to find his perfect woman so he drew up a list that included everyone from Boudicca to Cleopatra to Elizabeth I to Marie Curie to Audrey Hepburn to Lady Gaga to Sharon Cordova (captain of the winning team in the 2046 football World Cup, the first to have teams including both men and women) and a dozen other names. He then made it his business to meet them one by one and keep their name on the list or cross it off.

Boudicca was too vitriolic; Cleopatra had some commitment issues; Elizabeth I had just awful hygiene; Marie Curie was much too intelligent for him; Audrey Hepburn took a disliking to him almost immediately and thought he was a stalker; Lady Gaga scared him; Sharon Cordova was too physical and just wanted them both to exercise all the time. And so it went on, until every name had been crossed off and he was back to square one.

He was almost resigned to never finding the right person when he happened to be in Washington DC for an event at the White House. He was a guest of the then president, Franklin Delano Roosevelt. The year was 1937. Also at the dinner was Amelia Earhart, the intrepid explorer, first woman to fly solo across the Atlantic and a whole host of other achievements. It was love at first sight for both of them. Amelia was married at the time but not happily so, and she was shortly about to embark on a flight around the world. The flight would never be completed. Amelia Earhart was about to vanish off the face of the planet somewhere over the Pacific Ocean and the rest of the world would never know what became of her.

What became of her is that Sznarzel Otravinicus saved her from her plane as it ran out of fuel and plunged into the ocean. When she woke, she was in the Room of Doors and Otravinicus revealed that he was a time traveller with access to all of history at his fingertips. In Amelia Earhart, Otravinicus had found his perfect travelling companion and soulmate. From that day forth, they travelled everywhere together, exploring time hand in hand.

13

The stone steps went down a long way, curving to the right then the left. Junk, Lasel and Cobe walked in a line, hugging the wall. After the first dozen or so steps the fingers of moonlight that reached into the open grave, illuminating their path, faded to nothing and they carried on in darkness. Junk led the way, feeling for each new tread before putting his foot down. It was slow going. He held out his left hand, using the light from the countdown clock on his palm to try to see where they were going, but the light was dim and flat and didn't offer much in the way of help.

'I could use the Antricle to light our way,' he suggested.

'No,' said Lasel. 'Espa said Sbey would be able to find you if you used it.'

'But that's not really *using* it, is it?' said Junk. 'It's only using it as a torch.'

'You don't know that,' said Lasel. 'It might be all he needs. It's not worth the risk.'

'She's right,' said Cobe, 'and besides, I can see . . .' He paused. 'Something. There's light ahead.'

Junk strained to focus, but he couldn't make out anything at all. No shapes. No difference in light and dark. It was just dark. Just then, however, the wall started curving again towards the right and there was a distinct change in the acoustics as if they had just entered a much larger cavern.

'You hear that?' asked Junk, his voice echoing around them.

'Yeah,' said Lasel. 'It's colder too.' They could all feel an icy breeze cooling their skin and ruffling their hair (those who had hair).

'Go slower, Junk,' said Cobe. Junk listened and reached out with a shaking hand, his fingers brushing against the cold, crumbling rock wall, his foot scraping on the ground as he edged onward.

'Uh-oh,' said Junk suddenly.

'Uh-oh?' asked Lasel. 'What's "uh-oh"?'

'Wall's stopped,' said Junk.

'What do you mean, it's stopped? Walls don't just stop.'

That wasn't true of course, and this one had. Junk reached out, stretching, swinging his arm back and forth in a broad arc, willing his fingertips to connect with something solid, but there was nothing.

'I can't feel anything at all,' said Junk. 'The wall just stops here.'

'Are there any more steps?' asked Lasel.

'Hold on to me,' said Junk, and Lasel and Cobe both grabbed on to the back of his collar. Junk extended his right foot and lowered it to where the next step, if there was a next step, should be. There was nothing. He lowered it a little further, pointing his toe like a ballet dancer, bending his left knee, lowering himself slowly. He felt his balance faltering and stood upright again.

'Damn it! I can't feel anything,' he said.

'We should go back,' said Lasel. 'Go back up top and get torches and whatever else we might need, then come back down here properly equipped.'

'I guess,' said Junk, but his reluctance to turn back was apparent in his voice. He felt that he had been moving towards Ambeline. Turning around and going back would mean going in the wrong direction, even though he knew Lasel's suggestion was the most sensible one.

'Wait!' said Cobe, 'There! See? Light . . .'

'Where?' said Lasel.

'It's not like I can point,' said Cobe. 'Straight ahead, look down, less than a body's length ahead, I think.' Just having the one eye meant that depth perception wasn't his strong point.

Junk and Lasel followed his directions and peered into the blackness. It took them a few moments to make out some very faint tiny blue lights. There were dozens of them, all moving from right to left in a roughly straight line a short distance ahead of where they stood. It was hard to say exactly how far. Junk thought the individual lights were small, no more than five centimetres each. They moved at a uniform pace and the more he concentrated on them the more he could make out.

'They're insects of some sort,' he said. His eyesight was adjusting gradually and he could see what they were: scorpions or something very much like scorpions. They had a dimpled carapace and one large pincer on their left side. They had segmented bodies ending in a curled pointed tail. He had seen some scorpions in a zoo once back home. He remembered they lit up under ultraviolet light and there had been a button on their enclosure, which when pressed would bathe the little creatures in black light and they would glow bright blue. 'They look like scorpions.'

'Daccun,' said Cobe. 'Plenty of them in Cul Sita. We call them daccun. They can be dangerous. Give you a nasty sting. Kill you, some of them.'

'Sounds much the same as in my time,' said Junk. 'But they don't fly.'

'Fly?' said Cobe.

'I mean they're on something. On solid ground. They're not just floating, are they? Means the ground doesn't just stop.'

'But there could be a gap and we wouldn't know,' said Lasel. 'We should go back.'

There was silence then. Even though she couldn't see his face, Lasel knew Junk was debating what to do: go on or go back? The procession of arthropods had passed and their faint light was fading, but Junk still knew roughly where they had been. The sensible option was to go back, but he wasn't listening to that part of his brain. Suddenly Junk sprang forward, launching himself into the darkness, jumping from a standing position. Lasel let out a scream that was half surprise and half frustration as he landed where the scorpions had been marching past just a moment before. His feet touched solid ground and his hands reached out for something to grab on to, but found nothing and he started to overbalance. He compensated, struggling to get his footing. He was breathing hard, more from adrenalin than from the exertion of the jump. His heart was throbbing in his chest. Lasel let fly with a whole gamut of Jansian curses and Junk was grateful he wasn't fully fluent in the language.

When she calmed down there was a moment of silence.

'Idiot,' she said in English.

'I know,' said Junk. 'Sorry.'

'No, you're not. Saying sorry implies you won't do it again, but we both know you will.'

'What's around you?' asked Cobe, interrupting before Junk and Lasel's disagreement could boil over into something else.

'Where I'm standing feels solid enough,' said Junk, 'but I can't feel anything around me. No walls or structures or anything. I felt like I dropped a little when I jumped. It's not much of a drop. Half a metre maybe.

Stretch a foot out straight ahead,' said Junk. 'I'll come to you.'

'Go steady,' said Lasel. She reached out with her right foot, waving it slowly from side to side. Cobe grabbed the back of her jacket and held it tightly in his big hand.

Junk turned on the spot, keeping his movements to a minimum. His shoulders were hunched and his body stiff. He reached both hands out before him and moved them in much the same way as Lasel was doing with her leg. Then he took a very tentative step forward. It wasn't actually a step because his foot didn't leave the ground. Instead he shuffled one foot forward, testing the solidity of the ground with a prodding toe. When his first foot had moved half a dozen centimetres, he brought the trailing foot up behind it, still maintaining contact with the floor. He edged forward in this manner until he felt the tip of Lasel's toes. Both gasped in unison.

'That you?' asked Junk.

'It's me,' said Lasel as she reached down and their hands joined. For a moment they forgot their caution and stepped together. They had a split second to realize the ground was giving way beneath them before they fell. Both cried out. Cobe, who hadn't let go of Lasel's jacket, reacted instantly and braced himself, ready to support the pair of them. Lasel was gripping Junk's hands and he held on to her. Cobe pulled and for a split second it felt as if he was going to be able to pull them back, but then his balance shifted and, before he knew what was happening, he was pitching forward too.

All three cried out in terror as they plummeted through the fragile ground. They still couldn't see anything as they fell. Down and down they went, freefalling. They lost hold of each other. Three bodies dropping into nothingness, a bottomless pit. And then suddenly they reached the bottom.

Without warning, water enveloped them as they splashed into an underground river. Cobe hit head first and the impact knocked him out cold. Junk and Lasel were luckier and went in feet first. All three were pulled under. They were dragged down for several metres until their descent slowed and then they began to rise again. A violent current grabbed hold of them and pulled them along. Junk and Lasel were struggling to break the surface. When they had hit, the air was knocked out of their lungs and now instinct was telling them to breathe. Junk felt his head break the surface of the water and he took a big gulp of oxygen. The roar of the fast-moving water filled his ears but maybe because his other senses were compensating for the lack of sight, he could hear the sound of Lasel coughing.

'LASEL!' Junk shouted. 'WHERE ARE YOU?'

'JUNK!' He heard her scream, but had no idea which direction the sound came from. Was she behind him? Ahead of him? Right next to him? He thrashed about, grabbing at the water around him, praying that he would get lucky and snag hold of her, but there was nothing.

'LASEL!' he called again. 'COBE!'

'Junk!' It was Lasel again, but this time her voice was fainter, more distant. They were moving apart.

'LASEL!' Junk was panicking.

'Junk!' He heard her again, but further away still. Her voice was drowned out by the bellowing water and after that he couldn't hear her at all. He called to her and to Cobe but there was no reply. Exhausted by shouting and fighting the current, Junk had no option but to give in and let it take him.

As the river dragged Junk downstream he lost all sense of time and direction. It took what energy he had left just to stay on his back so he could keep breathing. Gradually he became aware that the world around him was starting to brighten. Very slowly at first but it was persistent. The current started to slow and after a little while longer he was floating gently, though the flow still propelled him forward. He started to see the roof of the cavern high above him. Ancient stalactites dripped down, emitting a pale phosphorescence like in the caves of the Valuda. It grew in luminance the further he went, until it reached the point where it was so bright it was like being outside. Junk was gliding peacefully along considering this, when he went under a bridge. It took him a moment to process what he had seen and then he thrashed his arms about to stop his progression. He bobbed in the river, treading water and looked back. It was a bridge all right. A covered wooden bridge. He swivelled to look around.

There was no sign of Lasel or Cobe but some fifty metres downstream he saw another bridge, and a third one beyond that. On the banks either side of the river were buildings. Lots of buildings. There were flickering lights in some of the windows and on the streets. There were streets, Junk realized then. Underground streets, houses, lamps, bridges. That makes a town. And then he noticed the people. Dozens of them. Hundreds even. They were walking along a road that bordered the river. They crossed the bridges ahead of him. He could hear chatter: voices engaged in commerce. Street vendors barking out lists of their produce; arguments; friendly banter; somewhere someone was singing.

Junk turned and swam to the nearest bank. He hauled himself up on to rough, slippery rocks that were covered with a buttery film of turquoise-coloured lichen. He struggled to gain any purchase on them, but persisted and eventually dragged himself on to drier rocks beyond. He pulled himself into a small hollow and lay there for several minutes as his energy level recovered.

He looked at his palm and the mysterious yellow symbols embedded there. The first six sectors of the circle in the diamond in the square were now just a faint outline and the seventh was flashing slowly. Before, Junk hadn't been too concerned about the symbols under his skin. He knew that was strange, but when he had thought Ambeline was dead, after everything he had been through, he had nothing left in him to worry about the true implications of what Dras Sbey had done to him. He'd been resigned to whatever would happen next. What could he do about it? But now there was a chance that Ambeline wasn't dead. That she was down here somewhere, wherever here was. Now Junk felt the urgency implicit in those symbols on his hand, that countdown, that nightmare clock. He didn't doubt that when the symbols were all gone, something was going to happen to him. He was going to be taken back to Sbey or maybe he'd just drop dead on the spot or maybe something else entirely. What was going to happen didn't concern him, but finding Ambeline before the clock ran out did. He didn't have any time to waste.

He was shivering. It was cold here. His breath condensed in front of him. Hypothermia would set in in no time if he didn't get out of his sodden clothes. The town ahead offered his only hope, but as people from down here had taken Ambeline, he had to proceed with caution.

Junk's every step squelched as he headed towards the town. He kept to the shadows and thankfully the outskirts were not busy. He saw an open doorway ahead. Inside was a raging fire in a pit and Junk could hear the clanging of metal against metal coming from within. Maybe a blacksmith's forge. He moved slowly and warily towards the door. Glancing inside, he saw movement in the back of a large cluttered workshop. He could feel the heat bubbling up from the heart of

156

the forge and he couldn't resist. He ducked inside and stood over the open fire. Steam rose from his clothes and his hair. The fire was so intense that it was drying him off in seconds. The cold he had felt after dragging himself out of the river had permeated to the very centre of his bones, but he could feel them thawing. Sensation returned to his fingertips. He spotted a thick jumper that had been tossed casually over the back of a chair. He knew it was stealing, but he needed warmer clothes. He grabbed the jumper and went to put it on. It turned out to be way too small. He couldn't even get his head through the neck-hole so he threw it back on to the chair. More movement from the back of the workshop. Junk retreated into the shadows as the blacksmith came towards the forge holding a twisted piece of blackened metal in a pair of tongs. Junk frowned as he stepped into the light. The blacksmith was a child. A boy of about eleven or twelve. He had light ginger hair and pale skin blackened by soot. He didn't see Junk as he thrust the tongs into the forge and released the length of metal. He returned to the back of his shop and Junk took the opportunity to leave.

Junk carried on, but the warmth that the forge had imbued in him quickly dissipated. He stopped in another doorway and wrapped his arms around himself, trying to hug some heat in. He looked ahead at the bridge he had seen from the water and saw it was bustling with people. This one was made of stone and there were stalls set up along its length. As Junk looked closer, he saw that most of the people on the bridge were small of stature. The shopkeepers and their customers, like the blacksmith, were children. There were some adults. Two, to be precise, that Junk could see. He saw them from a distance. They had their backs to him as they stood over a juvenile baker. Junk watched as one of the adults grabbed a loaf of bread from a basket, or at least something that looked very much like bread from where Junk was standing, and ripped it in two. He handed one half to his companion and they both started to eat. They turned then and walked on. Junk saw their faces. Both were Bone Faces. They wore masks made from skulls. One was an animal skull, something with a long snout, like a dog or a wolf. The other one appeared to be wearing a human skull. The front section had been cut free and several thick bands of leather secured it in place, tied at the back. The skull masks came down to just below their noses so their mouths were exposed, though shielded by the skull's teeth or fangs.

The two Bone Faces left the bridge. They were heading in Junk's direction. He sank further back into the doorway so he was concealed by the shadows. However, he needn't have worried as the Bone Faces turned a corner before they reached him and disappeared from view. Junk stepped out from the doorway and moved on. He paused at the mouth of the alleyway that the Bone Faces had gone down but there was no sign of them. Junk was about to carry on when he heard a crash, followed by angry shouts. As he looked again, he saw a tall, skinny young man being kicked out of a building, followed by the two Bone Faces. The skinny young man wasn't a child but he wasn't quite an adult either. He was maybe fifteen or sixteen years old. The two Bone Faces advanced on him, standing over him. When he tried to get up, first one kicked him down, then the other, both of them laughing. The lanky boy sat cringing on the ground but the Bone Faces each drew a short cane from their belt and started to whip him. The boy curled into a ball, trying to protect himself, but one Bone Face would strike the back of his legs, causing him to twist backwards, exposing his front, which the other would hit. Junk knew it was none of his business, maybe this skinny kid had done something to warrant this abuse, but Junk found it impossible to ignore. He looked at the Antricle. If he used it, the fight would be easy, but he knew he couldn't. Instead his eyes rested on a stout piece of wood lying on the ground by his feet. He picked it up and it sat in his hand comfortably. He sighed and headed into the alleyway.

As Junk drew closer to the lanky kid and his attackers, he could hear the two men laughing at their victim. Junk couldn't understand what it was they were saying but their tone incensed him. He came up behind the Bone Face wearing the animal skull without being seen and hit the man across the backs of his knees. The man screamed in pain and fell to the ground.

The other Bone Face, with the human mask, paused

for a moment and Junk could sense his surprise, maybe even disbelief. Junk knew already he was making a big mistake. The Bone Face said something, which of course meant nothing to Junk, so instead he just struck out at him with his club. He got the man between the legs and watched him crumple.

The man in the animal mask was beginning to struggle to his feet but Junk didn't let him. This time he hit him in the face with enough force to crack the wolf skull in two. The man's feet kicked up in front of him in an almost comical way and he crashed to the ground, landing on his back, already unconscious.

There was a moment of calm then. Junk looked at the young man the Bone Faces had been attacking. He was staring open-mouthed at Junk.

'You OK there?' said Junk, speaking Jansian but not expecting an answer. He looked at the two unconscious Bone Faces and saw they both wore warm clothing. One had on a heavy three-quarter-length leather coat and the other a pair of stout boots. Seeing this as the obvious solution to his dilemma, Junk crouched and started to unlace the boots.

'Are you crazy?' said the lanky young man, also speaking Jansian, which took Junk by surprise.

'Hey! Criptik te Jansian,' said Junk. *You speak Jansian.*

'You can't do that.'

'I'm cold,' said Junk.

'Who are you?'

'Junk,' said Junk. 'Where are we, by the way?'

The young man frowned. 'How do you not know where you are?'

'Well, I was in Dajja, and then I fell into an underground river –' he gestured behind him – 'that river, and now I'm here.' Junk had the boots on already and he stood putting on the heavy coat. 'That's better,' he said. 'What's your name?'

The young man assessed him. Finally he sighed. 'You should come with me,' he said. 'You don't want to be here when these two wake up.'

14

Lasel woke to find herself face down on a crescent of waterlogged shingle on a bend in the river. The powerful waterway flowed behind her, sloshing over her feet. It was light enough to see, though it was a dull, muted light and her first thought was that she was outside on a cloudy day, but when she lifted her head and looked around, she saw that she was still underground. The walls glowed with phosphorescence here too. Small stones clung to the side of her face and she brushed them off as she got her bearings. The rock walls around her were different shades of red, orange and yellow, built up in thin strata. They were perfectly smooth, as if the water had rubbed away all imperfections. It was rather beautiful. However she saw straight away that there was nowhere to go. The walls loomed above her, almost vertical. Climbing up them would be impossible. The opposite bank was practically identical to the one she was on. She got to her feet, but was dizzy and took a moment to steady herself. She realized then how hot she was. She crouched and dipped her hand into the water.

It was like a bath. She could smell sulphur in the air. Hot springs. She felt her clothes. They were almost dry, and she could see the steam rising off her. It was better than being cold, she thought.

She was debating her next move and thinking that she would need to wade or possibly swim further downstream when something caught her eye. The layered rock looked flat, but when she tilted her head she could see that just beyond where she was standing, it wasn't. The striations were acting as camouflage, concealing a narrow ridge. It might be nothing more than an outcropping but it was worth investigating.

The shingle crunched underfoot as she moved to the projecting wall. The ridge was twice her height but there was a bloated rock sticking out at the base and up close she could see one or two blemishes that weren't apparent at a distance. Plus she had been climbing her whole life. She took a short run-up, leaping on to the base rock and springing up and to her left where a small nodule jutted out. She got a hand to this and propelled herself upward, anchoring her foot on another small pimple of rock. She didn't pause and her momentum took her up to the ridge, where she managed to snag the lip of it with the fingertips of one hand. She hung there for a moment to get her breath back. If her tenuous grip failed she would drop to the uneven ground below and landing well would be tricky. She would probably turn her ankle or worse. It was important that didn't happen. She took a deep breath, centring her strength and swung her other arm high. Now she was holding on with two hands and she raised herself up. Her purchase on the lip of the ridge improved and she was able to haul her whole body up and over. She lay on her back and gave herself a moment to recover. Her biceps were throbbing. When the aching started to lessen she took a look around. The ridge was deep and disappeared under an overhang. She had to get down on her belly to investigate. It was dark inside, but when she squinted she could see light beyond. She made a decision and crawled in.

After pulling herself along, staying flat to the ground, for about ten metres, the passageway opened up considerably and she found herself looking into a deep well. Below was a drop of about five metres into water and above stretched up but she judged it an impossible climb. However directly opposite was a tunnel, easily big enough for her to climb through, and beyond she could see more light. Maybe not daylight but light nonetheless. It led somewhere. Hopefully. The well was about two metres in diameter, maybe a little more, so it wouldn't be an easy jump but she felt confident she could make it.

She looked down into the well again and noticed several smaller holes running up the shaft. If she was to fall, the water would break her descent and then the openings would act as hand- and footholds to allow her to climb up and have a second go. There was little to lose.

She pressed back against the wall, giving herself

as much of a run-up as she could, and then sprinted forward. The heel of her foot hit the edge of the well, rocks dislodging beneath her, and she leaped in the air, arcing gracefully over the well to the opposite wall. She was going to make it with ease. But just as she was reaching out to grab a hold of the cave mouth, a fat white snake reared up in her path. It had been lying just inside the mouth of the tunnel. It hissed and snapped blindly. Its dead eyes were as white as its skin, a result of living underground, but its forked tongue was flicking wildly. It had sensed that something living was nearby.

Fear and instinct took over and Lasel faltered midflight. Her feet hit the facing wall first and she dropped fast, splashing down into the water below. A maelstrom of bubbles whirled around her as she started to rise. She broke the surface, her heart pounding, panic starting to cloud her judgement. She forced herself to focus before she was lost. She looked up and to her horror saw movement everywhere. Her arrival had woken the residents of the well and all of the smaller holes she had thought she could use as handholds now had fat reptilian heads emerging from them. Snakes, dozens of them, were roused from their slumber and coming out to investigate. Then one of them came out so far it overbalanced and fell, landing in the water with a heavy splash. Now he was in the well with Lasel. Then a second dropped and a third. She looked left and right, scouring the water beneath her for signs of the serpents. She felt something brush against her leg. It was all she could do not to start crying. She had never been so frightened in her whole life.

Lasel knew if she gave into panic she would surely die. She made herself concentrate on working out what to do now. Climbing up was not an option – that much was clear. Her only other choice was going down. She knew that staying where she was would be pointless, so she took three short breaths and one big gulp and then dived.

The light was almost non-existent and she could see nothing beyond a metre. She looked around, hoping for a miracle. Something long and white wriggled past in her peripheral vision, but when she turned it was gone. Then she saw something else. Something black. It was the mouth of another tunnel. Most of it was below the point where the light reached so she would be swimming blind, but it was her only hope. She kicked her legs, powering down towards the opening. She caught the top edge of it and pulled herself in. She could be swimming into a whole nest of snakes for all she knew, but what choice did she have?

She kept her movements contained, no thrashing arms or hands reaching too far forward. She didn't want to touch something in the dark. Her lungs burned and the hot water stung her eyes, but she kept going and after maybe twenty or thirty seconds, which felt like a whole lot longer, she saw a pool of muted light above her. She swam up and emerged into a cave.

She scrambled out of the water without hesitation.

At least on dry land she could see what was near her. And what was near her were about a hundred or more snakes. They were everywhere. She was in a small cave about ten metres across, where the walls glowed and the inhabitants slithered in great intertwined masses of fat, scaly white skin. But that wasn't all that was in there. The floor was littered with bones. Lasel looked up and saw that high above her was an opening. She knew instantly that people had fallen down here or been pushed maybe and this was where they had died. There were skeletons everywhere, their bones picked clean. Some were still wearing clothes. Clothes that had rotted to rags, but still identifiable as clothes.

The snakes seemed subdued just then. She thought they weren't even aware of her presence, but that wouldn't last forever. She had to get out of there. Going back the way she came wasn't an option. She looked up to the opening high above. There were small holes in the wall all the way up the shaft as there had been in the well, but she assumed they all contained more snakes so that wasn't an option either.

Then she saw a tunnel leading away from the snake pit. She crouched, keeping her movements to a minimum, and she could see through to the other side. It wasn't that far. But there was movement in the tunnel. More snakes. She couldn't go back, she couldn't go forward, she couldn't go up. She was trapped.

Think, think, think, she told herself. Her eyes looked down on the dead bodies littering the floor and an idea started to form. It was a horrible idea. One that would probably give her nightmares for the rest of her life, but if it worked it would mean she had a rest of her life. She took a tentative step forward and one of the serpents suddenly reared up, blindly hissing and snapping. This set the others off and soon the small cavern was full of angry noise. It abated however, just as quickly as it had started.

Lasel reached down to the bones on the floor, the bones of people who had died here, and grabbed a piece of clothing. She lifted it free. The stitching fell open as she raised it, but the fabric itself was still intact. Moving slowly so as not to anger the serpents, Lasel wrapped the cloth around her lower leg, covering herself from knee to ankle, then used another strip of cloth to secure it in place. She grabbed at some more rags, but as she pulled them free a writhing, hissing mob of angry snakes tumbled out, encased in a naked ribcage. Lasel let out a short, sharp scream and froze, terrified the noise would attract the attention of all the other reptiles.

The snakes in the ribcage stayed put, but they were agitated and wound tightly around one another like a Celtic knot. Being even more cautious now, Lasel continued. There was more than enough material for her to cover her arms and legs in multiple layers until her limbs were padded to double their normal size. Then she covered her whole face, leaving only one eye exposed so she could see where she was going. The smell as she wound the cloth around her head was almost unbearable and it made her gag. It smelt of rotten meat, but she knew that was impossible. The flesh had been stripped from these corpses long ago. It was just the memory of rot.

Once she was completely covered, she picked up a long bone, once someone's thigh bone, and used it to flick aside any snakes that were between her and the mouth of the tunnel. When a path had been cleared she crouched down and stared into the dark passage that stretched ahead. One last short prayer and then she crept inside, moving forward, keeping her belly pressed flat to the ground. Even then the roof of the tunnel was so low she could only just squeeze inside. She could hear movement: the sound of thick, muscular bodies slithering over one another. There was hissing everywhere. The tunnel widened a little and Lasel was just beginning to feel slightly less panicked when she felt something drop on to her back and she fought the urge to scream and shake it off.

A snake reared up without warning right next to her face and her exposed eye. This time she couldn't help it; she did scream, and the snake attacked. It rocked back and then hurled its gaping mouth forward, its lips pulled back, its fangs exposed and it struck. It bit into Lasel's bicep, but the extra padding absorbed the bite and the venomous points didn't reach her flesh. She kept going, scrambling forward until she could see freedom beyond the tunnel. The tunnel however was starting to narrow again and Lasel pulled her shoulders in to make herself as thin as possible.

Her head emerged and she didn't pause. She kept going. Powering on. Her shoulders pushed through and after that the rest of her followed with ease. But the rags covering her left foot snagged as she came out and they were torn off. Her ankle was exposed and one last snake snapped, striking out. It sunk its fangs into the flesh of her ankle. She cried out in pain and jerked her foot forward, dislodging the reptile, but it was too late. She had been bitten.

She kept crawling forward, instinct telling her to put as much space between her and the tunnel of reptiles as possible. She was moving over smooth, gently undulating rock. She ripped at the protective covering, trying to tear the corpses' clothes from her, but she didn't get very far. She was dizzy. The world around her was spinning. Her ears were filled with the sound of white noise. Her mouth was dry and her heart was racing. She was starting to feel very sleepy. All the energy was leaving her body. Her arms gave out beneath her and she collapsed. The rock felt cool against her cheek. Treacle-thick blackness started to creep into her vision, but before it completely consumed her Lasel thought she heard footsteps. She had a feeling that there was someone standing over her, but she didn't have the strength to raise her head to look. The world around her vanished.

'Alfred?' said Junk. 'Like the butler in *Batman*?'

'I don't know what that is,' said the lanky boy. He spelled his name for Junk.

'Oh, Al-*frid*. OK,' said Junk. Alfrid led Junk through twisting, turning narrow streets. It was a maze, and Junk knew there was little chance of him ever finding his way back. It reminded him of the slums in Mumbai or the favelas in Rio, both places he had spent time in back when he was working on boats. Here, as in Rio and Mumbai, there were a lot of people packed into a small area. Every street they went down, Junk saw people, mostly children, sitting on the threshold of shops or tiny one-room shacks that had been cobbled together from anything that could be scavenged. This was not a happy place. The residents stared at him with hollow dark eyes. Their skin was pale and lifeless. They looked drained.

'Why were they beating you?' Junk asked Alfrid.

'It's what they do,' said Alfrid.

'What is this place?' asked Junk.

'You're a long way from Dajja. How long were you in that river?'

'I don't know,' said Junk. He glanced at the countdown on his palm. The final piece of the circle was pulsating now. The rest was all blank.

'Well, this is the Underland,' said Alfrid.

'Underland? How come you speak Jansian?'

'My family came from there. My father brought us to the Upworld.' He gestured above them and Junk glanced up at the roof of the cave looming high overhead. He knew that *Upworld* meant the world above ground. 'He had heard that fortunes were to be made there.'

'How did you end up down here? Are your family down here too?'

'No, they're dead.' He said it without any hint of emotion; just stating a dull fact, like grass is green or water is wet. 'The Bone Faces killed them and brought me down here.'

'Why did they do that?'

'It's what they do.'

'They take children?'

'Mostly. I was six when I came here.'

'Why children?'

'To work or to sell. They're slavers, you see. Children are easier to control than adults. Don't eat as much. I don't know. It's not like they explain it to us.'

'And what did you do? How did you survive?'

Alfrid shrugged. 'I just did. If you work, they give you food.'

Junk looked around at the children in the doorways. They were all ages, some as young as two or three, but they weren't crying. Junk got the feeling that they had long realized crying didn't help. They looked resigned to their fate.

'Have you never tried to escape?'

'Where would I go?' Alfrid sounded genuinely perplexed by the very notion.

'I think they brought my sister down here. Where would they take her?'

Alfrid laughed. It was not a happy laugh. 'It could be anywhere. I've been here ten or eleven years maybe and I've only ever seen a little bit of the Underland.' He stopped outside one of the small shacks. 'This is me.' The doorway was covered by a blanket, which Alfrid pushed aside and entered. Junk followed.

Inside was tiny. So small that Junk would not be able to lie stretched out. The walls were lined with shelves and on all the shelves were toys. Some were animals or model land-ships carved from wood. Junk thought back to the little figurines Garvan made when he first met him. That seemed like such a long time ago now. Others were dolls with painted clay heads and rag-doll cloth bodies or soft stuffed animals.

'Did you make all these?' asked Junk. Alfrid nodded. 'Is this a toy shop?'

'Well, it's not a shop. I don't sell any of them. I just make them and give them to the little ones.'

'That's nice,' said Junk.

Alfrid shrugged. 'It's important that they remember they're children. That's hard to do here.'

Junk thought about his own childhood. It had been heavenly for the first twelve years, which was a lot longer than most of the children here had had. Twice as long as Alfrid. Junk wondered what his life would be like now had Jacid Mestrowe not stolen Ambeline, but he dismissed the thought as soon as it surfaced. It was pointless to fantasize.

'I can offer you some tea,' said Alfrid. 'But it doesn't taste very nice.'

'No, you're OK,' said Junk. 'I was with some friends

when I left Dajja. We all fell into the river together. At least I think we did. It was dark. Any idea where they might have ended up?'

'It could be anywhere. Between here and Dajja there are lots of tributaries. Least half a dozen I know of, but I don't know where they all lead.'

'Great,' said Junk. 'Now I've lost my sister and my friends.'

15

The child was barefoot and his limbs were stick thin.
He stared down with eyes set deep within his emaciated
face at the strange young woman lying unconscious on
the rocks. His name was Vil. He wore a blank look, as if
nothing could evoke emotion in him. The young woman
was covered in tattered old rags, layer upon layer of
them. He could smell her from where he stood, but his
face didn't register disgust or surprise or interest. He
prodded her with his toe, but she didn't react. He saw her
ankle was exposed and he could see she had been bitten.
The skin was turning black and starting to blister before
his very eyes. A bump appeared on her ankle, inflated
and burst, oozing pus mixed with blood. It happened in
seconds. She was going to die, Vil knew, unless someone
helped her straight away. He should probably go and
get help, he thought, and he turned and started to walk
away. After a few seconds it occurred to him that it was
slightly more urgent than that so he should speed up. He
broke into a sedate jog.

*

'Look, Alfrid,' said Junk, 'I don't have long. I don't have time to be subtle. The Bone Faces took my sister, which means someone somewhere down here must know where she is. Where would I find the Bone Faces? Do they have a headquarters or something? Do they have a leader?'

Alfrid laughed but quickly realized Junk was being serious. He scowled, trying to fathom what Junk was suggesting. Although he understood the words, it made no sense to him.

'N-no one goes to the Bone Faces. Not through choice.' He shook his head vigorously. 'No! That would be crazy. No. They won't help you.'

'That's not what I asked. Do they have a headquarters? Do they have a leader?'

'They live up in the Temple. It's not a temple. That's just what they call it.'

'And their leader?'

'She's called the Tul, or least she calls herself that.'

'Tul?'

'It's an ancient word, thousands of years old.'

'I'm older than that,' muttered Junk.

'What?'

'Never mind. You were saying it's an ancient word.'

'It's an ancient word for "God".'

'The leader of the Bone Faces thinks she's a god? Well, I've kicked the arse of emperors. Nowhere to go but up. How do I get to the Temple?'

'I can take you, but I don't know how to get in.'

Alfrid paused and Junk could see he was debating whether to say something or not. 'But there is someone who might help.'

Junk followed Alfrid to the northern edge of the town. It was much warmer here and Alfrid explained that there were hot springs all around this area. Junk was just about to ask why the townsfolk didn't live here rather than the colder area further south when the smell hit him. The smell of sulphur was almost overwhelming and it brought tears to his eyes. As he struggled to breathe, he understood why no one chose to live here.

'Here,' said Alfrid, and he handed Junk a square of blue cloth. He folded a similar one in half and wrapped it around his nose and mouth, tying it in a knot at the back. It gave him the look of a highwayman. Junk did the same. It didn't block out the sulphuric fumes entirely, but it muffled them sufficiently that Junk could function.

'Take shallow breaths,' advised Alfrid. They continued on their way.

'So who are you taking me to see?'

'Her name's Tyva. She's not the friendliest person you'll ever meet but she hates the Bone Faces more than anyone I know. They took her sister from her, so she'll understand what you're going through. Her sister's dead though so there's no saving her. Tyva spends her time attacking the Bone Faces, but she's just one person. She can't take them all on, but she hurts them wherever and whenever she can. They've been trying to catch her for months but so far no luck.'

'And she knows how to get into the Temple?'

'I don't know,' said Alfrid with a shrug, 'but if anyone does, it's going to be Tyva.'

Alfrid led Junk into a narrow crack in the rock. It was so slender an opening that most people would never consider it a potential entrance and move past. That was the point. Junk was almost too big to fit through. He had to breathe in and think thin thoughts. The opening led into an equally narrow passageway that ran for longer than Junk would have liked. By the time he was only halfway through he was already feeling a rising sense of panic brought on by claustrophobia, which was not something he had ever suffered from but he couldn't shake the feeling that any second now the passageway might become so tight that he would be stuck and unable to go forwards or backwards and would die a slow, agonizing death between two walls of red and orange striped rock no wider than his head.

And then without warning the narrow corridor opened up considerably and he was able to breathe normally again. He found himself in a round antechamber with six separate passages leading from it, including the one they had come through. The walls glowed.

'This way,' said Alfrid, walking on. Junk looked at his palm as he followed. The first symbol had faded away completely, leaving just a faint outline. Now the first triangle in the second symbol, the eight-pointed star, was flashing.

'How do you know this Tyva?' asked Junk.

'I used to know her before.'

'Before?'

'Before they took her sister. Before she became . . .' he paused, choosing his words carefully, '. . . what she is now.'

The passageways they followed were almost identical. Junk wondered how Alfrid managed to remember the way. One passage would lead to a fork, which would lead to another antechamber, a crossroads, another fork. They went deeper and deeper into the heart of the rock until they came to an incredible room that had dozens of passageways, on multiple levels, leading away from it. Alfrid stood in the middle and shouted: 'TYVA? MAWS CHI, ALFRID. N'CALA PON TRUMAH.' He spoke in a local dialect that Junk didn't understand. His voice bounced off the walls, echoing around them. It disappeared down passageways and came back through different ones. Then Alfrid sat down, leaning his back against the rock.

'Now what?' asked Junk.

'Now we wait,' said Alfrid. 'She'll have heard that. She'll come to us.'

Junk looked at his palm. 'Can't we go to her?'

'I don't know the way beyond this point,' said Alfrid. 'Don't worry, she'll come.'

And so they waited. Junk looked at his hand every few minutes. He watched as the first triangle faded to nothing more than an outline and the second triangle started to throb. He was debating how long he could wait before having to try something else when suddenly he heard a voice. It was a girl's voice.

'Ha munna tatuma, Alfrid?'

Junk was on his feet immediately and turning in a tight circle, looking all around, trying to work out where the voice was coming from. He had no idea.

Alfrid got to his feet and addressed the room in general. 'Hadge no.' And he pointed to Junk.

'What are you saying?' whispered Junk.

Alfrid whispered back: 'She asked what brings me here, and I said it was you.'

'N'fila, Alfrid. Culla. Dulla nuala.'

'Goge!' Alfrid seemed more animated than Junk had yet seen him. 'Goge. Maws tratram. Binja Junk. No casi ta Juntry. Ta Nusk Fooder tush trally nol solge.'

Silence hung in the air. Junk was wondering if Tyva was even there any more.

'What did you say?' he asked Alfrid.

'I said it was urgent, that you're from the upland and the Bone Faces took your sister.' Junk and Alfrid waited, looking around at the dozens of possible passages, waiting for Tyva's response. Tyva's response came in the form of a talon-shaped blade that appeared from nowhere and took up residence under the handkerchief tied around Junk's mouth. He could feel the cold metal of the blade against his skin. Junk froze. She had made no sound.

'Pon solge, hadge nu tush porum,' said Tyva.

Junk flicked his eyes towards Alfrid, looking for help.

'She wants to know, does your sister have red hair?'

Junk frowned. It was a strange introduction. He could feel a vein throbbing in his neck directly beneath the blade. He spoke quietly.

'No, said Junk, 'she's blonde.' Alfrid translated. 'But,' Junk added, 'one of my friends I was separated from in the river, she has red hair. Her name's Lasel. Long red hair.' Alfrid relayed Junk's words to Tyva and after a moment the knife was removed. Junk pulled away from her sharply, turning, rubbing his throat. He was surprised by the sight that greeted him. Tyva was a child. She might have been twelve or sixteen or somewhere in between, he couldn't say. She was small and thin. Lank black hair hung down over her eyes. Her pallid skin, like that of so many down here, never saw sunlight. She spun the knife she had held to Junk's throat expertly and deposited it into a sheath hanging from her belt. Junk noted a second sheathed knife on the other hip. She said something to Alfrid and started to walk away.

'Hey! Where's she going?' said Junk.

'She says she doesn't know anything about your sister but your friend is in her camp.' Alfrid looked at his feet then and Junk could tell there was more to it.

'What?'

'I'm sorry,' said Alfrid. 'She says she's going to die.'

Junk knelt beside Lasel and took her hand. If it wasn't for the fact she was shivering uncontrollably Junk would have thought the worst the moment he had entered Tyva's home.

Tyva lived deeper still in the labyrinth of caves. Aeons of erosion had fashioned a series of tunnels and anterooms that she had put to good use. As they had entered, Junk was immediately aware of the children. There were dozens of them. He wasn't sure how many exactly. Most stayed hidden from the stranger, peeking out from behind rounded corners to catch a glimpse.

Lasel was lying on a pile of woven mats. Tyva had stripped her of the rotten rags she had insulated herself in and removed the rest of her clothes too. She was plastered in a dozen thin wet towels that covered her from the neck down, plus one over her forehead. Only her eyes, nose and mouth were left visible. Vil, the skinny boy who had found her, sat at her side, systematically swapping the towels for fresh wet ones as the ones on her started to dry out.

'What happened?' asked Junk, his voice thin. Alfrid relayed the question to Tyva and she answered, lifting the towel covering Lasel's left ankle to illustrate what she was saying.

'Tyva says she was bitten.'

'Bitten?'

'By a manok. It's a long, thin creature with no arms or legs. The caves are full of them. Much venom.'

'Isn't there an antidote?' asked Junk, and Alfrid repeated the question to Tyva.

'Zo,' she said, nodding, 'ja gum ta Nusk Fooder trun.'

'She says there is, but only the Bone Faces have it.'

'Well, that's why we're here anyway. Ask her to take me to the Bone Faces. Please! How do you say *please*?'

'Paranto,' said Alfrid.

Junk looked at Tyva and put his hands together in a begging gesture. 'Paranto,' he said. 'Paranto.'

When Alfrid explained what Junk was asking her to do Tyva frowned, looking at Junk like he was crazy. She shook her head, but it wasn't a flat refusal, just a gesture to show how stupid she considered him. She sighed and said something to Alfrid.

'What did she say?' asked Junk. Alfrid looked reluctant to translate but did anyway.

'She says you're selfish and not bright. You will get caught and your friend will die alone.'

'She's wrong. Lasel's not going to die. I'm not going to let her.

Tyva guided Junk and Alfrid through the warren of tunnels. Some of the children who had been hiding in the shadows joined them but stayed a little way behind, as if they were following secretly though they made no effort to hide themselves.

183

'Who are all these kids?' asked Junk.

'Just children who have got away from the Bone Faces. Tyva takes care of them.'

'Why do they all stay here? Shouldn't she get them further away from the Bone Faces?'

'And take them where? This is the only home any of us know. Here Tyva knows how to get food and water. They have beds to sleep in. In the Upworld . . .' He didn't finish the sentence. He just shrugged. Junk didn't press the issue. They carried on walking as a thought occurred to him.

'How will I know what the antidote is?'

Alfrid considered the question and shook his head. He called ahead to Tyva, asking her. She answered and Alfrid translated: 'She says she'll be able to show you the medical area. The antidote will be a powder. It'll be yellow and will probably have a picture of a manok on it.' All of a sudden, Tyva changed direction and leaped down into a small ravine. Alfrid, Junk and the children stopped to watch what she was doing. She was crouching down by a small hole just underneath a large boulder. She put her hand inside and pulled it out just as quickly. She was holding one of the white, sightless snakes that had attacked Lasel. She had it by its tail and it was swinging about furiously, hissing and snapping at the air in an attempt to sink its fangs into her.

'Manok,' said Tyva.

'That's a manok,' said Alfrid, translating rather needlessly. Tyva tossed the serpent aside and it slithered

184

quickly back beneath the rock. Tyva scrambled up out of the ravine and they continued their journey.

The Bone Faces' headquarters was vast. It was built into a cliff-face that rose 250 metres high. Junk had to marvel at the sheer size of it. The underground cave system they were in was absolutely huge. There was an entire other world down here.

The construction of the Bone Faces' headquarters was basic. The cliff-wall was pockmarked with about fifty or so irregularly-shaped holes, placed at apparently random locations so it was hard to know for sure if it was natural or manmade. Either way the Bone Faces had made it their own. There were walkways and ladders criss-crossing the cliff, connecting the various entrances.

The area was crawling with Bone Faces. There were at least thirty that Junk could see, male and female, each wearing a unique mask made from a skull.

Junk, Tyva and Alfrid were watching from a distance. The rest of the children had stayed well away on Tyva's command.

'Why do they wear the masks?' asked Junk.

'Because it's scary,' said Alfrid. Junk felt a little foolish for asking such an obvious question.

'I'm going to have to get me one of them,' said Junk. 'Shame I didn't keep one from the pair who attacked you.'

Tyva explained what they were looking at, and Alfrid translated for Junk.

'She says the doorway on the ground level, third along, that's the medical room, which is where the antidote will be. She also says to be quick. We'll wait back where we left the children, but she says we won't wait long because she's sure you'll be caught almost immediately.'

'Tell her thanks for the vote of confidence,' said Junk, and Alfrid translated.

Tyva frowned and shook her head. She said something else to Alfrid.

'She says you've clearly not understood what she was saying. She—'

Junk cut him off. 'It's OK. I get it. I'm doomed to failure. I won't be long. Don't let her leave.' Junk was about to move out from their hiding place when Tyva grabbed his arm to stop him. She reached into a bag strapped to her back and removed a skull mask, which she handed to Junk. It looked like it had once belonged to a large sheep. Not particularly scary but it would do the job.

'Oh, you star!' he said, grinning. 'That makes it so much easier. Where did you get it from?' Alfrid relayed the question as Junk fitted it over his face.

'She says she has several,' said Alfrid. 'Probably best not to ask.'

Junk looked inside the skull and saw a human tooth embedded within. Clearly the previous owner had not given up his mask without a fight. Junk grabbed the tooth between his thumb and forefinger and yanked it free. He flicked it away and then refitted the skull over his head. Tyva secured the leather laces at the back, fixing it in place.

'How do I look?' asked Junk. Tyva and Alfrid looked him up and down. Tall and broad-shouldered, Junk was still wearing the long coat and boots he had taken from the two Bone Faces who had attacked Alfrid. He looked just like any other Bone Face. Tyva grimaced and was about to say something when Alfrid gasped.

'Look!' he said. He nodded his head, gesturing. 'It's the Tul.' Junk followed his line of sight to see a tall, imposing, powerfully built woman. Her arms appeared to be flabby, but her bulging musculature was apparent beneath. She wore an animal skull that once belonged to something that had small tusks, a wild boar maybe.

'That's the leader of the Bone Faces, huh? The woman who thinks she's a god?' said Junk. 'Doesn't look so tough.' They watched as the Tul promenaded through her subjects, who were going about their daily chores. All bowed their heads subserviently. The Tul gave off an air of aloofness, as if she was floating above everyone else.

Keeping low, Junk edged his way towards the Bone Faces' domain. He got as close as he possibly could while staying hidden, but eventually he reached a point where there was no choice but to step into the open. His only hope of success was to walk tall and look like he belonged. Alfrid had given him a selection of three phrases he could employ in case anyone spoke to him.

Of course, Junk would have no idea what was being said to him so he would just pick one of the three phrases at random and hope it made sense in context, but really he was hoping he'd be lucky enough to get in and out without anyone noticing him.

As he went he kept an eye on the Tul. The Bone Faces' leader seemed to be just wandering aimlessly, surveying her troops maybe. She didn't talk to anyone and no one talked to her.

Junk wound his way towards the medical room. If any other Bone Faces looked as if they were about to cross his path, he would subtly change direction so he didn't get too close. However, as he neared the cliff-face that became increasingly difficult; there were Bone Faces everywhere.

A Bone Face wearing the skull of a large bird with a hooked beak stepped into Junk's path and nodded as they passed.

'Manandra,' he said, which, thanks to Alfrid, Junk knew was simply a casual greeting.

'Manandra,' he said in reply, and made sure not to slow or quicken his pace. He carried on, trying hard to look casual, grateful that his face was hidden. He neared the room where Tyva had said he'd find the antidote, and approached from an angle so it wasn't readily apparent that that was where he was heading until, at the last second, he ducked inside.

The room was dark with a low ceiling. It stretched back into the rock further than Junk would have guessed from the outside. There was a series of cot beds – eight of them, arranged into two facing rows of four, at the back of the room. All were empty. In the front was what appeared to be an examining table and surrounding it on three sides were cabinets and drawers. All were marked, but unfortunately Junk couldn't read any of the labels. He opened the first drawer he came to and found it full of small, white paper packets, about the size of a seed packet back home. The envelopes sat in individual slots so it was easy to flick through them. Each envelope bore a scribbled inscription explaining what was inside. Junk's heart sank almost immediately when he saw that none of them had any pictures. It was all well and good Tyva showing him what a manok looked like, but it turned out that it didn't help.

He started to open the packets, looking for a yellow powder. He was in luck and the fourth one he tried was yellow. But then a thought occurred to him and he tried some more. After two more, he found another one containing yellow powder. He kept looking and found two more in quick succession. He looked at the front of each of the packets. The writing on each one was different and of course Junk couldn't read what any of them said.

The drawer he was looking in held around sixty small packets and there were twelve drawers in total. That was a lot of packets. He couldn't take them all. He had to think of a plan B.

16

The bird-skull Bone Face with whom Junk had exchanged a polite greeting was moving past the medical room when Junk appeared in the doorway.

'Manandra,' said Junk, beckoning the man closer. 'N'cala pon trumah.' He hoped he had correctly remembered the phrase Alfrid had taught him. He hoped he was asking for help. 'Manok,' said Junk.

The man in the bird skull scowled. 'Manok?' he repeated.

Junk nodded. 'Zo.' *Yes.*

Bird-skull man started talking animatedly then. Junk knew from his tone that he was asking if someone had been bitten and where they were. All very reasonable questions when someone requests a snakebite antidote. Junk just nodded. The Bone Face hurried to a specific drawer and pulled it open. He flicked through the packets within until he found what he was looking for and held it up to show Junk. He was asking more questions, more questions Junk couldn't answer. Junk took the envelope from his hand.

'Puna,' he said, remembering a word that Tualla had used. He was pretty sure that it meant *come* or *this way*. Bird Skull followed Junk outside and Junk pointed off to an area opposite where Tyva and Alfrid were hiding, as far away from them as possible. 'Puna, puna,' said Junk again and started to run. Bird Skull started running too. Then Junk stopped and turned back, as if he had forgotten something. He waved the other man on and, caught up in the excitement of the moment, the Bone Face didn't think. He just kept running. The manok emergency at hand demanded immediate action.

Clutching the envelope containing the antidote, Junk hurried back the way he had come. He moved quickly but not so quickly that it would look like he was running away. Bird Skull however had no such compunction about drawing attention to himself. He called out that there was an emergency and everyone in the vicinity turned to look at him. No one paid Junk any attention as he scurried away to rejoin Tyva and Alfrid.

Tyva was frowning and shaking her head when Junk returned.

'Caparmana,' she muttered.

'What's that mean?

'Lucky,' said Alfrid, then frowned. 'No – more than that.' He struggled to find a suitable word.

'Jammy,' offered Junk. 'The word you're looking for is *jammy*, and yeah, I know.'

*

They got back to Tyva's cave in double-quick time and Tyva started to prepare the antidote. She needed boiling water and sent young Vil off to see to that. Junk knelt by Lasel, who was looking even paler and sicker than when they left. He held her hand, taking the opportunity to glance at the clock on his palm. The second symbol was already half gone. He didn't have long left, only about forty hours, and he still had to locate Ambeline.

Vil returned then with the hot water and Tyva produced a thick clay bowl. She emptied half of the powder into it, then added the water slowly, mixing the powder to a thick, gloopy paste and adding more and more water until it became a liquid. She barked an order at Junk, which Alfrid translated.

'Hold up her head.' He gestured to Lasel. Junk did as instructed and gently raised Lasel's head. As Tyva touched the bowl to Lasel's parted lips, a scream rang out. A child's scream. Everyone froze. More screams. Tyva thrust the bowl into Junk's hand and ran to see what was happening. Junk started to tip the antidote into Lasel's mouth, but as Tyva reached the entrance a crazed Bone Face burst into the room, swinging a cudgel. He hit Tyva and she collapsed backwards, falling into Junk. The bowl was knocked from his hand and it clattered to the ground, smashing into a dozen pieces and splashing its contents across the floor.

'NOOO!' Junk howled as he watched the antivenom soaking into the dusty ground. He had only managed to get a tiny amount of it into Lasel. More Bone Faces surged in now. They grabbed the screaming children. Junk saw Vil being picked up by his ankle. Alfrid was punched to the floor and kicked. Junk moved to help but the Bone Face who had attacked Tyva turned on him. Junk saw the cudgel coming at him but he could do nothing. The world turned black.

Lasel half opened her eyes. She tried to focus but everything was blurry. There was silence. The Bone Faces had gone, taking Junk and the others. Lasel had been slipping in and out of consciousness for a while and had been vaguely aware of what Junk had been trying to do. She saw the pieces of the smashed clay bowl on the floor. She knew she had to get more of the medicine or she would die. She tried to move, but it was no good. She couldn't lift her arm more than a few centimetres, and that tiny attempt at movement exhausted her. Her head slumped and her breathing was laboured. She was dying. The last thing she saw as her eyes started to close was a giant standing over her. Some sort of animal come to devour her, no doubt.

When Junk woke, the world was all skewed. Everything was the wrong way round. It took him several moments to realize the world was fine, he was the one who was upside down. He had been strung up by his ankles in a cage. His mind flashed back to something similar that had happened in Cul Sita when he had first come up against Jacid Mestrowe and the League of Sharks. He had gone through most of his life without being hung up by his ankles and now it had happened twice in a matter of a few months. Life was strange.

Alfrid was hanging next to him, still unconscious. Junk managed to swivel his body, though every little movement sent a marching band of pain straight to the centre of his brain. There were three more people hanging in the cage with them: a woman of around fifty and two men, both of whom looked to be in their thirties. All were unconscious. He didn't recognize them. There was no sign of Lasel or Tyva.

Then he glanced at his wrist and discovered the Antricle was gone. He felt a surge of panic in the pit of his stomach. He looked at his palm, hoping the nightmare clock would be gone too, but of course it wasn't. It was still there, glowing yellow. The first two symbols were now just faint outlines and the third symbol, the circle made up of circles, was the bright focus. That meant he had been unconscious for over eight hours. Time he didn't have to waste.

'BAH!' He heard a shout from behind him and turned to see a Bone Face approaching the cage. He unlocked the door and entered, bending to look Junk in the eyes. 'Nabo gani,' said the man from behind his skull mask. He stood up straight and turned to a fellow Bone Face standing by the door. 'Mutta ta Tul.' Junk didn't understand what they were saying, but he recognized that it had been about the Tul.

What the Bone Face had said was 'Tell the Tul', and shortly afterwards Junk had been unshackled and brought down from the roof of the cage. His legs were like jelly and he found it impossible to walk. The two Bone Face jailors half dragged, half carried him to an audience with the Tul.

They found her in a great hall in the heart of the caves behind the cliff-face. The entrance was only a handful of openings away from the medical room where Junk had acquired the manok antivenom. They walked down a long wide passageway that opened out at the end into a single room the size of a football pitch. In the centre was a round pit about twenty-five metres in diameter and twenty metres deep. The floor of the pit was stained red, and from where Junk stood he was pretty sure the stains had been caused by blood. Large quantities of it being emptied. He didn't like to think what had happened to cause large amounts of blood to be spilled like that.

Junk saw the Tul up close for the first time. She was far more imposing than she had been from a distance. She wasn't wearing her skull mask and she had a wild thatch of white-blonde hair cut short. Her eyebrows were also white-blonde, which meant, on first glance, that she didn't appear to have eyebrows at all. That gave her face a somewhat unsettling, alien quality. The Tul approached Junk, studying him closely. His legs were still wobbly but he was managing to stand unaided now. Junk was tall, but she towered over him. She reminded him of Cascér, the Pallatan who had travelled with them. She had the same combination of masculinity and femininity. Though there was something else in the Tul, something in her eyes that hinted at a level of cruelty that Cascér didn't possess.

'Ha pon mlu?' she said, leaning in close to Junk, examining him in minute detail. Her breath smelt like rotten eggs and rancid milk. It made Junk gag. She sniffed him.

'MLU?' bellowed one of the jailors who had brought him, using a thin cane to whip the back of Junk's legs. Junk cried out and had to fight hard to keep standing upright.

'I don't know what you're saying,' said Junk through gritted teeth.

The Tul and the jailor exchanged a frown and then a few words. The Tul turned to Junk and grabbed him roughly, pressing her large calloused fingers into his cheeks and squeezing his jaw. She barked words at him that he did not understand.

'You'd think with you being a god, you'd be able to speak any language,' said Junk.

The Tul pushed him away, infuriated by his insistence on speaking this strange, incomprehensible dialect.

Just then, there was a commotion behind them. Junk turned to see Alfrid being shoved viciously into the hall by another of the Bone Faces. Words were exchanged between the Tul and her minions, and although Junk didn't understand them, he could tell that Alfrid was the subject of the conversation. Then Alfrid was pushed forward. He lost his balance and stumbled to the floor. Junk moved to help him up, but his jailor whipped him with his cane once more and Junk stopped.

The Tul spoke, addressing Alfrid. He replied, nodding, and whatever he said made the Tul happier. She grunted, gesturing to Junk.

'I am to translate for the Tul,' said Alfrid to Junk. 'Her celestial greatness –' Junk rolled his eyes – 'wants to know who you are. What do you want me to say?'

'Tell her . . .' Junk considered how to phrase things. 'Tell her I'm a traveller from the Upworld and I'm here looking for my sister. Tell her I don't mean any harm.' Alfrid opened his mouth to relay Junk's words, but then Junk thought of something else. 'Or disrespect. Add that too. Do you have a word for *disrespect*?'

'Of course,' said Alfrid. He turned to the Tul and relayed Junk's message. When he got to the part about not intending to cause any harm or disrespect, several of the Bone Faces nearby chuckled derisively: *as if one scrawny boy could cause them any harm.*

'Tell her I just want my sister and my friends and we'll get out of here, you, me, Tyva . . .' He paused as his mind turned to Lasel. 'What happened to Lasel?'

'I'm sorry, Junk,' said Alfrid. 'They took us before we could give her the antivenom. She'll be . . .' He didn't finish his sentence. He didn't need to. Despair threatened

197

to overwhelm Junk but he fought against it. He had to focus on the here and now.

'Tell her I just want my sister and my friends and we'll get out of here and never come back.' Alfrid translated Junk's words and the Tul nodded, smirking, making it clear she wasn't taking Junk seriously. He was an amusement for her. She barked out an order over his head and the colour drained from Alfrid's face. Junk noticed it. 'What is it? What did she say?'

'There's a game she likes to play. I've heard about it but never seen it. She likes games.' The look of mounting horror on Alfrid's features was scaring Junk.

'What's the game, Alfrid?'

'I think she wants you to play it,' said Alfrid. Before he could explain any further a large terracotta pot was carried in and set down on a table in front of the Tul. The pot stood about a metre high with five holes the size of tennis balls arranged near the top. Then the other three people who had been in the cage with Junk and Alfrid, the older woman and the two men, were pushed into the hall. They stood shivering, with fear rather than cold. All three were muttering what Junk took to be prayers under their breath, but as he didn't understand the words, they could have been saying anything.

'Binja maj N'far ho mutta Rung pa Cunna,' said the Tul, looking at Junk with a wicked smile on her lips. The Bone Faces nearby were sniggering. They knew what was coming.

The Tul gestured to Alfrid to translate.

'She says, "This is a game she likes to call Pure of Heart."'

The men and the woman who had been brought in started to sob then and Junk turned to see another Bone Face approaching, carrying a covered box. He put it down on the floor and reached inside, drawing out a fat, furious manok that was hissing and snapping to show its displeasure. The Bone Face held him just behind his head and at his tail and he turned to display the serpent to the Tul. The Tul bowed her head, signifying her approval. The Bone Face moved around the hall then, showing the manok to one and all, taking particular enjoyment from the whimpers elicited from the other prisoners. He showed it to Junk, who didn't flinch. The man prodded the snake's gaping maw at Junk, but still Junk showed no sign of weakness. It wasn't that he wasn't scared, but he was determined not to give them the satisfaction.

The Bone Face gave up then and stepped away from Junk. He took the reptile to the terracotta pot and dropped it inside. Junk could hear it thrashing about within, its fat solid body slapping against the walls. The Tul started to speak, explaining what was going to happen, and Alfrid translated. However, Junk was only half listening. He had already worked out what the game involved. It was obvious.

The Tul produced four shiny coins, each about the size of a poker chip, and dropped them into the pot. They rained down on the manok, enraging it even more than it was already.

'First round, there are four coins in the pot,' said Alfrid. 'Five people put their hand in. If you get a coin, you can take your hand out; if you get bitten . . . you lose. The game keeps going till there's just one winner.' The woman and men from the cage were pushed closer. A Bone Face came up behind Junk to propel him forward but Junk stepped up without assistance. Then to Junk's surprise the Tul took her place opposite him.

'You're playing?' said Junk. A thought occurred to him. 'Alfrid, I want you to translate this. Tell her I'll play her game, but where I come from we always play *for* something.' Dutifully, if nervously, Alfrid told the Tul what Junk was saying. 'If I win,' Junk continued, 'then *all* my friends and my sister and me are free to leave.'

As Alfrid was speaking the Tul's face grew increasingly darker, and before he had even finished she started to bellow, her fury directed at Junk, who stared at her impassively, which made her all the madder.

'The Tul says that it is not your place to dictate the rules. You came here uninvited and stole from the Bone Faces. You will do as you're told or she will –' he faltered, '– take *my* eyes as a punishment.'

Junk glowered at the Tul, not shrinking under her murderous gaze.

'Tell her if she doesn't think she can win, then she shouldn't play the game,' said Junk.

'Junk, please,' said Alfrid, his voice cracking with fear.

'Tell her.' Junk took his eyes off the Tul and looked

200

at Alfrid. 'Tell her, Alfrid.' Alfrid took a deep breath and translated Junk's words. He could see the anger welling up within the Tul, but after a handful of very tense moments she relaxed and nodded her head approvingly, looking at her Bone Face soldiers, none of whom knew how to react so they nodded because she was. The Tul laughed but it wasn't a happy laugh. She spat out a few words in Junk's direction, which Alfrid translated.

'She says you're either very brave or very, very stupid. She thinks probably the second one. She agrees to your wager.'

The five players stood around the terracotta pot and the Tul put her hand up to the hole facing her. Junk did the same. Each of the other three players needed a Bone Face to prod them in the back or the back of the head to make them put up their hands.

'Corsant jop,' said the Tul, pausing before adding, 'Throom baan lono vanty na yawsty na unup.'

Alfrid translated: 'She said on three, and if anyone pulls out they lose their other hand.'

'Lim . . .' said the Tul.

'One . . .' said Alfrid.

'Fis . . .' said the Tul.

'Two . . .' said Alfrid.

'Jop!' With that, the Tul and Junk plunged a hand into the jar. The other three each took a whack on the shoulder from a Bone Face before doing the same.

In the jar, the blind manok could smell the five hands, could feel them hitting its flank, it was excited, knowing there was a kill looming, but which one to choose? Fingers found coins and four hands pulled out. The manok thrashed its head from side to side and then struck at the one remaining hand.

In the hall, one of the two men screamed. He snatched his hand out, but with the manok attached firmly to his wrist. The snake was pumping its venom into the man. The Bone Face snake handler stepped up and detached the serpent and dropped it back into the jar. The screaming man was led away and after a few moments his screaming stopped abruptly.

'Mollo fis,' said the Tul.

'Round two,' said Alfrid, and the Tul dropped the coin she was holding back into the jar. Junk did the same and so did the other woman. The man next to Junk was about to drop his in when the Bone Face behind him leaned forward and plucked it from his hand.

'Just three coins this time,' said Alfrid, translating for the Tul. The prisoner next to Junk was struggling to keep his tears at bay. Junk glanced down and saw that the man was standing in a pool of his own urine. Junk took a small step to the side. He caught the terrified man's eye and gave him an encouraging nod. It didn't help, and the man started to sob uncontrollably. His Bone Face minder cracked him on the ear with a cudgel so the man was terrified *and* in pain. The woman was just staring into space. Her face showed no emotion at all.

'Lim . . .' said the Tul.

'One . . .' said Alfrid. Junk looked at him and shook

his head. He didn't need him to translate this again. He understood.

'Fis . . .' said the Tul. 'Jop!' Junk was ready and plunged his hand in first this time, just ahead of the Tul. The other two followed a second later. The Tul was the first to remove her hand with a coin held between her forefinger and middle finger. Junk was just behind her. The sobbing man was next. He held out his hand, the third coin displayed in the middle of his palm. He was laughing but there was something unhinged about it, as if the experience had broken him, which it probably had.

The expressionless woman drew her hand out with the manok biting into the fleshy heel of her palm. She didn't react. She didn't scream or cry out in any way. She just continued to look impassive.

The snake handler separated the reptile from the woman's hand and she was led away. She didn't make it out of the hall before she collapsed and started convulsing. Junk turned back.

'And then there were three,' he said. Alfrid opened his mouth to translate but Junk shook him off.

Two coins went back into the jar along with the snake. The man next to Junk had a thousand and one different emotions playing out over his face, seemingly all at the same time. He was laughing and crying and muttering to himself. He looked excited, then confused, then excited, scared, excited and so it went on.

'Lim . . . fis . . . jop!' said the Tul, and all three pushed a hand into the pot. Junk got hold of a coin almost immediately and started to pull his hand out, but before he could the man next to him pulled his hand out clutching the manok. It wasn't biting him. The crazed man was holding the snake around the middle and he raised it to his mouth. He was going to bite the snake before the snake could bite him. Unfortunately his plan was flawed, in that the manok could strike much more rapidly than he could. As the man raised the serpent to his mouth, the manok launched itself forward and sunk its fangs into the man's cheek, just beneath his eye. He screamed and started whipping his head back and forth to dislodge the creature, but the fangs were buried deep. The Bone Faces had to knock the man to the floor and hold him down before the snake handler could retrieve the reptile and return it to the jar as the groaning man was carried away.

The Tul looked at Junk and smiled. She took one coin and dropped it on top of the snake.

'Lim . . .' said the Tul.

'Fis . . .' said Junk.

'Jop!' said the Tul and Junk together, and both thrust a hand into the pot. Junk felt the bottom of the jar and his fingers brushed over the surface looking for the coin. The manok was now writhing apoplectically, twisting itself into furious knots. It was not enjoying this game at all. Then Junk felt the cold metal of the coin, but as he was about to take a hold of it he felt something clamp down on his hand. At first he thought it was the snake biting him, but then he realized it was the Tul. She had grabbed his hand and was holding it in place. They locked eyes and Junk pulled back but she was too strong for him. The longer they stayed in there the more chance there was of one or both of them being bitten. And that's what happened. Junk was aware of the manok snapping wildly and he cried out as he felt the fangs prick his skin. He pulled his hand back sharply and now it slipped through the Tul's sweaty grasp. He drew it out, and he was clutching the coin, but on the back of his hand were two prominent puncture marks with two bubbles of blood swelling up out of them. Junk stared at his hand.

The Tul removed her hand and Junk saw the manok had bitten her too. In fact, it was still attached to her thumb. The Tul gripped the creature in both hands and twisted sharply, ripping it in two. The snake handler let out a cry of despair as he watched his pet bisected. The Tul discarded the two halves, dropping them into the jar and sucking at the wound on her thumb. She spoke to Junk, and Alfrid translated.

'She says not to worry, the manok's venom will be totally depleted after the second or third bite. You won't die.'

'OK,' said Junk. 'Then tell her I won, so I want my sister and my friends and we'll go.' Alfrid relayed Junk's words. The Tul smiled and turned her back on them.

'Hey!' shouted Junk. He stepped forward and three Bone Faces got between him and the Tul. 'I won!'

The Tul turned around and shook her head, tapping her hand.

'You were bitten,' said Alfrid, translating.

'So were you, and I got the coin,' said Junk, holding it up. The Tul wasn't interested in a translation. She turned her back on him again, dismissing him with a wave. 'NO!' More Bone Faces descended on him, whipping him to the floor with their canes.

17

When Cobe landed in the river, he was knocked unconscious immediately and carried downstream. The group had been split: Junk went down one tributary, Lasel down another and Cobe down a third. He was completely unaware of his journey or of being fished out of the water.

The next thing he was conscious of was waking up in a large stone-built cabin. It took him a few minutes to regain his senses, and when he did the first thing he realized was that he was naked. He looked around and saw his clothes sitting in a sodden pile in the corner. The second thing he realized was that he was manacled around the wrists and shackled around the ankles and was attached to a large table, meaning his movement was considerably limited. He heard humming and twisted his head to see a short but extremely overweight man enter the room. The man was so plump that he clearly found it difficult to move and perspiration rained down his face. Every action, no matter how insignificant, required a tremendous amount of effort on his part. He smiled when he saw that Cobe was awake but his face was so fleshy that it was hard to distinguish the facial movement as a smile. It was more a thinning of his small eyes and a swelling of his already swollen cheeks.

The fat man moved to the door, breathing hard, and shouted. Cobe heard a stampede of heavy footsteps approaching and soon four more short, obese people entered. All four had curly blonde hair and tiny eyes marooned in the ocean of puffy flesh that was their faces. They were the fat man's family: wife and three daughters. They crowded around Cobe and all clapped gleefully. Their well-padded hands made little sound. The father of the family made the introductions and even though Cobe could not understand the language he did manage to get all their names. The man was called Holf, his wife was Jarta and their three daughters were Muju, Tatra and Jundy. He also understood, more through circumstances than words, that they were planning to eat him.

Holf and his family started to bicker. Cobe got the idea that they were disagreeing on how they should cook him. Then Holf unveiled a selection of very sharp, effective-looking knives and he pulled a handle on the end of the table so it tilted to a forty-five-degree angle, head down. There was a gutter built into the table and Holf set a large tub on the floor to collect the run-off blood.

Cobe tried talking to them, to persuade them not to do what they were about to, but they didn't understand him any more than he understood them. They just nodded and kept smiling as Holf sharpened a cleaver-like blade. Cobe wondered for a moment if this was all some crazy hallucination and maybe he was still floating down the river, but then Holf was leaning over Cobe's face smiling down at him, speaking, saying incomprehensible words and miming the fact that he was about to cut Cobe's throat.

Cobe realized two things at the same time. The first was that the table he was chained to was big but not quite big enough. His feet projected off the end and it was not wide enough to contain his shoulders. The second thing he realized was that that meant that the table, as big and sturdy as it was, had not been designed to accommodate someone quite as big, sturdy and strong as him. With that he let out an almighty roar that made Holf leap back, startled, clutching his cleaver. Cobe focused all his strength on the restraints around his wrists. At first they seemed totally solid but he vibrated them rapidly and very quickly he started to feel some give in them. He increased his efforts and in just a few seconds he heard the wood of the table crack and Holf and his family starting to panic.

They were right to panic. If Holf had had the wherewithal to finish his task swiftly, the day might have had a very different outcome for everyone there. Instead he concentrated on ushering his wife and daughters out of the room, which gave Cobe time to break out of his bonds.

209

Holf attacked him then, brandishing the cleaver, but it was too late. He was no match for Cobe in hand-to-hand combat and he ended up with his head on back to front.

Cobe got dressed into his still damp clothes and was feeling quite miserable when he left the cabin. That sort of violence was a thing of his past, and even though he had had no choice in the matter, he felt he had let himself down.

Junk and Alfrid had been taken from the hall back to the cage they had been in before. They had been strung up by their ankles once again and left there, dangling helplessly. Hours passed. Time Junk couldn't afford to lose, but his calls for attention went unanswered. He kept snatching glimpses of the symbols on his hand. He watched impotently as the third symbol faded and the fourth, the Rorschach-like lines, became brighter. The eight lines moved randomly but always contained in an area just two centimetres square. One by one, those lines started to disappear too and still no one came. There were now only five lines remaining. Less than ten hours left until the countdown ran out. Not long until he found out what it would mean when it did expire. He hoped he had enough time to finish what he'd started, but it was looking increasingly unlikely that he would be able to find Ambeline now. However, he was certain Garvan and Cobe would carry on with the search. After all, they had, along with Lasel, continued looking for Ambeline when Dras Sbey had taken Junk the first time. This time, whether he was taken again or dropped dead on the spot or exploded or had his mind wiped or any of the dozens of scenarios that Junk had imagined would occur when the countdown ran out, he knew his friends would finish his quest for him.

He thought about Lasel. There was part of him praying for a miracle, praying that she had somehow, despite everything, survived, but he knew it was unlikely. She had been left behind and alone. He was sure none of the Bone Faces would think to administer the antivenom, and he had only managed to tip the smallest amount into her mouth. He kept telling himself that it might have been enough, but the rational part of his brain knew that probably wasn't true and Lasel was dead. He shook the thought from his mind. If he was about to die, he didn't want to be thinking those thoughts at the end. He would die ignorant of what had really happened to Lasel.

Occasionally the cage would open and a new prisoner would be brought in and hung up by their ankles. There were men and women, ranging in age from a couple in their late teens to a seventy-something-year-old man. He was weak and feeble and Junk wasn't sure he would survive the inverted hanging, let alone whatever was going to happen next.

He tried to speak to him, with Alfrid's help, but the old guy just shook his head and refused to engage. A woman in her thirties tried apologizing for him, saying he was frightened, as they all were. Only then did the old man speak. He corrected the woman, explaining that he wasn't staying quiet because he was frightened but because they were all destined for the arena and very soon he was going to have to try to kill everyone in the cage so he didn't want to get to know them.

'It will make killing you harder,' he said.

'What's the arena?' asked Junk.

'The big pit in the hall,' said Alfrid. 'It's another of the Tul's favourite games. Ten, twenty, however many people go into the pit; only one's allowed to come out.'

'What?' said Junk, horrified.

'It's a fight to the death.'

'And you didn't think to mention this before?'

'I didn't know it was going to be relevant, and you didn't ask,' said Alfrid with an inverted shrug.

'I'm not killing anyone,' said Junk.

'Then you'll die,' said Alfrid. 'Some of these people have chosen to be here.'

'What? That's crazy. Why would they do that?'

'The one who wins gets to become a Bone Face.'

'Who the hell would want to be a Bone Face? I don't want to have to wear a dead animal on my head!'

'They get to live here,' explained Alfrid. 'They get fed, they're feared. For some people, that's worth the risk.'

'But I don't want to be a Bone Face. I need to get out of here,' said Junk.

Alfrid laughed. 'There's no getting out of here, Junk. We're at the whim of the Tul now.'

'I had a metal bracelet on my wrist when we arrived. If I can get hold of that, I can get us out. All of us. Did you see what they did with it?'

'No,' said Alfrid. 'But you won't get it back. The Tul considers everything here to belong to her. You belong to her, I belong to her. We're her playthings. Her trinkets. So's your bracelet. Forget about that. You need to focus on surviving.'

Two more lines on Junk's palm went out before they were taken from the cage. They were led, single file, back to the hall. As they approached the massive cliff-face punctured with holes, entrances to all the different rooms, Junk scanned the wrists of every Bone Face they passed, hoping to spot the Antricle, but he had no luck. The thought had occurred to him that even if he did find it, how was he going to get it back? From what he had seen of the Tul, she was unlikely to just hand it over.

As they drew near, Junk saw a Bone Face holding a bag out for each of the participants in turn. Each person in line reached their hand inside and drew out a slip of paper bearing an ideogram.

'That decides which weapon you'll get,' explained Alfrid as they stepped closer to the Bone Face with the bag. Ahead a man of about forty and of similar height to Junk, though his torso was twice as broad, bloated with muscles like a steroid-ravaged bodybuilder, reached into the bag. The paper he drew out bore a crescent-moon symbol. He snatched another paper from a twitching, nervous man ahead of him. This paper bore what looked like an animal tooth. The bodybuilder considered it before throwing it back. He turned to watch as the man behind him drew out his paper. It had a circle on it. The bodybuilder laughed derisively and resolved to keep his original choice. Junk didn't have the first clue as to what the symbols represented, but clearly others did.

When it was Junk's turn, he drew out a piece of paper bearing what appeared to be a letter S and its reflection. Alfrid's had just three vertical lines.

'The trident,' said Alfrid, explaining what his meant. Junk held out his. 'Hooks,' said Alfrid.

As they lined up to enter the passageway leading to the hall, the hairs on the back of Junk's neck stood up and a shiver ran down his spine. He felt as if he was being watched. He turned to look. There were plenty of people nearby, all Bone Faces, watching the procession of prisoners heading to the slaughter, but no one who stood out. Then Junk was jostled from behind and he heard a commotion. He turned to see what was wrong, but there were too many people in his way.

'What's going on?' he asked Alfrid.

'I don't know. Someone trying to run away, I guess.'

'I thought you said they'd chosen to be here.'

'Not everyone. Some, like us, are just picked by the Tul.' Junk watched as some more Bone Faces headed to the back of the line to see what the problem was as the prisoners continued into the hall.

A ramp had been added to the pit and they stopped at the head of it and waited. A Bone Face, wearing the skull of a big cat, something like a panther, walked the line, counting. As far as Junk could tell, he appeared to be unhappy about something. He was shouting at other Bone Faces.

'What's going on?' whispered Junk to Alfrid.

'It seems like they miscounted. There's one too many.'

Junk frowned. 'What does it matter?' Maybe the man in charge had some form of OCD and wanted an even number of people to fight to the death. Whatever the reason, the Bone Face in the panther skull walked the line again, recounting. He got to the end nearest Junk and Alfrid and started to shout again. Then he walked towards Junk and grabbed the woman next to him, pulling her from the line. She was lean and muscular. Her hair had been shaved at the sides and she had leather straps wound around her arms. She started protesting immediately, screaming and pulling away from him.

Alfrid explained quietly to Junk what was happening. 'He wants someone out of the group. He picked her, but she doesn't want to leave. She's one of the ones who wants to be here.'

An idea occurred to Junk as the woman rejoined the line next to him.

'HEY!' shouted Junk, getting Panther Skull's

215

attention. Then he gave Alfrid a shove and he stumbled forward. 'Choose him,' said Junk, stabbing a finger at Alfrid. Panther Skull marched towards them and Junk could tell he looked angry under his mask.

'What are you doing?' demanded Alfrid.

'How do you say, "Choose him"?' Junk asked Alfrid.

'Sussa nol,' said Alfrid, who'd grown so accustomed to answering Junk's translation enquiries he replied automatically.

'SUSSA NOL!' shouted Junk, pointing again at Alfrid. 'SUSSA NOL!'

'Junk, no. I—' But Alfrid didn't get to finish his sentence. Panther Skull marched over and grabbed Alfrid by the arm, pulling him out of the line. Alfrid locked eyes with Junk.

'Just do it, Alfrid, please!' Alfrid could see the pleading in Junk's face. 'The Tul's not going to let me out, is she? It's crazy for both of us to end up in there.'

Alfrid could not argue with Junk's logic and allowed himself to be led away. Junk was on his own.

Panther Skull seemed satisfied now and he bellowed out another command. Half a dozen Bone Faces moved down the line, their arms loaded with various weapons and shields. Each participant handed over their scrap of paper and received the relevant weapon in return. Junk was given a pair of gruesome-looking hooks. Each had a handle that was perpendicular to the hook and each hook ended in a vicious point.

Once all were armed, the order was given for the

line to descend into the pit. Junk shuffled forward with the others. He searched the crowd as he went, looking for the Tul. If only he could get his Antricle back, then he could get out of here. He looked down at his hand. Only two lines left now. He was surely going to die in this pit, so using the Antricle couldn't possibly make things any worse. If Sbey was able to track him and take him back to Pirestus Octonary, then so be it. He'd escaped once so he could escape again.

It seemed to Junk that every single Bone Face had gathered to witness the fight to the death in the arena pit. There were more than a hundred of them. But he still couldn't see the Tul.

Once the prisoners and volunteers were in the pit, the ramp was hauled up so there was no way out. The Bone Face in charge, the one in the panther skull, stood on the edge of the pit and bellowed something Junk could only assume was a request for silence, because all the hubbub and chatter in the hall died down, punctuated by only the occasional cough and some whimpering from one or two of the participants in the pit not there by choice. Panther Skull started to explain what Junk guessed were the rules, but seeing as he didn't understand a word of it, he didn't pay attention and looked around the arena instead.

The walls were embedded with stones, something sharp and smooth like flint. Junk knew it would hurt to come into forceful contact with any part of the walls. He could see gouges in the stone where weapons had struck or terrified competitors had tried to climb to safety. The walls were vertical. They would be impossible to climb. The place made him think of gladiators in an arena in ancient Rome. Of all the things to survive the passing of so much time, it would be the barbaric desire to hurt and maim and kill and watch others doing so.

He looked down at the stained sand beneath his feet. It was dark red. He scored a line through it with his toe and saw that the red had soaked down a long way, getting darker the further he went until it was black. This wasn't the first fight to the death this arena had hosted. Nowhere close. Junk glanced up then, looking around at the others in the pit with him. They were mostly men, a few women. Some wore blank, glassy stares, as if trying to block out the reality of what was about to happen to them; some were weeping quietly with building fear and disbelief; others were giving themselves muttered pep talks, barking out muted whoops of self-encouragement (clearly those were the ones who had chosen to be here). He saw the woman with the sides of her head shaved, the one who had refused to leave the line earlier, standing near him. She was armed with a double-bladed axe and was practising her 'moves', swivelling at the hips and ducking to avoid an imaginary attacker. She performed this routine over and over again; it was smooth and flawless.

A short distance beyond her was the bodybuilder Junk had noticed earlier. His weapon was a scythe. Junk watched him nodding to himself, his lips moving quickly, reminding himself how much of a warrior he was, Junk assumed. Then he started to punch his own biceps, which took Junk by surprise.

Next to the bodybuilder was another man of a similar age but that was the only thing they had in common. He was thin and weedy-looking. His shoulders were hunched. He looked defeated already. He was acting out something imaginary too but it wasn't offensive, or even defensive, moves. He seemed to be pretending to put his arms around someone only he could see, someone standing in front of him. More than one person. He crouched down to do it too. He was saying goodbye to his family, Junk thought. He stood again to kiss someone invisible, his wife perhaps. Junk saw his lips move, and even though Junk didn't understand the language he knew he was saying, *I love you*. Junk looked away, feeling the moment was a private one.

In the opposite direction, Junk caught the eye of a man of maybe thirty who was staring directly at him. The man was shorter than Junk but he had a lean, strong torso. His arms were covered in scars and ropey veins, his nose had clearly been broken more than once, and as he opened his mouth to sneer in Junk's direction, Junk saw he was missing most of his teeth. He reminded Junk of a boxer, maybe a welterweight, or even a middleweight. Junk's dad had been a big boxing fan, a spectator rather than participant, but Junk knew a few things about it. Unfortunately the one thing he didn't know that might now have proved useful was how to actually box.

219

Next to the boxer was a man in his fifties, who looked more like a professor than a killer. He had neat salt-and-pepper hair, parted at the side. He looked as if he usually wore glasses and the world appeared mighty strange without them. He was blinking continuously and screwing up his eyes as he glanced around the pit. He was sizing up his opponents and, Junk thought, ranking them. He pointed with one finger to the boxer to his left first. Then with two fingers to someone to his right whom Junk couldn't see from where he was standing. Three fingers to the bodybuilder, four to the woman with the sides of her head shaved. Five fingers to a tall, flabby man who was chuckling to himself under his breath and nodding. He appeared to be quite insane, which was understandable considering the circumstances and quite possibly an advantage.

The panther-skull Bone Face was still talking but seemed to be coming to an end. Finally he took a deep breath and said something about the Tul. All heads turned to the opposite side of the hall, where the many Bone Faces clustered together at the edge of the pit parted, moving aside to create an avenue. The Tul appeared then. She gazed down into the arena, assessing the competitors one by one. When she looked at Junk she smiled, and to his shame he looked away, averted his eyes, cast them down to the ground. He was immediately annoyed with himself. He should have held her stare.

The Tul started speaking and Junk's mind wandered to the fight that was about to ensue. What was he going to do? Junk had never killed anyone . . . Well, that wasn't quite true. Some of the Nine Emperors' soldiers had died because of him. He might not have killed them personally, but he had set a herd of stampeding dinosaurs loose on them, crushing them underfoot. He had plucked the Spitfires and Messerschmitts from the Battle of Britain and transported them to the plains beyond Versailles with their machine guns blazing. He had diverted a train from the frozen wilds of Alaska and caused it to run over dozens of soldiers. But this was different. This would involve picking up a weapon (he glanced with dread at the hooks in his hands) and forcing that weapon into the body of another person. He would be looking at them when he ended their life. He didn't think he could do that or live with himself afterwards if he did. Of course, at least half the people in the pit with him would have no similar reservations about ending his life. There can only be one survivor from the twenty. That means that it was likely he wouldn't have to kill just one person to survive, but at least three if not four. Twenty would become ten; ten would become five; five would become two or three; two or three would become one. And if that was the case, if he was sure he couldn't bring himself to end the lives of four people, then what was the point of participating at all? Maybe he should just sit down now and wait for the killing blow to come to him. The skinny family man appeared to have done just that. He was on his knees with his head bowed, waiting for death. He'd said his goodbyes, so now his business was done.

The Tul finished speaking. She spread her arms magnanimously and an explosive cheer shook the hall as the Bone Faces stomped their feet and started to chant. They wanted blood and they wanted it now. It was time for the main event.

18

A band started playing. Their instruments were strange trumpet-like contraptions that sounded like a lot of cats being poked with sticks while bouncing in a vat of jam. The music (or din) built and built, racing towards a crescendo, and when that crescendo came it was deafening and it signalled the fight was on.

In the pit, the bodybuilder, the woman with the shaved head, the boxer, the professor and a few others charged into action. They each had a game plan. The boxer had been armed with a wicked-looking iron mallet, but he let it drop to the ground, preferring to rely on his fists. And then he turned and fixed his eyes on Junk.

Junk was aware immediately that the man was running straight at him, but it took his brain a few seconds to wade through the debilitating panic and consider how to react. He remembered the professor had picked the boxer to be his first kill. Junk looked to see where the professor was now, hoping he was about to leap into the boxer's path and run him through with the spear he had been holding. Junk saw the professor was on the ground, with the laughing lunatic sitting on top of him laughing wildly as he pounded the professor's lifeless body with his meaty fists.

The boxer reached Junk and leaped into the air, pouncing like a tiger, one arm pulled back, his fist ready to strike. Junk couldn't move out of his path in time. The man looked so crazed that it would probably only take him one blow to finish the job. The boxer let rip with his clenched fist and it rocketed straight at Junk's face.

But then the strangest thing happened. The boxer's arm extended fully. His aim was true and his reach should have been more than adequate, but instead his fist stopped just short of Junk's nose. There was a split second of inactivity and then the boxer's eyes widened in surprise and he started to retreat. It took Junk a moment to understand that the retreat was not through choice. The boxer was being forcibly restrained by another of the fighters. The boxer lifted off the ground, levitating like some unbelievable magic trick. He twisted his body and launched a crushing right hook that would have decimated most opponents. The punch hit his assailant square in the jaw. Junk couldn't believe what he was seeing. Cobe barely flinched from the force of the blow and the boxer looked scared then.

Junk had not seen Cobe as they entered the pit, which was strange because Cobe was hard to not see. Cobe hurled the boxer at the wall behind Junk and he hit with a sickening crack. He slid to the ground and didn't move again.

'How are you here?' shouted Junk in the midst of the mayhem going on around them.

'Chance,' said Cobe. 'I came out of the river west of here. I was wandering, looking for you and Lasel, when I saw the crowds and decided to see where everyone was going. I came across this place just as you were being led inside. I didn't know where you were going, but it didn't look good so I joined near the back of the line, figured I'd tag along.'

Junk realized that that must have been the cause of the commotion he had heard as they were entering the hall and the reason there was an extra body in the group.

'Where is Lasel?' asked Cobe, but before Junk could answer they were attacked again.

It was the bodybuilder. Cobe pushed Junk aside just as a spiked club sailed past them. Half a second slower and the spikes would have impaled the side of Junk's head. Junk found himself on the ground looking up as Cobe and the bodybuilder clashed. The bodybuilder was the only person in the arena who could challenge Cobe in size and strength. He had the added advantage of two weapons, the spiked club in one hand, which he must have acquired from an earlier victory, and the scythe that he had been allocated to begin with. What's more, he clearly knew how to use both.

The bodybuilder roared as he swiped the club and the scythe first one way and then back again. Cobe was instantly on the defensive, moving to avoid being skewered and slashed. The bodybuilder swung both weapons again. This time Cobe sidestepped them and the scythe struck the rock wall and jumped out of the bodybuilder's grasp. Using this advantage, Cobe let fly with a punishing jab that caught his attacker on the side of the head. Unbelievably the man just shook off the blow and kept coming.

Still clutching the spiked club, he swung again and this time Cobe raised his arm to parry the blow. The spikes dug into his flesh and Cobe bellowed in pain.

Junk couldn't just sit and watch his travelling companion being hacked to pieces. He ran at the bodybuilder, leaping on to his back before he had a chance to think about what he was doing. He snaked his forearm around the man's throat and started squeezing as hard as he could.

'JUNK! GET AWAY!' shouted Cobe. The bodybuilder backtracked rapidly, running into the jagged wall. The blow knocked the wind out of Junk and the razor-sharp flints lacerated his back. He lost his grip and as he fell to the ground he was half aware of the bodybuilder swinging the spiked club at his head. Junk reacted without thinking and flung himself to one side. The spikes hit the wall, creating a shower of sparks.

Turning, the bodybuilder saw Cobe coming for him again. He swung the club back the other way. Cobe grabbed a hold of a smaller competitor, a crazed, almost feral twenty-something-year-old man who was awash with blood, seemingly none of it his own. Cobe picked the bloody man up and used him as a shield. The spiked club speared his ribcage, and when Cobe threw the smaller man aside, the club, embedded deeply in his body, went with him and was wrenched from the bodybuilder's grip.

Cobe and the bodybuilder went up against one another then, both empty-handed, trading blows. Junk saw the woman with the shaved head run her long sword through the throat of the chuckling lunatic, who was still chuckling as he fell face down on the sandy floor.

Junk was shocked to discover that the arena was strewn with corpses and now only the four of them remained. The woman turned to see Junk and Cobe and the bodybuilder fighting. She raced up behind Cobe with the intention of sticking her blade through both him and the bodybuilder while they were distracted, killing two in one go. That would only leave Junk to deal with.

'COBE!' shouted Junk, as the woman thrust the sword forward. Cobe didn't even turn to see what was happening, apparently aware the instant Junk cried out. He took a step to his left, exposing the bodybuilder to the sword, which went straight through his belly. It took the woman a moment to understand she had only got one out of two, but she didn't have enough time to do anything about it. Cobe turned sharply, swinging his arm straight. It connected with the woman's jaw and Junk heard her neck snap. By the time, Cobe had completed the move she was dead and on the ground, as was the bodybuilder, and Cobe was left holding her sword.

Cobe moved to Junk and pulled him to his feet. Junk was dazed. It had all happened so quickly his head was spinning. He wasn't aware that Cobe had slapped the hilt of the sword into Junk's hand or that he had curled his fist around it. Junk was trying to take in the unbelievable carnage surrounding them. They were the last two standing. Everyone else was dead.

'Is it over?' said Junk breathlessly. 'Are we finished?' He looked down and frowned as he realized for the first time that he was holding a sword. He looked up at Cobe, who was standing in front of him. Cobe smiled at Junk and then let himself fall forward.

The sword went straight through him.

'NO!' Junk cried out. Cobe dropped to his knees and Junk went down with him. 'Why did you do that?'

'Only one . . . can –' the words did not come easily but he persisted –'. . . survive. Find your . . . sister . . . and take her home. For me. Put right . . . what I did wrong.'

Junk stared down at Cobe as he sank further to the bloody, sandy floor. The Pallatan was too heavy for him to support, so he sank down with him. The light in Cobe's one good eye faded until it was gone. He was dead.

Junk was crying and he realized in that moment that the man who had been Jacid Mestrowe had become his friend.

Junk became aware of the ramp behind him being

lowered. The master of ceremonies, the panther-skull Bone Face, descended. Beside him walked three body-guards. Panther Skull surveyed the massacre, making sure everyone else was indeed dead, before he gripped Junk by the wrist and yanked him unceremoniously to his feet. As Junk stood dazed, Panther Skull raised his hand to signify they had a winner. He announced this fact to the crowd and there was as much cheering and excitement as booing and anger. Money changed hands and it was apparent that few had bet on Junk to win, and those who did had won big.

Junk was pulled away from Cobe and marched up the ramp. Nothing seemed real. Everything was happening so fast. At the top of the ramp, the swarms of gathered Bone Faces parted to allow him and Panther Skull through. Looking up, he realized they were en route to another audience with the Tul. Junk was aware that she was smiling, nodding, looking impressed with him. He was also aware that she was speaking, but he wasn't listening, not that he would have been able to understand anyway. Alfrid was pushed up next to him.

'Junk, I can't believe it,' he was saying, beaming ecstatically. 'I can't believe you survived.'

'Me neither,' said Junk. Then Alfrid gestured for Junk to be quiet as the room hushed and the Tul was speaking again. Alfrid translated as she spoke, speaking softly into Junk's ear.

'She says you fought like a warrior and have earned your place alongside them. You are a true Bone Face.'

The Tul gestured to someone behind Junk and all eyes turned to see a group of three Bone Faces approaching. The first carried a skull mask, the second a sheathed knife, the third a long leather coat. Junk hadn't even noticed that all the Bone Faces wore the same sheathed knife. This was clearly one of their traditions. He looked around and saw that about half wore long leather coats. He remembered then that he was wearing one already, the one he had taken from one of the Bone Faces who had attacked Alfrid. The coat he was wearing was peeled off him and he cried out. The back of it was in tatters from where he'd slammed into the jagged rock wall in the pit. If the coat looked like that, he shuddered to think what his actual back looked like. As the new coat was put on him, his reaction to the pain that shot through him was resolutely ignored by everyone around him.

Then the Bone Face carrying the sheathed knife stepped up and presented it to Junk. He took it but was already shaking his head. Then the skull mask, *his* skull mask, was brought forward and raised in front of him, ready for Junk to step into it. Junk pushed it away, eliciting gasps from the crowd.

'What are you doing?' hissed Alfrid.

'I don't want any of this,' said Junk angrily.

'You must!' said Alfrid, sounding worried and glancing at the Tul, who was already frowning.

'I want my sister! I want Tyva and the children they took. I want my Antri— my bracelet,' he corrected himself, 'and I want to get out of here.' He looked at the palm of his hand. There was only one line left. 'I want to get out of here now.'

The Tul spoke, addressing her question to Alfrid. 'She's asking what's wrong,' said Alfrid to Junk.

'Well, tell her.'

Alfrid looked into the Tul's glowering face and he felt his legs threatening to liquefy beneath him. He considered how to respond. He decided the truth was the best option, but a more palatable truth. He told the Tul that Junk was exhausted after the battle and, with all due respect, he would, if the Tul saw fit, appreciate seeing his sister and friends and getting back a bracelet that he had had when he arrived. The Tul stared at Junk while she considered what Alfrid had said. She was feeling in good spirits and she had had plenty of fun with this newcomer, so she decided to grant his requests.

'Yaso pon solge?' she said.

Alfrid relaxed slightly then, letting out a brief sigh of relief as he smiled at Junk. 'She wants to know who your sister is?'

Junk described Ambeline and explained that the Bone Faces had taken her from Dajja several weeks earlier. The Tul looked to an advisor, who approached and whispered in her ear. They had a short, hushed exchange and then the Tul turned back to Junk but spoke to Alfrid. Again Alfrid translated.

'She says they have your sister, but she's not here. They will send for her and she'll be here within the hour.

In the meantime, you are to get cleaned up. When you come back she will have your bracelet for you too.' Alfrid looked shocked. 'She clearly likes you,' he said to Junk, 'or else you've caught her on a very good day. She's never this nice.'

'Tell her I want the bracelet now.' Junk knew he sounded like a petulant child but he didn't care. 'And find out where Tyva is and—'

'No, Junk, don't be –' Alfrid forced a smile on his face and a calm tone into his voice so no one else would question Junk's attitude. 'She could change her mind back just as quickly. Don't be stupid about this. Just be patient and you'll get what you want. Annoy her and you won't.'

Junk considered this and he had to admit that Alfrid was right. He nodded his agreement and then turned to the Tul and bowed, smiling his thanks. She smiled back.

Junk was led away to a room where a tub of hot water was waiting for him. His hands were tacky with blood. Cobe's blood. A Bone Face entered and explained, via Alfrid, that he was there to tend to Junk's wounds. The man bathed the cuts on Junk's back and then applied an ointment that hurt more than the initial injury. Junk howled with pain, but the Bone Face said that was a good sign. It meant the ointment was working.

Once he was cleaned up, he got dressed. Alfrid insisted that he put on his skull mask. It was a human skull. Junk didn't want to wear it but Alfrid reminded him that he needed to keep the Tul happy until he got everything he wanted from her.

Junk glanced at his palm. The last pulsating line of the fourth symbol was still burning brightly, still flashing steadily. He didn't know how much longer he had, but he was sure it wasn't long. He couldn't dwell on what was going to happen when that final part of the final symbol disappeared. He needed to focus on the present.

Less than an hour had passed and Junk, with Alfrid at his side, was back in the hall. The energy in the room was high. The gathered Bone Faces treated Junk as their new friend now; there was no more aggression towards him. Instead there was much backslapping (not one of them noticed how he flinched every time they did it) and plenty of being overtly friendly, trying to engage him in conversation. Although Alfrid was a vital part of the conversational process, not one of them acknowledged him.

The Tul wasn't in the hall when they returned and Junk kept sneaking glances at the yellow line on his hand. Maybe it would keep pulsing forever. Or just stop and his hand would go back to the way it was before. Maybe it was harmless after all. Just an experiment number as he had originally thought. But deep down he didn't believe that for a second.

The arena was empty now. The corpses had been removed. Cobe had been removed. Junk was just beginning to wonder who he should talk to about claiming Cobe's body so he could give him a proper burial, when there was a build-up of excited chatter and Junk turned to see that the Tul had entered the hall and she wasn't alone. There was a child with her. Junk was immediately alert. He couldn't see her clearly yet. There were too many bodies between them, but from a distance he could tell she was blonde and about the size that Ambeline would be now.

The Tul and the child drew nearer and came to stand before Junk and Alfrid. The little girl had her head bowed, looking at the floor so Junk could see only the top of her hair. His heart was pounding. His mouth was dry. Was his journey really almost over? The Tul started speaking and Alfrid translated:

'You fought bravely and you deserve your reward. The Tul says it is her honour to present your sister.'

With that the Tul put a hand on the little girl's back and guided her forward. Junk took a step forward as well.

'Ambeline?' he said softly. For a moment the little girl didn't move, and then slowly, hesitantly, she started to raise her head. Junk was shaking as adrenalin surged through him. And then the little girl's head shot up, taking him by surprise, and instead of looking into Ambeline's sweet young face he was looking at the lined, ragged face of a small man. He opened his mouth and let out a hoarse bark. Junk pulled back. It wasn't a child at all, just a midget in a wig. The Tul's idea of a joke.

And she found it very funny. She laughed, the midget laughed, the Bone Faces laughed. Only Alfrid and Junk weren't laughing.

Pure unadulterated rage coursed through Junk and he leaped at the Tul. Her soldiers reacted in the blink of an eye. Junk and Alfrid were grabbed, held roughly and weapons were drawn.

'Faush nol,' said the Tul, staring straight at Junk with wicked delight. Somehow he knew that meant *Kill him*, and he was right. The panther-skull Bone Face drew out a long, thin dagger and advanced on Junk. Junk looked down at his palm. The last line was still there. That wasn't going to save him. He knew this was the end of the road. He had felt certain that Ambeline was close. Despite everything, some small pilot light of hope still burned within him. There had to be a way out of this, but at that moment he had no idea what it might be. Panther Skull touched the blade to Junk's throat and was all ready to slice him open. Junk knew he had to do something right then . . . but his mind was blank. He couldn't think of anything to say or do. It was over. Panther Skull drew back his arm, ready to make the killing slash when, all of a sudden, the bolt from a crossbow thudded right into the middle of the skull mask's forehead with a resounding thwack and the man dropped to the floor.

Chaos ensued. Huge soldiers clad in black and orange armour filed briskly into the hall. All of them towered over the Bone Faces. Some sported multiple-barrelled crossbows, others had four-bladed broadswords, others wore massive metal fists over their hands. The soldiers subdued the Bone Faces in seconds. Orders were barked out and then their commander-in-chief entered the hall. He wore gold and black armour and stood near enough four metres tall. He removed his helmet.

Junk couldn't believe what he was seeing. He dropped to his knees, crying and laughing at the same time. Catching his breath proved difficult. Garvan crouched down next to him and put a massive comforting hand on his shoulder.

'Your Majesty is a long way from where he should be,' said Junk finally when he regained the ability to speak.

'He's exactly where he should be,' said Garvan.

Junk moved and threw his arms around his big friend and hugged him. 'How did you find me?' he asked.

'Went back to Versailles and picked up your trail, followed it all the way to Dajja and then here. Found this one first.' Garvan turned, guiding Junk to one of his soldiers. The soldier stepped aside to reveal Lasel. Alive and well. She ran to Junk and they threw their arms around one another.

'I thought I'd lost you,' said Junk.

'Never,' said Lasel. 'Garvan found me not long after you and the others were taken. He gave me the rest of the antivenom.'

Junk's mind was spinning. He was so happy, but

there was so much to say. He needed to tell the others about Cobe, but that would have to wait. Instead he turned to the Tul.

'Alfrid, tell her if she wants to see another day, then she needs to tell me the truth. Does she have my sister or not?'

Alfrid translated Junk's words and the Tul, her face rigid with anger, considered her answer carefully. Finally she nodded.

'Zo, n'tush nul.'

'Yes, she has her,' said Alfrid.

Junk closed his eyes for a moment. He opened them as he remembered something else: 'And my Antricle?' said Junk. 'The bracelet.' Alfrid relayed the question and the Tul nodded to one of her lackeys, who stepped forward with a box. He lifted the lid and there was the Antricle. Junk picked it up and slipped it on. He felt better, stronger, when he was wearing it. This was almost over.

'Junk?' Lasel was frowning at him. 'What's happening to you?'

At first Junk didn't know what she meant, but he quickly became aware that his heart was starting to beat faster. He was feeling light-headed. He looked down and his hand was starting to turn transparent.

What?! He held up his hand and he could see straight through it.

'Not now!' he said, and rotated his hand to look at his palm. The last line of the last of the four symbols was now just a faint outline. The yellow glow had faded. And now he was fading too.

Everyone watched open-mouthed. Junk was dematerializing before their very eyes. 'What are you doing?' Alfrid sounded understandably dumbfounded.

Junk raised his arms and discovered his hands had vanished completely. His arms ended just below the elbows, but even that wouldn't be the case for long. His arms were disappearing, unravelling like a cardigan in an old *Tom and Jerry* cartoon.

His whole body vaporized, and then Junk was gone.

19

Everything was white. No, even less than that. Everything was absolutely devoid of colour or depth. Junk was floating in nothingness. He wondered if he was dead. *Is this what being dead was?* The Antricle was no longer on his wrist, but his limbs were back, visible again, along with the rest of him. He could turn his body. He felt his muscles contracting, his bones moving, his skin stretching, his tendons flexing or whatever it is tendons do, but as he was in nothingness there was no demonstrative result to that turning.

'Hello?' he called. He could hear his own voice. It floated away from him, quickly diminishing to nothing, and absolute silence was left in its place. He had never heard absolute silence before. No sound at all.

He stretched out his arms, moving them in a wide circle 360 degrees around him, twisting at the waist, first one way and then the other, as if he was doing exercises. There was nothing to feel. He pushed down with his feet. He couldn't sense anything underneath him either. He reached up. Again there was nothing.

It was an odd sensation. He didn't really feel like he was floating. It wasn't like being underwater or back in Sbey's tank. There were no forces, gravity and what have you, acting on him and he had no impact on the world, or lack of, around him. He didn't feel like he was standing upright any more than he felt he was reclining, but when a person is in the middle of a big pile of *nothingness*, he could be doing both at the same time.

He inhaled deeply. He could breathe. There was oxygen here apparently. Unless of course he was dead and then he wouldn't need oxygen. He wasn't hot and he wasn't cold. He was in a state of pure nothing. It was the only way he could describe it to himself. He felt a tang of panic then. He could move but he couldn't go anywhere. He couldn't see anything or hear anything other than himself. But he was conscious and aware. What if it was just this? For eternity. He would surely go insane. On the positive side, if that did happen, then he probably wouldn't worry too much about his predicament because he'd be too busy chasing unicorns or playing Rock-Paper-Scissors with Napoleon or whatever it was crazy people did.

He thought about St Jude's then. That was a building full of crazies, even though Dr Oak would have frowned at him for using such a *dangerously pejorative* word. He still didn't know what that meant. Of course there was no Dr Oak, so it didn't really matter what he thought or didn't think, seeing as he didn't actually exist and therefore didn't think about anything. Junk was starting to suspect he was already crazy.

Was this due to Dras Sbey? This place? He was pretty sure it must be. Had Sbey put the nightmare clock in his hand? The clock had timed out and this was where his countdown had been leading. Maybe this was another tank in Sbey's laboratory on board Pirestus Octonary. He had figured out how to escape the first tank, so what did Sbey do? Put him in a tank with nothing for him to utilize to fracture his reality. No way out.

But of course that wasn't true. Dras Sbey wanted something from him. He wanted to know how to use the Antricle. He didn't want to punish Junk or merely imprison him. Keeping him here would mean that Sbey wouldn't get what he wanted.

'DRAS SBEY?' Junk shouted. He waited. No reply. He tried again, quieter this time, more conversational. He turned his head as he was speaking, addressing different areas of nothingness for no particular reason. 'Look, I know what you want from me and I have no issue with telling you how it works. You need to understand what the Antricle is. How it works is not something that I can put into words necessarily. And you've tried that already with St Jude's.' He paused now to give Sbey an opportunity to respond. Nothing. So Junk continued:

'I just want to get back to my friends and my sister. Please. I was so close. Just talk to me. I'll show you how the Antricle works. Anything you want.' He paused again but there was still no reply. He didn't know what else to say.

So he hung suspended in nothingness for more time. He had no idea how long. It might have been hours or weeks. He didn't think he had fallen asleep, though he didn't feel remotely tired. Nor did he feel hungry or thirsty. Every now and then he would call out to Sbey and suggest they discuss this man to cyborg or, as time stretched on and Junk grew increasingly bored, he would suggest they 'discuss this face to face to face to face to face'. He was the only one to laugh at that and only the first time he said it.

He didn't understand why Sbey was just keeping him here. It served no purpose. Or maybe it did. Maybe Sbey was working away at him on some psychological level. Breaking down his walls of resistance through sheer and utter boredom. Junk decided he could give up or fight back. He chose the latter, though reserved the right to give up later.

His way of fighting back was to keep himself occupied, which he did by reciting facts. He listed all the members of the Galway Hurling team (albeit last season's team). He named all the James Bond books in order of publication (the ones written by Ian Fleming only) and all the official James Bond films in order of release. Then he remembered all the theme songs and their singers, the villains and Bond girls. He had seen the last Bond film in a crumbling but still majestic cinema in a town called Tampico in Mexico. The person sitting next to him had brought a parakeet in a very large ornate cage along to watch.

Then he did the same for all the Sherlock Holmes stories, the ones by Sir Arthur Conan Doyle, anyway. He named the novels with ease. Everyone knew them, apart from maybe *The Valley of Fear*, but there were only four in total so it wasn't exactly hard. However there were fifty-six short stories and naming those was much harder. These he did not try to do in publication order. He managed fifty-four, but the final two got the better of him and he had to admit defeat. (For the record, they were 'The Adventure of the Reigate Squire' and 'The Adventure of the Retired Colourman'.)

After that he recalled the name of every boat he had worked on, from the time he had arrived in Spain all those years ago up until he found his way into the Room of Doors while diving from the *Pandora*. He wondered, not for the first time in the last few months, what his eccentric Russian skipper, Timur, was up to now.

He did countries and capitals, counted to 1,257 in Gaelic and tried to remember all the lyrics to *Everybody's Got Something to Hide Except Me and My Monkey* by the Beatles, which had been Ambeline's favourite song in the world when she was four. An odd choice for a child. After that he was thoroughly sick of the sound of his own voice and so stopped. He emptied his mind then and closed his eyes. He still didn't feel tired, but because he wasn't thinking about anything at all he wasn't aware that he wasn't tired right at that particular moment.

And that was the moment that Dras Sbey chose to appear. He made absolutely no sound on arrival so Junk wasn't sure how long he had been standing in front of him. Junk had opened his eyes and let out a yelp of surprise. As he felt his heartrate spike the thought flitted through his mind that he couldn't be dead because he could still feel it beating.

He studied Sbey. He'd changed. The most startling difference compared to the first time Junk had seen him was that Sbey was no longer thirty metres tall. Now he was only about two metres, if that. Another difference was that instead of caterpillar tracks for legs he had legs for legs. The were long and elegantly sculpted in the same seamless red substance as his robotic arms, which he had crossed behind his back, along with his organic ones. The smaller pair that had been sprouting from Sbey's belly and typing at a keyboard that last time Junk had seen him were now absent.

'You have been a most interesting subject to observe, Mr Doyle,' said Sbey. 'You are astonishingly adaptive for an aberration of nature.'

Junk scowled. 'I'm not keen on being called an aberration. Considered a bit rude where I come from. And while we're on the subject, also considered rude is the whole kidnapping me thing. Twice.' He held up two fingers to emphasize that.

Sbey dismissed his objections with a wave of one of his red robot hands. He started to walk in a circle around Junk. Junk wondered how he seemed to be able to move about when Junk could not.

'How come you're so small now?' Junk asked.

'I'm not actually here,' said Sbey.

'And here is . . . ?'

'You're on board Pirestus Octonary again. In a projection tank.'

'Is that what you call the thing I was in before when you made me believe I was at St Jude's?'

'That's right.'

'But there's no real point putting me back in now I know how to get out.'

'Unfortunately that is true. Thanks to your friend Espa Hara-kayan. He was a disappointment.'

A chill ran down Junk's spine. 'Was?'

'I had expected more from him. He was a promising student once upon a time.'

'What did you do to him?' asked Junk, fearing the worst.

'Nothing. Yet. But his betrayal cannot go unpunished.'

'You don't have to do any of this. If all you want is to know how the Antricle works, I'll show you. I'll teach you.'

All four of Sbey's faces cringed. He flushed with anger.

'How dare you! There's nothing you can teach me.

245

You are an inferior life form. You're an abnormality. A freak occurrence. A mistake of nature.'

'I'm a mistake of nature who knows how to use the Antricle, and you don't.'

'There is an explanation for why you are able to manipulate the Antricle as you do.'

'Which is?' Sbey was silent. Junk laughed. 'Sure. There's an explanation – you just don't know what it is.'

Sbey fumed silently but it was true.

'You want to be able to use the Antricle like I can, so let me show you. I can't describe what I do when I'm using it. You had me locked up in one of these things for weeks trying to get me to do that. I'm a freak occurrence. I don't have the capacity to articulate my method. We'll go out, I'll use the Antricle and you can observe. You're a scientist Espa said. That's what scientists do, isn't it? I assume it's the same here as on Earth.'

One of Sbey's mouths smiled thinly. 'Your plan is so transparent. If I let you out of here, you think you'll just be able to run away, escape into the Rammaniac.'

'Well, seeing how you've already nabbed me twice, even a dumb inferior life form like me knows you can just get me again.'

'Yes, that is true. And you would be wise to remember that I am superior in every way.'

'So I'm no match for you. We're agreed.'

Sbey considered this for a few moments. It felt like Junk was manipulating him, but of course that would be impossible on account of Junk being of such a lesser species.

'Very well,' said Sbey. 'We will try. Why not? Though if it fails then I will have to try something more invasive. Of course, the drawbacks there are if that doesn't work, then you'll be dead and I can't experiment on you any more. Still, I'm willing to take the risk.'

With that, Sbey blinked out of existence. Junk waited but nothing happened. Nothing continued to happen for quite a while, though Junk realized being in this tank deprived him of his sense of time. It might have been a day since Sbey was here or maybe only a minute. It was impossible to tell.

Suddenly, everything changed and Junk found himself on a table as big as a room in a room as big as an aircraft hangar. Dras Sbey stood over him, back to his natural height of thirty metres. He still wore the red metal legs rather than the caterpillar tracks. He was also wearing an Antricle of his own. Espa had told Junk once that there used to be hundreds of Antricles. They were standard issue for Espa and Sbey's race of universe builders. They were a skeleton key used to sneak behind the scenes of a maturing planet and make adjustments to the simmering ingredients needed for a world to evolve. Most Antricles had been recalled; some had been lost along the way. Sbey's one was in the form of a glove covering his organic left hand. The thought occurred to Junk that if Sbey was unable to manipulate the Antricle, unable to make it alter its shape as Junk could, then it made sense that the glove was its initial shape, its factory default setting. The first time Junk had seen his Antricle it was in the shape of a cube. Since he had learned how to communicate with it, it had been everything from a sphere to a pyramid to a full armoured bodysuit. Junk's musings were cut short when Sbey held up a 'small' black box (about the size of a car to Junk).

'Do you know what this is?' asked Sbey. Junk shook his head. 'Before I woke you up, I injected a small explosive device into your bloodstream. It is currently making its way to your heart. When it gets there it will attach itself to the outer wall of the right ventricle. If you try anything, I will activate this –' he wobbled the black box in his hand for emphasis – 'and your heart will explode. Also the rest of you. It was the smallest explosive I had, but as you are so ridiculously puny it will obliterate you. You have been warned.'

'Listen, I don't want to trick you—'

'And you can't.'

'And, yes, as we've established, anything I can think of, you will already have planned for because you're superior and I'm inferior.'

'Quite right.'

'Look, I really would just like to get back to my friends and my sister and I figure the only way I can do that is if you let me. So if I give you what you want, I'll be no use to you any more. Right? And then I can go back to my life.'

Sbey smiled. He almost felt sorry for this poor little trusting creature.

Junk looked around the laboratory. It was not the same room he had been in previously. There were five tanks lined up along one wall. What had Sbey called them? Projection tanks? Whatever they were called, they were the same type of glass repository that Junk had escaped from before. Four were empty. The fifth however was full of the same pale pink translucent liquid that Junk had previously woken up submerged in. And Junk could see now that there was someone in the tank. He shifted, moving along the tabletop until the front of the tank came into view. Junk's jaw opened as he saw who was inside.

'Dr Otravinicus!'

Sbey moved silently on his long red metal legs. He glanced at where Junk was looking.

'Yes. I picked him up shortly after I first got you. I was hoping he could give me the answers I'm looking for, but unfortunately he's rather useless. He uses the Antricle in a very basic way. He just doesn't have the same connection with it that you do.'

Junk stared at Otravinicus floating helplessly in the pink liquid, hooked up to a ventilator. Junk wasn't sure how he felt about it. He and Otravinicus weren't friends. Otravinicus had proved himself to be duplicitous and untrustworthy too many times, but no one should be imprisoned like that.

A drawer slid out of the table Junk was on. He

looked over the edge and saw that it contained an Antricle. *His* Antricle. Sbey removed it and Junk held out his hands, eager to get it again, but instead a small compartment opened up on Sbey's robotic thigh and he put the Antricle inside. It snapped shut and Junk felt a stab of disappointment.

Without a word to Junk, Sbey spread the fingers of the Antricle glove he was wearing and a huge doorway of green light appeared before them. It was enormous. Much bigger than the ones Junk was used to. This one was big enough for Sbey to pass through.

Sbey's eyes flicked to his rear face so he was looking at Junk. He tapped one of his long, elegant red fingers on a specific part of the tabletop.

'Stand there,' he said. Junk did as he was told, crossing to the spot Sbey had indicated. Nothing happened. Junk shifted awkwardly.

'Now what?' he said, and the words were only just out of his mouth when the table beneath him opened up and clamped around his feet. It took him by surprise and he cried out. Then a circle about a metre across revealed itself and a flat, thin disc rose up, lifting Junk with it. He put out his hands to steady himself but it wasn't necessary. The hovering disc felt totally solid and he felt secure on it. He grew increasingly confident and tested the disc's limits. He leaned back a little and the disc stayed level. He leaned forward and from side to side and still the disc was flat. He tried a little jump and the disc was steady.

'This is so cool,' said Junk.

'It is not cool,' said Sbey priggishly. 'It is necessary. Your tiny legs would mean we would never get anywhere.'

'Yeah, all right,' said Junk. 'So how do I control it?'

'You don't,' said Sbey. 'I do.' With that Sbey moved towards the portal and Junk on the floating disc went with him.

20

They passed through the portal and Junk found himself in the Room of Doors for the first time in a long time. It felt like coming home. The shimmering green-black floor spread out before him in all its iridescent beauty. The Room itself looked the same as it always had, but with one very noticeable exception. Everything was on a massively increased scale to what he was used to. There were still thousands of individual doorways, lined up in row upon row reaching away as far as Junk could see ahead of him and behind and above, stretching up endlessly, vanishing into the gods, but now each one of them was in proportion to Sbey, so twenty times the size they had ever been for Junk.

Sbey stopped and Junk's hover-disc did too. It hung in the air near Sbey's shoulder so he and Junk almost shared an eye line. The compartment in Sbey's thigh opened up with a hiss and Sbey took out Junk's Antricle.

'Remember,' he said to Junk, and tapped his own chest.

'Yeah, cos I'm likely to forget the bomb attached

to my heart,' said Junk. Sbey nodded in agreement and held out one of his huge metal hands, Junk's Antricle presented on the end of his index finger. Junk savoured the moment and then reached out and took it.

'Hello, old thing,' he said to the Antricle. Almost immediately it melted, losing its bracelet form and slithered serpent-like up Junk's arm. It curled around his forearm before solidifying.

'How did you do that?' said Sbey, his eyes wide with wonder, his voice thick with desire.

'I didn't. The Antricle did,' said Junk. 'But surely you can do that too. Yours is in a glove.' As he said that his Antricle morphed once again, turning liquid and trickling down his arm, collecting around his hand and covering it like a glove. It was just the same as Sbey's. The cyborg covered his gloved hand subconsciously. He sounded embarrassed when he spoke.

'No,' he said, 'it was this shape when I got it.' Just as Junk had guessed.

'Oh!' said Junk. 'OK. Well, first thing you need to do is clear your mind.' Junk closed his eyes, inhaled deeply and mimed errant thoughts or whatever drifting off into the ether from the top of his head, carried away by jazz-hands.

Sbey closed his eyes and took in a deep breath, his organic chest expanding. He didn't do the jazz-hands, and Junk toyed with the idea of insisting. It might be amusing, but he decided it wasn't worth it.

'Now with your mind clear,' said Junk, 'listen to the

253

Antricle.' An extended moment of silence hung in the air.

'I don't hear anything,' said Sbey.

'That's because it's not making any noise,' said Junk. 'You need to make exactly the same amount of no noise.' Junk let that one hang for a moment and then half opened one eye to peek at Sbey, who was frowning deeply, trying to work out what that meant. Junk closed his eye again. 'Can you hear its heart beating?' said Junk.

'No,' said Sbey.

'Then you need to listen with better ears. Boom-boom . . . boom-boom . . . boom-boom.'

His eyes still closed, Sbey focused harder. Straining to listen. And then he heard it. It was very faint but he smiled.

'I can hear it,' he said, excited like a child.

'Good. Now hear your own heartbeat.' Junk paused. 'You do have a heart, right?'

'I have three,' said Sbey.

'Hmm, OK. Well, you need to synchronize them with the Antricle.' Sbey placed both of his flesh-and-bone hands on his chest. One right in the centre, the other a little down to the left. Then one of his red robotic hands came around and cupped his right hip, just above his metal legs.

'Boom-boom,' whispered Sbey, almost inaudibly, 'boom-boom, boom-boom.'

'Now, when you're ready,' said Junk, 'make your Antricle change. Make it move up your arm.'

His eyes firmly shut, his left robotic arm outstretched before him, Sbey concentrated deeply. All four of his faces were the very definition of focus. For several moments nothing happened. Junk glanced at Sbey from the corner of his eye and could see one of his brows just starting to furrow. Junk could tell he was threatening to lose his patience, which was in short supply to begin with. Just then Sbey's Antricle glove started to move.

'I'm doing it!' barked Sbey. There was a thrilled giggle in his voice. The glove started to spread up his arm until it encased the whole appendage in a thin, flexible layer of bronze. Sbey opened his eyes; they were wide with glee. 'I'm doing it!'

'Yes, you are,' said Junk. 'What do you want to do next? You want to open a door?'

Sbey had a bright, wondrous smile on each of his four faces. Though the ones without eyes made it look more like he was in pain than ecstatically happy. 'Yes! Yes! Let's open a door.'

'OK,' said Junk. 'Where to?'

Sbey thought for a moment. 'We have to be careful when we visit your planet. We can't go anywhere too populated. We stand out. Well, I stand out among you puny little people.'

'You do,' said Junk, 'that's true. But there are still lots of places to go. How about the moon landing? 1969. We could go to Florida and watch Apollo 11 taking off, or we could go to the moon and watch Neil Armstrong landing. The Antricles will protect us.'

'It's not important where we go. It's just a test, and your moon landing was so massively insignificant, but it's fine. Yes. Florida, near Cape Kennedy. 16 July 1969. We'll go there.'

'OK, cool,' said Junk. 'So same as before: your heartbeat . . . beats and the Antricle as one. Boom-boom . . . boom-boom. Yeah?'

Sbey held up a hand as if to say, *I have this*. He closed his eyes, frowned with deep concentrating focus.

'Picture where it is you want to go,' said Junk softly, '*when* it is you want to go. Then picture the doorway you need.'

Sbey concentrated hard but nothing happened.

'Don't worry,' said Junk. 'Just think about what it is you want. Nothing else.'

Sbey took in a slow, deep breath, and as he did so a pinprick of green light materialized before him. It started to grow and grow and grow bigger until it became a massive sparkling portal standing before them.

'I did it!' said Sbey proudly.

'You're a natural,' said Junk. 'Let's make sure it takes us to the right place.' Sbey walked forward and as he did so Junk came with him, hovering by his shoulder. They passed through the portal. Junk felt the magnetic pull as he lurched inside.

A moment later the two of them were spat out on an area of flat, black rocks. The sky was full of furious storm clouds, crackling and flashing with fork lightning, and the rain was lashing down. Thunder roared angrily overhead. Junk looked over his shoulder and Sbey switched his eyes from one face to another. There was a growling volcano in the distance, spitting out balls of fire, belching smoke and flame. This was most definitely not Florida in 1969.

'This isn't right,' said Sbey.

'Nope,' agreed Junk.

'I didn't get it quite right,' said Sbey.

'You haven't got it at all,' said Junk.

'What? What does that mean?'

'It means you're proper useless, you superior moron. You know where this is?'

'No. Where?'

'This is the last day of the planet. This is when the Earth dies. When it erupts into a fireball, cracks into a billion pieces, turns to dust.'

'I was a little off then,' said Sbey. Then he was silent for a moment as a thought came to him. 'Wait. How do you know that?'

'Because I brought us here,' said Junk.

'What?'

'You can't manipulate your Antricle. That was me. I was doing it, not you, you useless lump.'

Sbey looked confused on all four faces as he played Junk's words back and forth in his head. It didn't take him long to realize Junk was up to something. His right hand, the one without the Antricle glove, shot to the compartment on his thigh and pulled out the black box. To begin with, he was thinking about threatening Junk

257

with it, but in the second and a half that it took him to extricate it he had already realized Junk was far more dangerous than he had given him credit for. He knew he had to end his life this instant.

The black box sat in his palm and his thumb moved to depress the button that would detonate the explosive attached to Junk's heart. In that quarter of a second, Sbey's Antricle sprang from his left hand on to his right and wrapped itself around the black box, enclosing it completely. Then, in the blink of an eye, it left Sbey altogether and flew through the air for some distance until it came to a massive pool of lava that had spewed from the volcano and dived in. It was burned away to nothing the instant it made contact.

Sbey was caught off guard but that didn't last long. The floating disc Junk was on suddenly lurched, moving straight towards Sbey. However, by the time it reached him, Junk's Antricle had encased him completely. Sbey grabbed him, detaching him from the flying disc, but even Sbey, big as he was, could not penetrate the Antricle's defences. He tried to crush him in his massive robot hands, but it was like a toddler trying to crush a pebble on the beach. Inside the Antricle, Junk didn't feel a thing. Anger and frustration got the better of Sbey and he hurled Junk's small Antricle-clad figure to the ground. Junk was up in a heartbeat and running. A doorway of green light opened up in front of him. Sbey saw it and realized what was happening. He threw himself forward, towards Junk, his arms, all four of them, outstretched. But he was not quick enough and Junk jumped through the portal. Sbey reached out, but he was big and the portal was small. His red robotic hand was all that would fit through. He grabbed at Junk as Junk slid across the floor of the Room of Doors, but he missed him and Junk slammed the portal shut. Sbey's metal arm was severed at the elbow and it clanged to the ground.

Back on the side of the volcano, Sbey howled in anger. He looked around. He couldn't believe it. Junk had beaten him. He was marooned on the last day of the planet's existence. Soon it would implode and everything here, including Sbey, would cease to exist. He controlled his panic and focused his mind. He was a far-superior life form to Junk and therefore he could not lose like this. All he needed to do was think things through, and he would . . . The planet split into a billion shards then and the ground opened up beneath Sbey. He dropped into an ocean of molten rock and was burned up to nothing.

In the Room of Doors, Junk's Antricle armour retreated and he looked at the disembodied red forearm and hand lying lifeless on the floor.

'Not bad for an aberration, I'd say.'

Dr Otravinicus and Amelia Earhart were standing by a roadside in Dallas, Texas. It was 22 November 1963. A presidential cavalcade was approaching. In about three minutes the thirty-fifth president of the United

States, John Fitzgerald Kennedy, would be assassinated. It was a momentous event in North America's history and Otravinicus and Amelia wanted to witness it. Otravinicus was strangely quiet. He was distracted. There was something he was about to do that he had never contemplated doing before. It was an old custom, a custom from Amelia's time, not his. He felt the small box in his pocket. It was about the three hundredth time he had checked it was there since they arrived. He decided it was now or never. He took a deep breath and turned to Amelia, but she wasn't there. Nor was the road, nor was Dallas. Dr Otravinicus found himself in a tank of pale pink liquid. The tank started to drain and the level of the pink liquid fell rapidly.

Beyond the wet glass of the tank, Otravinicus could see the most enormous-looking room. There was movement and a huge face leered up to the glass. Otravinicus cried out, but his voice was muffled by the oxygen mask covering his nose and mouth.

A short time later, Otravinicus was wrapped in a huge towel and was sitting in Dras Sbey's laboratory opposite Espa and Junk. Otravinicus could not take his eyes off the cyborg as Junk spoke. He had been speaking for a while, and the doctor had heard his words, but that didn't make them any easier to absorb. Junk had explained that everything Otravinicus had seen . . . everything he had witnessed . . . Amelia . . . was all imaginary. He was on a space station. The huge four-faced being in front of him was an alien from a race of universe builders. They had built this universe. It was all too crazy for words.

'So what happens now?' asked Otravinicus.

'I'll take you wherever you want to go. Take you home if you want,' said Junk.

'Can I have my Antricle?'

Junk looked at Espa for an answer. Espa shook his head.

'Oh.' Otravinicus looked downhearted. He tried picturing himself returning to his apartment in Arrapia. The prospect filled him with dread. Then he thought about going to 1937 and finding the real Amelia Earhart, but then they wouldn't have the Antricle so they couldn't be time travellers. He loved Amelia, but he also loved that he was a time traveller with Amelia. It was tremendous fun to have someone to share his adventures with. It was more than that. It was the most fun he had ever had. It wasn't real, but it felt real. And what was better: miserable in the real world or deliriously happy in a fake one?

'I wonder,' said Otravinicus demurely, 'if it's all the same to you, do you think you could put me back in the tank?'

Otravinicus turned. Amelia was standing next to him. They were by the side of the road in Dallas and the convoy of vehicles was approaching. Otravinicus went down on one knee and removed the ring box from his pocket.

*

261

Junk and Espa were looking at Otravinicus floating serenely in another tank of pink liquid. A smile crept across Otravinicus's face and, though his mouth was obscured by the breathing mask, they could see his eyes smiling.

'How long can he stay there?' asked Junk.

'I have no idea,' said Espa. 'With Dras gone and only a minimal crew left on board, maybe no one will notice him. Even if they do, they'll probably just think it's one of Dras's experiments. Who knows how long it will take them to notice Dras is no longer about.'

'Thank you, Espa,' said Junk. 'For everything.'

'I did nothing. Less than nothing. You beat Dras all on your own.' Espa smiled, fascinated as ever by Junk. 'Tell me where you want to go and I will send you there.'

A doorway of light shimmered in the hall of the Bone Faces' compound and Junk stepped out. The hall was empty, though the ground was littered with dead Bone Faces. Clearly there had been some sort of battle here after Junk left and the Bone Faces hadn't fared well. He stopped to listen and heard nothing. Just silence. He went down the tunnel to the front of the compound and the towering cliff-face. There was no one there either. No one living at least.

Another portal opened and Junk stepped through. He was on the bridge of Garvan's airship, the *Xcsso*. It was low-ceilinged and cramped for Cantibeans, but massive as far as Junk was concerned. Everything was black and slick. A thin window of tinted glass ran around the front and Junk could see they were flying over open sea. He couldn't see any land. The only thing within view was a massive land-ship that was cutting through the ocean below.

'Junk!' Garvan leaped out of his chair and ran to his friend, picking him off his feet into a hug. 'What happened to you? Where did you go? Again.'

'Long story. I'll tell you later. Fill me in – what's happened?'

'After you vanished, all hell broke loose. The Bone Faces fought back. Took us by surprise. We were more than a match for them, but some of them, including the leader – what's she called?'

'The Tul.'

'That's her. She and a few others got down into some tunnels. We were too big to follow. The tunnels led all the way to the coast. They had a ship. That ship.' He pointed to the land-ship in the water below. 'We've been following them, but they have a lot of weapons on there. We could easily blow it out of the water, but there are children on board.' Something unspoken passed between the two friends. Garvan knew Junk was praying that one of those children would be Ambeline, but there was no guarantee. 'Every time we try to get close, they open fire.'

'So,' said Junk, holding up the Antricle, 'we sneak in the back way.'

21

A portal opened up in a darkened hold on a lower deck. The doorway, which was the only source of light in the room, was larger than normal, wider and higher, because a hundred four-metre-tall armour-clad Cantibean soldiers needed to pass through it. They came first, making sure the coast was clear for Junk, Lasel, Alfrid and most importantly their king. Garvan's general, a man even bigger than Garvan, called Mosscos, was deeply unhappy about Garvan being here and had pleaded with him to stay behind, but Garvan would have none of it.

Before they had left the *Xcsso*, Junk had detailed the plan of action. Half the soldiers were to deal with the Bone Faces, put them out of action. Garvan and Lasel along with the rest of the soldiers were to free any prisoners on board while Junk and Alfrid found the Tul. Garvan wanted Junk to take some of his soldiers with him but Junk refused, and now that he could use the Antricle freely again, Garvan knew Junk was able to take care of himself better than any of them so he agreed.

The Bone Faces' land-ship was enormous. The Bone Faces, as Alfrid had once explained to Junk, were slavers. That's how they made their money. They would spend half the year raiding settlements in the Upworld, settlements like Dajja, amassing stock. Stock in this case being people. Children always sold well, so they took them whenever they could, but they took adults too. Generally no one too old; rarely would they take someone over forty, because there was little demand for them and the price was always low. Plus they took up more room and needed more food. Once they had enough mochu, which meant cattle, they would load them aboard their land-ship and sail from port to port in the great ocean, selling their merchandise as they went. As luck would have it, it had almost been time for another selling expedition so the land-ship was mostly ready to cast off. When Garvan and his soldiers invaded, the Tul was able to make a quick escape without leaving much of value behind. She was annoyed by the incursion on her territory, but it was a problem that she was sure would be solved by the time they returned in half a year.

The Tul stepped out on deck and felt the salt spray hitting her face. She closed her eyes and savoured its refreshing sting. She loved the open sea. Such a difference after being underground for months on end, but that was the way things had been done in her tribe for centuries. She would love to live above ground all year round, or even live on the water, but she knew it would be impossible to change the minds of her brethren. Bone Faces were under-dwellers. Always had been, always would be. The Tul had expanded the trade routes considerably since she took over from the last Tul, which meant they were away and at sea for longer than in her father's day. Her father had always dreamed of being Tul, but he had not been a leader. She was reflecting on this, reflecting on what an utter disappointment her father was to her, when she suddenly noticed the airship was gone. The big black bird that had been dogging them for days, that had become a fixture in the sky, was nowhere to be seen. The giant aggressors had given up, as she had been sure they would. The Tul was a brilliant strategist. Everyone said so. Well, OK, she said it and everyone agreed, as was her rule, but she was certain they meant it nonetheless.

Once the Tul had drawn the captain's attention to the fact that the aggressors had given up and flown away, the captain decided to make a ship-wide announcement. The Bone Faces had been under a lot of stress for too long and the captain knew from experience that such stress would build and build until it had no alternative but to find a release. The Bone Faces were used to being the biggest, meanest and scariest ones around. That was true in the Underland, but the soldiers that had invaded their stronghold were twice the size of their biggest man and had clearly had more combat training than any of them. In a straight-up fight, the Bone Faces would have lost.

That was hard for warriors of their ilk to accept. The stress that fact engendered could have terrible consequences. It could lead to fighting from within. So when the captain made the announcement he exaggerated the brilliance of their victory. He had heard of the Cantibean army; who hadn't? And he decided to add some stories about their lethal reputation. Stories about how they had lain waste to entire armies, entire nations. It wasn't true, but the Bone Faces had beaten them so that meant they were the greater. They had beaten an invincible foe.

The captain's announcement had the exact result he intended. With the Bone Faces thrown together as they were, things were building to a detonation and it wouldn't be pretty. There was a huge collective sigh of relief when they heard the aggressors had given up. Percolating tensions were instantly forgotten. A sense of release flooded across the ship. Those on high alert relaxed. This next stage of the journey was everyone's favourite. There was nothing to do for a few weeks apart from some minor housekeeping. Making sure the mochu were clean, fed and exercised. No one would want unhappy, unhealthy or dead stock when they reached the markets. Those tasks were done on a strict rota, which meant everyone had some periods of downtime.

Junk, Lasel, Garvan, Alfrid and the Cantibean soldiers ascended five decks until they reached the point where they would separate. Junk and Alfrid carried on going

267

up, while Lasel and Garvan and their troops went aft to the slave quarters, and the rest of the army, led by General Mosscos, went forward to the crew deck.

They were unsure how many Bone Faces were watching over the children, but the plan of action was to let Mosscos and his troops overrun the Bone Face crew first, utilizing the element of surprise.

The crew quarters, where the majority of the Bone Faces were to be found, was an entire deck. A long corridor ran the length of it, with dormitories towards the back and large recreation areas nearer the front. In the middle were the bathing area, a large gymnasium so the Bone Faces could work out, kitchens and some private rooms for anyone who wanted some solitude. Solitude was on a strict rota as well. The problem for Mosscos and his troops was that there wasn't the open area needed for a mass attack. The Cantibeans, being the size they were, would have to attack in single file. This was extremely dangerous for whoever was leading the attack.

Fortunately there were stairwells the entire length of the ship. So Mosscos got his soldiers to spread along the deck below and wait until everyone was in place. Then Mosscos gave the order, which was relayed all the way along the corridor, and the attacks, twelve separate attacks, happened simultaneously. The Bone Faces were not expecting it. They were not able to mount any sort of effective defence. The battle was short and, for the most part, bloodless. None of the Cantibeans were injured. A few of the Bone Faces were killed, though most were captured, the majority capitulating almost immediately under such obviously overwhelming strength.

At the same time as Mosscos was unleashing his troops on the Bone Faces, Lasel, Garvan and the rest of the soldiers were moving into position to take control of the slave quarters. There were only five Bone Faces on duty, overseeing three hundred slaves. There was no real fight. However, there was only one access point into the entire slave area, which meant Garvan and Lasel couldn't use the element of surprise in the way Mosscos had.

They broke through the locked door with ease. Garvan led the way, much to the chagrin of Tyunkas, Mosscos's number two. He too had tried to convince Garvan to stay at the back, but it was hard to argue with your king. He generally won every argument.

Once inside the slave quarters, Garvan, Lasel and the troops hunted down and dealt with the remaining Bone Faces quickly and efficiently. Unfortunately, because of the way the place was set out, the Bone Face furthest from the entrance was able to raise the alarm before they got to him.

Of course, by then all the Bone Faces on the crew deck had been neutralized themselves so that wasn't a problem, but the Tul was alerted to the attack before Junk and Alfrid made it to her stateroom.

Lasel, Garvan and the soldiers moved quickly

through the slave quarters, unlocking and freeing all the mochu. In the third room she liberated, each room holding thirty or more people, Lasel found Tyva, Vil and the rest of Tyva's adopted children. Lasel, of course, didn't recognize any of them as she had been unconscious during their entire acquaintance. But Vil, the boy who had found Lasel dying in the caves, recognized her. When she unlocked the door and stepped into the room, Vil's face had lit up and he ran to her, throwing his arms around her and speaking in a language she didn't understand. However, Alfrid had told Lasel everything that had happened while she was unconscious, so Lasel was able to make educated guesses about who this animated little boy was, and the protective black-haired girl who watched them all like a hawk and looked ready to attack at the slightest provocation.

'Tyva,' said Lasel, pointing. Tyva nodded but glared back suspiciously. Lasel glanced down at the boy clinging to her waist. 'Vil?' she said. Vil answered with a breathless outpouring of incomprehensible words. Lasel opened her arms to Tyva, and for a moment the girl held back, but then she gave in and accepted Lasel's embrace. Once Tyva did, lots of the other children did too and they all crowded around Lasel. Some of those who couldn't get close to Lasel, and probably didn't understand why anyone was hugging but wanted to be in on the action, wrapped their arms around Garvan, though his cold, hard armour coating didn't make for a particularly pleasant experience.

'Stay behind me,' said Junk to Alfrid. It was an unnecessary order. Alfrid was no hero or fighter and wasn't planning on being the first through any door. Junk wore the Antricle as armour, covering his entire body up to his chin.

They stepped out of a bulkhead door and found themselves on the open foredeck. They saw the Tul standing on the next deck up, staring down at them, ready and waiting for them. To reach that deck, Junk and Alfrid would have to cross the foredeck to a set of metal steps. However, between them and the steps stood twenty Bone Faces, all armed to the teeth. Alfrid whimpered with fear. Junk, however, looked unfazed.

With a wave of his hand, twenty portals of blue light opened up under the twenty Bone Faces and the Tul watched in abject horror as her protection detail dropped out of sight.

'How did you do that?' Alfrid sounded amazed. He hadn't really understood what was going on when they had come through the large portal to board the ship, assuming it was some sort of Cantibean technology he wasn't aware of; he hadn't realized it was Junk.

Junk turned his head to look out to sea, and Alfrid and the Tul followed his gaze. Another twenty portals opened up a hundred metres off the port side and the twenty Bone Faces who moments before had been standing on the foredeck fell out, screaming in panic, arms flailing, as they splashed into the open sea.

'How did you do that?' said Alfrid again, probably not for the last time. Junk didn't answer him but turned back to the Tul and locked eyes with her. He could see the fear that she was trying to mask. The Tul put on her own skull mask then. She did it slowly, almost as if it was part of a ceremony, a build-up to the main event. Then she turned and went into her stateroom.

'Come on,' said Junk, and he started towards the steps. Alfrid was still struggling to understand what was happening but followed Junk dutifully nonetheless.

The Tul's stateroom was big, the size of a ballroom. There was not much in the way of furniture, just a large table and six chairs off to one side. An ornate candelabra stood in the middle of the table. It looked like a hand reaching up from out of the wood and at the tips of each of the fingers and the thumb was a long red candle. For some reason, it got Junk's attention and he thought it looked out of place around the Tul. Later, he would reflect on how odd it was to focus on a candlestick when, at the far end of the room, there were three children, each standing on a small platform raised about a metre above the floor. They were locked in place, shackled to poles embedded in the platforms. The children were all about the same size, all had long blonde hair that hung down below hoods that had been placed over their heads. All three were sobbing and shaking with fear, but their voices were muffled as if they had all been gagged under those hoods.

In front of each child stood a crossbow-like

contraption sitting on a tripod. The crossbow bolts were aimed directly at the children. Behind them, the far end of the room was bathed in impenetrable shadow. Junk heard the Tul's voice drifting out from there, but he couldn't see her, couldn't pin down exactly where she was.

'Na tush parsgu ramatartum,' she said, her voice deep and guttural, almost a growl.

'You have ruined everything,' said Alfrid from behind Junk, translating the Tul's words.

'Orum ki chi posko ta woko.'

'Now let me return the favour.'

The Tul started to speak quickly then from the darkness and Alfrid translated as she spoke, just one word behind. The Tul's voice was toxic, like a poisonous gas drifting on the breeze.

'Your sister stands before you. One of these three children is the one we took from Dajja as you described to us. You must choose one crossbow and pull the trigger. They are fixed so you cannot aim away. If you do this, the other two children will be freed. Or I will fire two crossbows and you may keep the one child that lives.'

Junk scowled into the shadows. He couldn't see the Tul, but he assumed she could see him. The Tul continued to speak and Alfrid continued to translate:

'Two live if you play my game, only one if you refuse.'

Junk shook his head. 'Still playing games.' Alfrid translated for the Tul's benefit now. 'You've lost. You

273

know that. Your crew, your soldiers, they're all gone. If you stop now, stop this ridiculous game, I'll let you be. Take you wherever you want. Take you home. Somewhere else.'

'Throom hadge ha?' said the Tul. The words were spat out with bitter indignation.

'And do what?' said Alfrid. He continued: 'You have taken away everyone I've ever known. All my people. My home. I am alone. Because of you. Now let's see if luck is on your side. Choose one. I will give you to the count of thirty. One . . . two . . . thr—'

Junk held a hand up to Alfrid, telling him he could stop translating now. Junk looked at the three girls on the platforms. Was one of them really Ambeline? Was he that close now? It was impossible to tell which one. He hadn't seen his sister in three years. She would be taller of course. She'd be almost ten years old now, maybe already ten. He'd lost track of the date back home. He wasn't sure how long he had been here. Without seeing her face, he couldn't know if any of them was really her.

Alfrid was counting out loud again: 'Twenty-seven . . . twenty-eight . . . twenty-nine . . . thirty! Time's up.'

'OK,' said Junk, squinting into the shadows. 'I've chosen. This one.' He pointed to the crossbow on the right.

The Tul spoke, her voice sounding cruelly amused. 'Are you sure?' relayed Alfrid. 'Last chance to change your mind.'

'This one,' said Junk again, and he stepped to the crossbow on the right. He looked at the little girl on the platform ahead. She was shaking wildly and he was sure the only reason she was still standing was because the restraints were forcing her to stay upright. It'll all be over in a few seconds, thought Junk. He curled his hand around the stock of the crossbow. The trigger was a long, gently curving lever hidden underneath the stock. Junk couldn't know how sensitive the trigger was until he started to depress it. He took a deep breath, held it and slowly started to squeeze.

'Junk!' He froze and turned to glare at Alfrid. 'You can't play her game.' Junk gave Alfrid a fierce look and the young man cowered. Junk turned his attention back to the crossbow. He took another deep breath and started to squeeze. It didn't take a lot of force to activate the mechanism, and the bolt shot out and travelled the short distance to its target in less than a quarter of a second. Before it hit the girl on the podium however, a small window of blue light snapped open in front of her, swallowing the bolt. Half a second later another window opened in the shadowy recesses at the back of the room, illuminating the Tul. The very same crossbow bolt flew out of that window and embedded itself in the Tul's back. She had only a moment to realize she had lost before she tipped forward and fell to the floor.

She was dead.

Junk moved quickly now. He ripped the bolts from the other two crossbows and tossed them aside, making certain they couldn't fire accidentally. He ran to the first girl, the one on the right, and unshackled her. He pulled the hood from her head. It wasn't Ambeline. There was a length of cloth wrapped around her mouth, which Junk pulled free and the little girl took in a deep gasp of breath. Her eyes were burning red with tears and she was shaking violently. Alfrid crouched down next to Junk and smiled at the girl. He spoke softly, telling her she was safe now. Saying they would take her home, asking her questions to distract her from her trauma.

Junk left her with Alfrid and moved along to the next child. Once again he unshackled her wrists and removed the hood. A pair of bright blue eyes were blinking at the light. Junk studied her as he removed her gag. For a moment he thought maybe it was Ambeline. He tried to imagine how she would have changed. Alfrid crouched next to her, the first girl still clinging to him, and he spoke gently to the second girl. She nodded in answer to his question. This wasn't Ambeline either.

Junk turned and looked at the third and final child. Could his quest be about to end? He removed the manacles and the girl massaged her wrists where they had cut into her skin. Junk paused for a split second and said a little silent prayer and then he removed the hood. Blonde hair was everywhere, covering her face. Gently, Junk reached up to brush it aside, first one way and then the next. Another pair of blue eyes blinked at him, but these were different. These held something else: recognition. A faint but growing memory. Junk removed the gag.

'Hello, Ambeline,' he said, his voice barely audible, cracking, tears starting to run down his face.

'Do I know you?' she said. She hadn't lost her Irish accent. 'You look like someone I used to know. Long time ago. In a dream.'

Junk shook his head. 'That wasn't a dream. That was real.'

Ambeline frowned, trying to make sense of everything. 'Junk?' she said.

Junk nodded and he had to bite down on his lip to stop himself from collapsing into uncontrollable sobbing. 'I've been looking for you for a long time,' he said.

Ambeline nodded. 'I always knew you'd come. One day. You're my knight.' With that she reached out her hand and stroked her brother's face, wiping away some of the tears, but the action opened the floodgates for Junk and he couldn't stop himself from bawling. 'It's OK,' said Ambeline sweetly. 'You'll be all right.' And Junk laughed. He was still crying. Crying and laughing at the same time.

22

Lasel and Garvan stepped out on to the huge foredeck, leading the Bone Faces' former prisoners into the light. All was frightening and new for them. Many of the slaves had never seen daylight before, or at least not so they could remember. None of them had ever seen the ocean. Little children clutched the hands and hems of older ones. Older children stayed close to the adults.

On Garvan's orders, his soldiers held back. Some returned to the *Xcsso* via the portal still active in the lower deck, while others combed the ship from top to bottom for any Bone Faces that might have been missed. They didn't find any.

Lasel was looking at the children tilting their heads up to the sun, closing their eyes and feeling the warmth on their skin. She wondered what would happen to them now. They could try and take some home, the ones who had homes or remembered their homes, but lots had nowhere to go but back to the Underland. It felt wrong to send them back there. An idea hit her and she looked around for Junk, eager to tell him.

Her eyes went up to the next deck and she saw Alfrid emerging with two young blonde girls. They started to descend the steps to the foredeck. Then there was movement behind them and she saw Junk. He was carrying a young girl and Lasel knew from the way she had her arms wrapped tightly around him, her face nestled into the crook of his neck, that this was Ambeline. Lasel gasped out a cry of joy. She had been on this journey with Junk for so long and knew the nightmare he had gone through, from everyone back in his home believing he had killed his sister to losing his parents' love. She knew how alone in the world Junk had felt, and it was a world much bigger than he or any of them had ever imagined. He had set out to do the impossible, and now he had succeeded. Happy tears started to stream down her face.

Garvan looked at Lasel and saw she was crying. He frowned.

'What's the matter?' he said, following Lasel's eye line as he said it until he too saw Junk and Ambeline. Garvan let out almost an identical exhalation of happiness as Lasel.

Junk saw them looking up at him and he smiled. He descended the steps, still holding Ambeline in his arms, and crossed over to his friends.

'Ambeline,' he said gently, 'I want you to meet my friends. I could never have found you without them.' He set Ambeline down and she looked at Lasel and then at Garvan, her mouth dropping open in shock as she saw how big he was. 'This is Lasel and Garvan. Garvan's a king, so be polite.'

Lasel crouched down in front of Ambeline and took her hand. 'I am so pleased to meet you, Ambeline,' she said, battling tears but losing. 'I've heard so much about you.'

Unsure what to say, Ambeline smiled at Lasel and looked up at Garvan. 'Are you really a king?'

Garvan knelt down but still towered over her. He nodded. 'I am,' he said, 'thanks to your brother.'

Ambeline looked proudly at Junk. 'He's a pretty good brother then?'

'You just wait till you hear. He climbed mountains to find you, fought whole armies by himself, battled man-eating birds and dived to the bottom of the ocean. Yeah, he's a pretty good brother.'

Ambeline turned and threw her arms around Junk again.

Junk looked at all the people on the deck and he frowned. 'What are we going to do with this lot?'

'I had an idea about that,' said Lasel.

A wide portal opened up and Junk, Ambeline, Lasel and Garvan led the Bone Faces' former slaves out into a bright sunny field. Ahead of them stood Versailles, exactly as it was after the battle with the Nine Emperors' army. Part of a wall had been destroyed, but Garvan could soon see to that and there was plenty of room here.

Alfrid and Tyva came through the portal with Vil

and the children Tyva had adopted. Behind them followed many more of the residents of the Underland. Junk and Lasel had explained, with Alfrid's help, that those who wanted to could live here. There was still plenty of food here that had belonged to the Nine Emperors and they could grow crops, farm animals. Whatever they wanted. If there was anyone who had a home to go to, then Junk would make sure they got there.

Alfrid looked at Tyva. She was smiling. He smiled back and they broke into a run, with Vil and the other children tagging along with them. Eager to explore their new home, they ran to Versailles.

Janice Doyle was sitting atop a ladder, painting the ceiling of the attic room. She wasn't the gaunt, bitter, unhappy woman that Dras Sbey had created. In fact, she didn't look very different from the way she looked all those years ago before her whole world came crashing down around her. She had had some bad times, some very bad times in the months following Ambeline's death and Junk's disappearance, and some people might not have been able to cope with such tragedy, but Janice Doyle was a strong woman. She had spent a lot of time in grief counselling, both in Ireland and back in the States. She and Dominic had separated for a time, but Ireland was her home. Her heart was here and neither she nor Dominic could bear to lose each other as well as their children. So Janice had come back. Back to Ireland and back to her husband. They thought about selling the house and moving on but something, instinct, a feeling, told them that they should stay. So they did. They had grieved for their dead daughter and accepted that she was gone forever. Even so, Ambeline's bedroom remained untouched, as did Junk's. Both Dominic and Janice truly believed that one day their son would come back to them.

Elton John's 'Your Song' came on the radio and Janice paused. She used to sing this song to Ambeline when she was a baby. Anything that reminded her of Ambeline was a good thing and she smiled, picturing her baby daughter cradled in her arms. She happened to glance out of the window just then and was surprised to see two figures walking over the field that bordered the house on one side. She thought that was odd, because there was no way to cross that field without first coming past the house and she had been up here all morning. Surely she would have noticed them going past earlier.

The song continued to play and Janice continued staring out of the window at the two ramblers approaching. Then an even stranger thing happened; the two figures broke into a run. They were running straight towards the house, there was something urgent about their movements. Not like an emergency but like they were desperate to get there.

As they drew closer, Janice could make out more detail. It was a man, tall and lean, and a child, a girl, maybe ten or so. Then the sun touched the girl's head and her long blonde hair blazed to life, a whip of golden fire. Janice's heart started to pound. The craziest idea was forming in her head. It was insane. Utterly insane.

Janice Doyle leaped from the ladder, upsetting it and it toppled over behind her, spilling the paint all over the floor but she didn't even notice. She ran down from the attic to the landing and raced down the main staircase.

'DOM?' She yelled out her husband's name at the top of her lungs. 'DOM?'

Janice reached the ground floor and sprinted outside, unlatching the door to the boot room. They had a pair of dogs now, a pointer cross and a Jack Russell. Both had been dozing in front of the Aga but, roused by Janice's excitement, they leaped to their feet and ran outside with her.

'DOM?' she called again, and Dominic Doyle stepped out from his workshop to see what all the commotion was about.

'What's wrong?' he said.

'Look!' said Janice, pointing. Dominic turned to see the two figures running towards the house. They were much closer now, so close that he could make out details. A shiver ran through him.

'It can't be,' he whispered. He so wanted to believe what he was seeing, but he knew it was impossible.

'It is!' shouted Janice, and she ran on, the dogs bounding ahead of her. And then he heard it:

'Daddy! Mummy!' A girl's voice. A voice he knew so well. A voice he had never forgotten. A voice he had never expected to hear again. His girl's voice. Ambeline's voice. Dominic Doyle set off after his wife and the dogs. His long, powerful legs meant he caught up to Janice in seconds. They raced through the gate just as Junk and Ambeline arrived.

Junk held back then and let Ambeline run forward. The dogs were bouncing up and down, barking excitedly even though they had no idea why. Ambeline threw herself at Janice and Dominic and the three of them collapsed in a sobbing, ecstatic pile.

'AmbelineAmbelineAmbelineAmbelineAmbelineAmbeline,' Janice Doyle said over and over again, squeezing her daughter one second, then holding her out to look at her face the next. Could it really be her?

Dominic looked up at his son now. After everything that had happened, and despite bringing Ambeline home and proving he hadn't done what they thought, Junk wasn't sure how his parents would react to him. There was a part of him that still expected to be rejected. Suddenly his father flew to his feet and hurled himself at Junk, taking him by surprise. Dominic grabbed him and wrapped his arms tightly around him. He was choking with sobs.

'My boy. My boy. My beautiful boy. How?' said Dominic. 'How? I don't understand.'

It was Ambeline who explained. 'It was Junk,' she said breathlessly. 'He found me. He never stopped looking and he found me and he rescued me.'

Ambeline struggled to get up, pulling Janice with her, and led her to Junk and Dominic.

At long last, the family became whole once again.

The Doyles went into their house and Junk and Ambeline told their parents the story of everything that had happened since the night Ambeline had been taken by Jacid Mestrowe. Of course the story sounded incredible, and of course Janice and Dominic didn't believe their tales of sharkmen and time travel, but Junk and Ambeline had already talked about that. Junk was all ready to take their parents on a whirlwind tour through history, but Janice said that wouldn't be necessary. Maybe they didn't fully believe their story, but they didn't need to. They had their children back and that was all that mattered.

Dominic did a roast for dinner and he made bread sauce especially for Ambeline. It had been her favourite. And Yorkshire pudding for Junk. His favourite.

That night, Ambeline slept in her parents' bed and Junk in his old room.

But Junk couldn't sleep. He knew he wasn't going to stay. There are some things that can't be undone, and Junk didn't feel like he belonged here any more. His heart was in another place, another time. With Lasel and Garvan.

He sat at the window at dawn and watched the sun come up. It was a view he loved and one he had never been sure he would get to see again. Now he had.

He wrote a note to his parents and Ambeline,

assuring them he would be back to visit soon but there were things he needed to take care of. Garvan's coronation for one. Garvan had asked him to be his 'Falamira'. It was a vital part of the coronation ceremony and a great honour to be asked, though Junk had no idea what it involved. He left the note in the kitchen, finished a cup of tea and said goodbye to the dogs. Then he left.

He walked to the cliffs. He wanted to see the sea again. He breathed in the salt air. Ireland smelt like nowhere else. Now or millions of years in the future.

The Antricle was on his arm and he turned, about to open a portal when he saw his mother hurrying towards him. She was in her dressing gown and wellingtons. She was holding his note.

'Don't go,' she said.

'I'll be back,' he said, 'all the time. I promise.'

'All these years I've wanted to make up for what I did to you back then, what I said to you.'

'It's OK,' said Junk.

'It's not,' said his mother. 'I did the worst thing a mother can do. I love you so much. Not a day goes by that I don't regret—'

'Ma!' Junk cut her off. 'It's OK. I'm not leaving cos of that.'

Janice nodded but she didn't look convinced. Junk took his mother in his arms and held her. He kissed the top of her head.

'I love you, Ma.'

Then Junk stepped back and touched his fingers

to the Antricle. A doorway opened up and Janice Doyle gasped. Suddenly she realized the incredible story Junk and Ambeline had told them was all true. Junk touched the Antricle again, and instead of a doorway of green light the portal became a transparent window. A window into another time. They were looking at Cantibea. There was movement on the other side, and Junk and his mother saw a girl. Lasel. She was wearing a long flowing dress and looked incredibly beautiful.

'That's why I'm going back,' said Junk to his mother.

Janice smiled then. She understood. She kissed her son on the cheek. 'Thank you for bringing Ambeline home.' She paused. 'Will you be back for Christmas? You can bring guests.'

Junk smiled. Then he stepped back, moving through the portal. Janice watched as Junk approached Lasel. When Lasel saw Junk she threw her arms around him. The portal started to close then. It grew smaller and smaller until it blinked out of existence and Janice Doyle was all alone on a cliff-top looking out over the Atlantic.

THE END

BOJOLO GLOSSARY

B

baan	if
babanda	home
binja	this is
bo	are
Bu	We

C

cala	need
camasir	marker
caparmana	extremely lucky or jammy
casi	from
chi	me
corsant	on
culla	sorry
cunna	heart

D

dulla	another
durt zha	all clear

F

far	like
faush	kill
fila	(to be) busy
fis	two

G

gani	awake
goge	no
gum	only

H

ha	what
hadge	does

ho	to
ho nabe	asked and answered

J

ja	but
jop	three
Juntry	Upworld

K

kamanana	have us see
ki	let

L

lijna	tree
lim	one
lono	anyone

M

ma	my
manandra	hi
marna na	boy
maws	it is
maj	game
mlu	name
mochu	cattle
mollo	round
munna	brings you
mutta	tell/call

N

N'	I
na	you
nabo	you're
no	he
nu	she
nol	him
nuala	time
nul	her
nungra	monster
Nusk Fooder	Bone Faces

O
orum   now

P
pa   of
paranto   please
parsgu   ruined
pon   your
porum   red hair
posko   return
puna   come

R
ramatartum   everything
rung   pure

S
solge   sister
soot   is
sunsee   circle
sussa   choose
susu   beneath

T
ta   the
tarnotsir   field
tatuma   here
throom   and
trally   taken
tratram   urgent
trumah   help
trun   it
trunna   would you
tush   have

U
unup   hand

V
vanty   pulls out

vebo	we see
W	
wesil	upside down
woko	favour
Y	
yask	understand
yaso	who is
yawsty	lose
Z	
zo	yes

ACKNOWLEDGEMENTS

I would like to thank Rachel Faulkner, Sarah Lambert, Roisin Heycock, Niamh Mulvey, Lauren Woosey and everyone at Quercus. Thank you for sending Junk and his friends out into the big wide world. A massive thank you to Talya Baker for fixing my mistakes yet again. And to James Fraser and Sam Hadley, who I have neglected to thank previously (mostly because we've never met), but I love your cover art. Thank you for making my books look so good.

Thank you to Eugenie Furniss and Liane-Louise Smith at Furniss-Lawton. And Lucinda Prain, Rob Kraitt and Isobel Pietsch at Casarotto-Ramsay for guiding the other half of my working life for me.

And a huge thank you to Katie Hills for Tyva (including the artwork) and to Gabie for Alfrid the toymaker.